I Could Ride All Day in My Cool Blue Train

PETER HOBBS

faber and faber

First published in 2006
by Faber and Faber Limited
3 Queen Square London WC1N 3AU
This paperback edition first published in 2008

Typeset by Faber and Faber Limited
Printed in the UK by CPI Bookmarque, Croydon, CRO 4TD

The right of Peter Hobbs to be identified as author of this work
has been asserted in accordance with Section 77 of the Copyright,
Designs and Patents Act 1988

A CIP record for this book
is available from the British Library

ISBN 978 0–571–21716–8

2 4 6 8 10 9 7 5 3 1

for Lee

Contents

I Could Ride All Day in My Cool Blue Train

Dream #84
20/11/__

She's called Annie; he doesn't have a name. She travels, socializes; he works in the city, though nothing too evil, his soul has survived intact and residually innocent. They're both staggeringly beautiful, air-brushed and freshly cut from magazines, made solid and somehow human. They play across the eye like slow-motion advertisements for inconsequential beauty products. They are a little older now and no longer as they once were, lingering somewhere in their mid-thirties like artefacts from miscarried youths. They haven't known each other long. It's a love story, of a kind.

They meet in the car park. He pulls up in a non-specific – though undeniably non-economy – car. Her car is red, sporty. She's already there leaning against it dressed in tennis whites, head tilted back to catch the sun, slick black shades over her eyes. A short skirt, acres of perfect thigh. The sky is blue or green. He's wearing his suit, silk and sharp, his tie loose and raffish. They greet each other with excessive and revealing and frankly unconvincing casualness. Something is going on here between them, something in its earliest, most pleasurable stages. He heads off to get changed. She loiters, magnetic and irresistibly sexy. In no time at all, time passes.

They have reconvened on court. The game is in progress. He has already sliced a plurality of shots embarrassingly low into the net and his forehand pass, his saving grace, the stroke that provides the illusion that he is a better player than he ever really could be (in secret he admits to himself his weakness) is being unerringly dismantled by the killer volleys of his net-loving opposite. The last time he probed along the

3

line, the ball decurving at great speed in a searing arc zenithing an inch above the tape, she moved early, impossibly early, and deflected the ball cutely down across the court where it didn't even bounce, merely rolled away, deft as hell. On her service game he has won precisely no points. He waits a yard or more behind the service line. In the distance the ball drifts high and straight, he sees her body curl in a gathering of potential energy, then there's a kinetic snap, and that is the last he knows of it, nowhere in its perfect path does the ball travel remotely near him. Six games to love, six games to love.

'Good game. Thanks.'

'So what's your ranking?'

'Three hundred,' she says with satisfaction. 'I'm resident pro here – you knew, didn't you?' She smiles. 'You didn't expect to win, did you?'

He denies it, almost convincingly. They retire to the clubhouse. He follows a little behind her so as to mop his forehead covertly.

The inside of the tennis club resembles strongly the inside of a gentleman's club once seen on TV. There is a bar, where they buy drinks. They stand around chatting delicately. Other couples do the same. They laugh discreetly. Despite, or perhaps because of, his incompetence on the court, things are going well. Their mouths twist wryly in absurdly exaggerated forms, and this passes for clever conversation, even flirting.

There is a calendar, or perhaps a diary, belonging to a full and satisfying life with numerous wonderful engagements strewn across its much-parsed pages. Without actually passing, time passes.

They are talking, as they often do these days, on the phone. She wants him to enter the Antarctic Games with her. The whole phone call is an expanse of snow, wide and white. Kayaking, she suggests. They could compete together and splash out into the freezing, unfrozen, black Southern Ocean against a background of icebergs. For some reason she feels he is up to the challenge. He num-nums the idea, as he has

4

done every time over the past weeks when she has raised the subject. Eventually, she does not let it go by.

'Well why not? Scared?'

'Absolutely not.'

'It'll be wonderful. Just think of it.'

'I've thought of it.'

'So why not, sweetheart?'

'Already done it.'

'No.'

'A long time ago.'

'No.'

'When I was at school.'

'NO.'

He really has. He tells her how his school – a private school, a boarding school, a school with its own chaplain, a lake in the grounds and innumerable rugby fields, a movie-fed cliché of a school – entered a team. He was eighteen at the time. There were two teachers accompanying the sixth form, flying in the school's private jet via the Falklands, where they paused briefly to undertake essential geography fieldwork regarding penguins. In the Games, they finished seventh, highest placed of all the youth teams. Uniquely, she has precisely nothing to say to any of this. He thinks a little more.

'We could do the cross-country skiing. I didn't do that last time. Not a very good skier back then.' He brightens. 'That might be fun.' Though they are still on the phone she looks at him, appalled.

In an instant, time passes. They don't see each other for a while. One, or both, are playing hard to get. She's seeing other men; he's seeing other women, but he's thinking of her. She's not necessarily thinking of him, and thus has the edge in this respect. In the middle of December he logs on to a swimming-club chat room and finds her there as *Xnnie2s*, deep in conversation with someone called *TheTasteOfFloom*. They are discussing wedding details, though both are certain they will not marry. He makes his presence known. She is casual, almost disinterested. But eventually, and only after enduring repeated mocking interruptions from *lohengrin29* and *applesnapple* – cyberfriends of hers, apparently – he extracts from her a promise to meet, a few weeks hence.

Time passes, perceptible but swift. With his eyes on the prize he begins to plan. He has grown a grand design, fertilized its seeds with love and cunning. The rest is foretold, he knows it, he can see it. They will be together. And though he is in love with her he does not need to see her in the meantime. He does not need to call her. There will be time enough for that. He knows that she is in love with him, and he knows too that she does not yet know this. He will enlighten her.

Time, inevitably, passes.

It ends happily. They are having dinner together, some-where sensational, outdoors at the Acropolis, in a log cabin beside a Norwegian fjord, at a charming Italian restaurant overlooking the Aegean, in the penthouse flat of a New York skyscraper. They are warm and laughing, a little drunk, pleasantly so. The dinner – or perhaps merely the place where they are eating – is red and gold. Curtains, possibly drapes, curl warmly around. Behind them, a man with a vio-lin plays impossibly beautifully and utterly soundlessly. They are sitting across a table, but they and the table appear to be snug in bed. It is precisely as he knew it would be. He leans over and whispers softly into her ear, 'Imagine that we're penguins adrift on an iceberg.'

Deep Blue Sea

I Could Ride all Day in My Cool Blue Train

I live in a town full of rain, a liquid city. We've got water up to our gills and I'm having trouble breathing. The bilge-pumps are struggling and the overflows are overflowing – hell, even the *air* is wet. Before today it rained for thirty-three consecutive days and the water level went up eight inches. The Stilt was cramped enough already, and now the water's pushing up and we're pushing out. The Fixers are getting ready to build another level and move us all upstairs again.

All this water, and we can't drink any of it. We're down to two cups of clean a day. It's probably a good thing. Sal joked the other day that one misplaced piss and we might all be swimming. The clean pipe which runs from the purifiers up to the kitchen is beginning to taste no different to the rest of it. The water in the showers is thick and coloured and you feel cleaner without it. After the rain, everything stinks. The purifiers can only do so much. The food situation though is just about stable. There are seaweed crops. Some days we eat fish and some days we eat *fish substitute*.

As of last week, downstairs became submarine. It's like someone drowned my youth, because we were brought up down there. That was back when there were still children allowed on the Stilt, before all of that was taken over to the Dries. I was eleven then. A big transport arrived and mothers and children made a mass exodus. Except for me, because my mother was dead and I was sick and didn't qualify. They left me to see if I'd make it. I tell myself that maybe now that I

7

have, someone will come back. They never do, though. Soon after that the travel permits came in, and no one goes now who isn't taken. People arrive, and are put to work. But they never leave, no one gets permits now.

Once when the water was lower, before the Overboards were even built, I sat on a step and watched the last swan anyone here ever saw, floating in the water like a long-necked lily, an opening fist of a flower. Then the thunderous snap of its wings in take-off. The immense clean span of its flight. Maybe it's gotten bigger as I remember it, but it was *huge*. Even then it looked like a creature from myth. No one dared kill it, not for food.

But now the Overboards are built, everyone else I knew then is gone, no one's seen any kind of a bird except seagulls for years, and even they've finally learnt to stay away from the rigged netting we set. From time to time a helicopter flies over, going this way or that. Out to the west the line that looks like the horizon is actually the start of the Dries – a great levee keeping the water at bay. Though with the weather lately, I don't want to think about the kind of trouble they're having over there.

There is Upstream and Downstream. The main currents run right past town, and lately there's something dark in the Wide Channel, like a slip of oil spooned into the river and threading along it. They've cut off the inflow for a couple of days while someone works out who's dumping what, but in the meantime everything is progressively stagnating, and after all the rain there are traces of black even in the water downstairs. There are rumours it's infiltrated the seaweed crop, though I haven't been to see. Can't stand the smell there, is the thing. And no one knows what the dark stuff is. A couple of people have grown sick.

But I've been sick a long time, since the beginning. Since I remember, which is always. I get chills which come and go and I natter my teeth with nausea for a day. All I can do is give the doctor a call, then curl up and wait for someone to bring pills. They bring pills.

Those days I stay in my bunk. We're berthed in a raised railway carriage, the insides torn out and the bunks built in, just the blue of the upholstery remaining. Most days I'm the only person in. Everyone else works. It sways on stilts in the wind. And with the noise of the bilge-pumps churning away on the lower decks below, you might just think you're moving, if you take your pills and close your eyes.

I could ride all day in my cool blue train
If my cool blue train would just stay in lane

I've been writing lately but it hasn't been going well. No one likes the stories I've finished, and I can't seem to get them out. For a few days now I've been trying to write a story I've called 'Trash'. It's about a world ruined by a Major Climate Event so that everyone who can has left the world. The fire-fighters and geriatrics have gone off to live on the sun. Anyone who can afford it has relocated to cooler planets out in the solar system. There's just an underclass left on the world living in these tiny cells which are part of one great machine, which gives energy and cools the temperature to bearable by recycling waste. Air and water are strictly rationed. Nothing is thrown away. There's terrible over-crowding, but strict individual segregation has been established by some unknown controlling body, to quell trouble and prevent breeding. So there are these tiny cells full of the inhabitants' own waste and rubbish, and in one of these cells there's a desperate man who feels he does not belong there, who is forming a plan to get up out of the cells, and thinks that he could survive it all if only this one girl were there with him. *If you were with me*, he thinks, *I could survive it all*. But she's not, and I can't work out how to end it. I'm really not good at science-fiction. But I think it's a pretty funny story, considering. One they'll appreciate.

Yet even with the pills I can't get it done. I just curl up and get as warm as I can, and still I keep shaking. Then before everyone else gets back, I fall asleep, riding all night in my cool blue train. You can get travel sick staying in the bunks too long.

One Day I Grow a Horse's Head

Today I take my pills and grow a horse's head. It's something I've been meaning to do for a long while. When everyone else is out of the bunks I take my pills and my forehead splits and lengthens. I look for a reflection in the murky glass window, and I'm a horse, I'm a horse. I stay that way all day and by the evening I've got a big old headache in my big old head. Still, the thing about horses is that they're honest above all, and some days you need to be that way.

I get dressed and go deck to deck until I reach the bar. The rain's holding off and it's a dry walk over. Heavy tarpaulins hang over the bar entrance and you have to slide in through them. The air inside is close and thick. Everyone's there, everyone who can be. They can't drink water so they come to drink the whisky.

By the entrance on the inside there's the Idol. The Idol's made from an old diving suit stuffed with plastic straw, the suit itself too ripped and the rubber too spoiled to be any use. The head is a round mask with black stone eyes, like an insect's, and has two old flippers for oversized ears. The Idol blesses the bar, and if you baptize it with whisky it'll bless you too. But there's always the weighing up to do – precious whisky or unlikely luck? I always choose the whisky. After all, how lucky can anyone get?

Sal's waiting behind the bar, a worn look on his worn old face. He's standing beneath a fading drawing of an alligator someone did once, charcoaling it onto the wood wall at the front. The alligator grins, and I grin back.

'Whisky, Sal?' I say.

'You're late,' he says. 'Maybe when you're done. If you're good.'

He bangs the bar and things quiet down, a little. Sometimes

they want to listen and sometimes they don't. Tonight they don't seem too sure either way.

I stand up on the bar and read out a story. It's an old one but they haven't heard it, and I couldn't write anything new. It's about a boy and a girl who meet and fall in love and generally cause each other completely inexplicable amounts of happiness. They get engaged and exchange vows of *undying love* one perfect day. They live Happily Ever After, until one day when she tells him she's leaving him. She takes her bags and starts to walk out on him and he can't believe it, he's in tears, I mean he's being completely *torn apart* here because very real pieces of him are going out the door with her and the horrible bitterness on his tongue is a foretaste of his own death, but he gets himself together enough to say, *but you said you'd love me forever.* And this at least causes her to pause at the door, and she turns round, and he's waiting for her to Come Back In and Realize She Made A Mistake, and to Make It All Alright Again. Or at least *explain.* But in fact all that happens is that she slips a puzzled look on her face and she says, *well gee, honey, it sure* felt *like forever.* And off she goes.

They don't like this one at all. Some of the Fishers and Fooders who have been struggling all day to gauge and gain resources don't want to hear this kind of thing. They do not like it one bit, and for a minute I'm in danger of being lynched by a couple of the larger thugs. There is a distribution of discontent, which can always get nasty. Then one of the Lazy Sunbathers stands up from where he's been sitting, holding up his bag of stones, and things calm down. Grateful, I'm merely kicked out of the bar, forbidden to read stories for a week, and told in whispered threats that whatever it is, it had better be better next time, or I'll be looking for a new career.

As I'm being dragged out the crowd disperses, dousing the Idol with whisky on its way out to purify the place after my disturbing of the peace. Bad stories will do that. I go back to skulk in the bunks for a while. Then the chills come over me

and I get a heat beating at the thin skull around my temples
and my teeth begin to natter.

> *I could sleep all night in my cool blue train*
> *If my cool blue train would just kill the pain*

Getting Back Together Was One Long Negotiation

At the end of the week a helicopter appears and hovers overhead. I was with the chills up in the bunks and didn't see it,
but Sal did, and he comes by to tell me about the hovering.
He says he saw ropes flung from the inside of the helicopter,
and four men in black leap out and slide down, landing on
the decks where the canoes are usually moored. Not that we
have any canoes any more. He laughs and tells me that one
of the men took one step and fell straight in, before the others dragged him out. They waved to the helicopter, which
flew off. With a lot of slipping they got off the decks onto the
ladders and clambered like lizards up to the Overboards,
heading, for sure, for powwow with the Lazy Sunbathers.
They'll be out in their deckchairs wrapped in thick towels
against the cold.

I feel a lot better after he tells me that. Men don't come from
helicopters just to stay. They come with reasons. Something
important. Contact with the others is always good for the
Stilt. You can go for months otherwise and think that you're
all there is in the world. And then they might just have come
for you. You never know. I think to go over to the main deck
to see what's going on, but I know I'll never get close.

By then my ban from the bar is over so I spend the rest of
the day writing a story which I read out that night. The bar is
full, as it's always full. Everyone's in. There's something
strange about the atmosphere that I can't quite place. They're
waiting for news from the Lazy Sunbathers, apart from
everything else. We like to be kept informed. But the Lazy
Sunbathers aren't here, which means they're still in counsel.

All the same I sense there's something I'm missing.

'They're expecting better,' warns Sal when he sees me. 'Don't disappoint, will ya?'

He gives me some whisky and I take a bitter sip to loosen my lips. Then I climb on the bar and begin to tell them a story. It's a story set over in the Dries. It's about a terrible earthquake which consumes a city, and how all these wonderful buildings with people in them turn into mass graves of rubble. I know they'll listen. They like to imagine the Dries, or have it imagined for them. They like to hear words like *concrete* and *skyscraper*.

It's about how after the tremors died down and nearly everyone's dead and buried, the rescuers are making a futile and endless effort to search for survivors. And how constantly hanging around them is this one little girl who's just in floods of tears because she's lost her mummy, and she's lost her dog as well, and no one has any time to pick her up and comfort her.

It's an affecting story, seriously.

So this girl is wandering around crying and eventually one of the rescuers, an exhausted fireman, stops from lifting rubble and bends down to face her, and in his weary way is about to tell her that *everyone's dead* but that they will keep looking for her mummy, even though he knows in his heart that her mummy is certainly and painlessly pancake-flat, but meanwhile she should follow the other people back to the assembly point where she can get some food, because isn't she really hungry? He's just gathering these words together when there's a bark, and he's back and focused in an instant because he thinks it's one of the rescue dogs that's found someone – probably a piece of someone rather than the whole of someone – but then he realizes that the bark was muted and suppressed like it came from beneath the rubble, from where nothing's been heard for many an hour. A dozen rescuers triangulate on the spot and start shifting wreckage, just to get to this possibly trapped animal, because frankly any sign of life is going to feel like redemption on a day like that. Behind the fireman, though he can't see, the little girl's face has just lifted because she knows she just heard *her* dog bark, no way in heaven she'd fail to recognize it. And she quietens down and sits, waiting for the rescuers to fetch her dog.

Then there are no more barks and I play with my audience a little. You know – maybe they've dug in the wrong place, maybe the dog's going to be dead by the time they get there, maybe it's not really the girl's dog after all, that kind of thing. Keep them rapt. Then there's a huge block lifted and in an impossible crawl-space beneath it is the little girl's beautiful dog, looking up anxiously at the sudden light and all the people. And the rescuers are completely stopped in their tracks, because what is more, the dog is being held in a woman's arms, and the woman, though covered in dust and suffering some obvious distress and a trapped foot, is not only alive but *conscious*, and when they pull her out the little girl stands up and in the happiest tired voice you can imagine, says: *Mummy*. And her mummy reaches out a hand for the little girl and when their hands meet she says, *Oh sweetheart, it's all right sweetheart, I've got you.*

I hear Sal sob just behind me. The regulars are in tears. I swear there's rainfall from eye level down. Like I've precipitated a microclimate localized in the bar. With absolutely no exceptions, except for these four guys dressed in black who I only just notice at the table at the back, just around the curve of the wall. Who have apparently finished consultation with the Lazy Sunbathers and have come to sample from our whisky still. And who are not crying. Though they appear to be listening.

These, though, are distractions I can't deal with now. I haven't finished my story, even though they think I have. I regain their attention. I speak with scorn. I go on to say that, because they're crying, they haven't understood a word of what I've been saying, that they don't seem to realize that it was a terrible story, that *thousands of people died*, that the end-

14

ing was not a happy ending but a false one, a jarring one, an ironic one. That their reaction is sentimental and naive and disappointing, that despite everything here they're still pumped full of illusions, that they still have illusions practically *flowing* out of them.

That what they think I meant to say was: *there's so much crap in the world, and then all of a sudden there's honesty and humanity and hope*.

Whereas what I actually meant to say was: *it's all just crap*.

The silence continues just a bit longer, while they weigh this up. Then there is uproar. *You little fucking shit. You little fucking cunt.* This time there are none of the Lazy Sunbathers here to calm it down. Something glass is thrown hard at me, a whisky glass heavy in the air as it whisks past my ear and shatters against the alligator drawing. They do not like being mocked. They do not like being made to feel stupid. I jump down quick behind the bar, but Sal steps away from me. I had him, too. One of the big Fooders from the kitchen leans over the bar and makes a grab for me. He has tears still smudged in the dirt of his cheeks, but he's looking ugly, murderous. He's balled his fist. It goes back to his shoulder and I curl up down on the floor waiting for the pummelling. One blow hits my back but it's soft, he's in an awkward position leaning over and I sense him readjusting for better purchase. But nothing comes except air, and the noise is no longer all around, but becoming isolated. Everyone was shouting and now there's just one person shouting. I get up to see who it is.

It is one of the men in black. A ripple of silence emanates from him, goes along with his voice. He *shouts* and they *quieten*. I can see it crossing the room, and it looks like fear to me. They are afraid of this man. Who does not even bother to reveal his gun. Everyone already *knows* he has it. Even if no one knows who or what he is. No one has ever explained. Some things we just accept.

'Quiet,' he says finally, when he no longer needs to shout, and the whole bar is already quieter than it's ever been before. He looks round to catch the eyes of the room, and none of them seem inclined to meet him. Then he looks at me, and I look at him and I can't look away. He's younger than I thought. Just about my own age. Then he smiles, so quick it makes me doubt I saw it.

'Just *pipe down*, all right?' he says as he looks at me.

Then he sits down with the others and they resume their drinking, all in silence. And so does everyone else, but only in fear, not because they want to. They don't dare look at the men in black, but they look at me, and they haven't forgiven.

I want to go over to the table where the men in black have settled back down. They are not looking at me. I want to see if I recognize the others, if one of the men is perhaps a woman. If they have new friends now. Not that it matters. But Sal has grabbed my arm and pulled me back behind the bar.

'You'd better go,' he says. 'You might not be reading any more, but you'll live, if you're lucky. There's always a job in the kitchens, right?'

He pushes me into the back room, the one with the still. A yellow liquid bleeds through thin tubes where Sal turns water into whisky. I think to go back into the bar but then Sal would probably kill me himself, so I lift the trapdoor and go down the ladder into the dank lower decks, the rank smell of salt and rotting seaweed, the fetid warmth.

Deep Blue Sea

It's all very well feeling safe where there are protective men with guns around, but outside the bar there's no certainty that a Fisher or a Fooder won't be hanging around, waiting for me with a meat hook. And seeing as dumping bodies is an A-list crime at the moment (it pollutes the water Downstream, causing diplomatic issues), there would only really be the kitchen to drag me to, and *fish substitute*.

So I hang out for a while, not below decks where it's dark and shadows and I can't see anyone coming, but up on a small disused fishing deck far from the bar, near the carriage. It's cold, but I can live with that. There's a moon, off-round, but big and white and silvering the water so I can almost see the black in it. The clouds are thin grey ghosts speeding by on the ethers. I sit and shiver, and it's not the chills for once, just the cold. No one comes.

I get to thinking I might have been a bit hard on them with the story. After all, everyone here lost their mother once. Maybe I was wrong to mock their illusions. I get quite miserable, thinking about it. It makes me think I should write another story for them, to make up for it. But they'll never let me read again now. Which gets me further down. So I try and work out whether I'm going to be able to get out or not. I give the men in black time to leave the bar. I stay crouched on my deck and then when I think it's safe I just shin straight up a stilt and over to the carriage.

Back to my bunk room, but there's no sign of anyone, which I'd half been hoping. Maybe they haven't come after all. Maybe I misunderstood. But then I see my bunk. There, wrapped with an outrageously inappropriate blue ribbon and topped with an enormous matching stick-on bow, is an aqualung. It's a little battered, with a dent in the tank, but there is a gauge and a tap and a mouthpiece and I know it will work.

Beside the aqualung is a lattice of dry sticks tied together with twine. It looks like a cat's cradle of string, except there's a nagging familiarity to the design of it. A larger stick down the centre with a tiny white shell glued beside it, another shell at the edge of the criss-cross structure. I turn it both ways, circle it round, and looking down on it eventually work it out. It's a map of currents. The large stick is the Wide Channel. The shell beside it is a big arrow saying You Are Here. The other shell represents Something Else. And for a while I'd thought all the clues were going to be in code, and I'd be always wondering if they were even there.

I take the last silver strip of pills from my stuff, and make to pop a couple through. So I can do it. But then I stop. Perhaps the pills are a bad idea, the last thing I need. It's not the time to be confused. No pills today, then. My cool blue train will have to stay away. I'll be going under my own steam.

I sort my stuff and listen for sounds. About the time I feel the bunks will start filling up I gather my stuff together then leave by the Overboards. No one takes the Overboards at night because they're not that safe. Even if I hit the water when I fall, I can't swim. The water's not clean, so who learns to swim? If you fall in and don't get pulled out, you drown, the way my mother did. If you fall in and get pulled out, the way I did, you get sick.

This time, though, I don't fall. I thought I'd have trouble hauling the aqualung but its weight balances me. I take the high boards all the way until I'm above the bar, and then I wait up there till it empties and I see Sal come out. And then I wait some more. The misshapen moon circles round for a better look and the wispy ghosts go by.

I slide down a stilt and push through the tarpaulins. Inside it's pitch but I find the bar with outstretched arms and make my way round it. I reach up to the shelf with my hands, careful not to knock anything glass. I take the waterproof torch from the tin over the bar and switch it on, so I can operate quicker. I put the tin back. I dismantle, as quietly as I can, the Idol by the door, ripping its flipper-ears off and pulling free too some strands of plastic straw I can use, to tie them to my feet. I tear patches off the rubber suit for warmth.

And then I drag everything back up the stilts, tie the flippers to my feet and the rubber patches round my arms and legs. I belt up the aqualung and suck hard on the mouthpiece. The needle on the dial flickers, but doesn't drop down from the FULL indicator. I pick up the torch and the stick map. Then I lean backwards, knowing I should probably have tried to get down the ladders so I was closer to the water when I fell, but knowing too that the only way of persuading myself to get into the water at all was to take myself by surprise, a pre-emptive strike. With the heavy lung on my back I rocket downwards, overhead and headfirst, and penetrate the water. There's an immense splash that consumes me before I leave it behind. I'm so shocked I forget to go to the surface, then as I start to sink I begin to panic, until I realize I can breathe just fine. I appear to be all there. All here. Just the map disintegrated in my hand – I think I crushed it myself in the fall, or perhaps it wasn't meant to be used underwater. But I don't need it. I am by the little shell. I am heading for the other shell. I give my flippers a kick and I'm propelled pretty effectively through the murky water. Somehow through all of that I managed to keep hold of the torch in my other hand, and even luckier, the torch works.

I never thought I'd be submarine again, not after the first time. There are two things about the underwater that overwhelm me, only one of which I was expecting and that's the cold. It's not like air cold. Wrapping up doesn't help. The rubber doesn't help. There are cold currents and warmer currents, but basically it's cold like death. It presses in. My eyes are wide with it. All I can do is keep moving.

The other thing is the possibilities. A world in three dimensions of a scope bigger than I imagined. Directly beneath the boards it's not so deep – I can see the muddy bottom where most of the stilts are buried, and where the bar's anchor is half buried. The torch can sort of pick them out. But where the Wide Channel is, the water floor just drops sharp away into a trench and it opens out all oceanic and limitless, the water cleaner and the visibility too improved. Then you feel like you're floating above a great space, rather than thinking about how deep beneath the surface you are.

I know I have to cut first across the Wide Channel. I can see the stain of black running thicker than ever above me but I glide right beneath it through clearer waters. Just little kicks of my legs, flicking the flippers, and I move right along. I've never felt so free. I go kick kick kick slide.

I could ride all day in my cool blue train
In my cool blue train I'll shelter from the rain

I've a head-full of shells and shelters. I get out far beyond the Wide Channel. It's difficult now to keep my bearings, to be sure I'm still going away from the Stilt. Sometimes I have to stop kicking, to see if I'm being moved by a current, to see if it's taking me left or right or forward or back. I check my air and it's still in the upper half. I slip into one of the current streams and slide along with it. I start to keep an eye out for the pipe, if it's there, if I don't miss it. If I go too far, how do I get back?

Keep quiet there. Pipe down. There is a pipe, and I will follow it down. Those were the directions. It's good for once to have instructions. After you decide to follow them everything is easy, you don't need to make anything up.

The dial is registering almost empty, less than a quarter left, when I find the pipe. It is large and iron and runs along the sea bed, then turns a corner and plunges over a cliff, going straight down to where the moonlight doesn't reach. I shoot down along it, kicking all the way. I keep my torch on the iron side of the pipe and soon that's all I can see. The pressure hugs me, squeezes me till I start to feel dizzy. I can see cold and black and just a tiny patch of light and this pipe still going down. I could surface, but I'd never get back so deep again. And there's nothing up above me anyway. The surface seems a lonely place to be.

Just before the pipe runs straight into the mud floor there's an oval opening. My torch shines into it, but it's just the inside of a pipe. A small compartment. I swim in. With one hand and the torch looking I feel round the edge of the opening and find a door. Some kind of airlock. A door on the outside and somewhere then a door on the inside too. The first door shuts infinitely slowly. The dial on my air reads empty. I pull a breath and it still comes out so I hold it for as long as I can. I look for the switch or the sign or the way out. The second door. I scan the insides of the pipe section, trying to orient which way is up, which way is out.

Then the torch goes out.

Then I take a breath that cuts out half way through.

The tank is empty. My arms and legs spasm in a panic which takes hold of me, I'm squirming and kicking out, thrashing and trapped, until I bash my arm and feel the pain from it, a numbness heavier than the one already overtaking me.

There is something on the wall. Some kind of a handle on the wall. A circular handle on a shaft. I grasp it in my left hand and pull myself to it, holding what's left of my breath. Too late now to surface. Too late for most everything. Not too late to decide which way the handle turns, if it even turns. Clockwise. I turn but can't move it. Too late to try the other way? Or should I just keep forcing it? It might not have been moved for generations. Too late for any of this?

I bring my legs up past me and plant my feet on the wall. I grip tighter, apply torque. The last of the breath bubbles out of me with the effort. I suck but nothing else comes and my chest leaps like a mad heartbeat.

And then there is a give, a definite slight give. And then a further turn. But there is no air, and my arms and head are rebelling, threatening to convulse.

Everything is already black, but the black is coming further inside now, into my blind eyes and my empty lungs. I force the handle one last time and there is a silent roaring which takes everything away in a long dark falling, save the blackness.

It's the shivering that wakes me. My body shaking like a Fooder has gotten hold and is rattling me like a bag of stones. But my lungs are going, clattering in and out. The air is awful, and I make to reject every breath, but I stutter and cough and carry on. I pull off the heavy aqualung, which was lying awkward beneath me, keeping my face out of the water I'm in. I stand up and choke, and kick something with my foot, which turns out to be the torch. I can hardly get my hand to close on it, it seems to take minutes to get my grip. Irritatingly enough, the torch seems to be working again.

I look around. I'm in a pipe, but not the one I was just in, because this one seems to go horizontally. My hands can't untie the flippers and in the end I just rip them off. Some of the twine digs in my foot and cuts through the skin. My feet are too cold to feel it. The skin is blue and no blood runs. I choose a direction and start to slosh along through the water.

The pipe tilts upwards, fractionally. The water is definitely getting shallower. The inside of the pipe is thick with slime. It is dark and cold and heavy and where I am I don't know. I walk for ages, until the torch dims and the water's down to my ankles.

There is another door blocking my way but it has a handle which twists it open to a shrieking of rust and metal. The tunnel beyond it is cleaner. Less muck, less slime, hardly any water on the floor. And then I realize I don't need the torch any more. It was dark and then it isn't. There's a light at the end of the tunnel, a faint light, but it reflects off the wet of the pipe and I can see where I'm going. I turn the torch off to save the batteries, and stumble on.

At the end of the tunnel there's a sealed door with a thick window in it. And through the window I can see someone standing there with his back to the door, apparently guarding it. He's dressed in black like his own shadow and is carrying a large gun. Beyond him I can't quite make things out. Things seem to be green. Things seem to open out a bit.

I bang on the glass with the butt of my torch and the guard physically leaps about a foot in the air. He pulls his face up to the window and peers through, blind in the darkness. His face looks weird pressed up to the glass, I can see every flattened pore, and the panic in his eyes. Then a shift of the light or his eye and I know he can see me. We stare at each other a moment, and I watch his mouth drop open in slow motion.

Then he is gone. The seal cracks, the hatch opens inwards and I tumble in, and for a second time black falls all over me, but this time I'm grateful for the body heat.

There is shouting in a language I don't understand. Pinned on the soft floor I can smell something. Not just the shock of outside air after the aqualung's rarefied mix and the stagnant air of the pipe, not just that. Something else. Something too beautiful for words, something that needed to be shared. Something you'd smell that would remind you of your youth, maybe even something that would cause you to go back. I'm too crushed to start laughing, but the shivering starts, and makes me feel warm.

Afterlife

The Divorced Person, long before she became divorced, left college without completing her degree to marry a man she had met and fallen in love with. Two and a half years later she sat on the floor of her lounge with her two boys, twenty months apart, and watched helplessly as they cried and bawled and wouldn't stop. One of them held a pacifier and the other a bottle; she had got mixed up for a second and given each child the wrong thing. This was the first time she remembered thinking that this wasn't how things were supposed to be.

With the subsequent failure of many of her other expectations of life, the Divorced Person came to believe that nothing worked out the way it was supposed to. Over the years she built a list of evidence to back this up:

Item 1 – When the Divorced Person was separated from her (still, but only just) husband, when she thought they were still trying to work things out, he arrived one time at her house to collect the boys with another woman in the passenger seat of his car.

Until that moment the Divorced Person had not for one moment believed that the Other Woman, who was later to become her children's step-mother, was real.

The Divorced Person grew to hate the word 'step-mother', because she, after all, was the mother, and no one else had any right to use any variation of the name. It marked the beginning of a slow process of usurpation. Several years later the Other Woman would feel sufficiently confident, or malicious, to phone the Divorced Person's home to talk to her sons. On the first occasion this occurred the Divorced Person had been speechless with horror, and had let the phone drop slowly back into its cradle. Eventually, though, she became able to deal with these calls, and prided herself on this found ability. She never stopped wanting to rip the Other Woman's eyes out, however.

Item 2 – Her husband, when he had just ceased to be her husband and had become her Ex-, was self-employed, and did not have money to pay maintenance for their sons. Within two years he had made himself into a millionaire, moved to a huge house in South Carolina, joined an elite country club and taken up golf. At the country club he networked, made some useful connections, and later took one or two walk-on parts in major Hollywood movies.

How the Ex- made his money: by selling household appliances. His firm, Home Run, sold sinks, ceiling fans, kitchenware, shower fittings, toilet seats, light fixtures, and anything and everything else he could buy in cheap and ship out expensive, even kerosene heaters, before they were banned as unsafe. Which left the Divorced Person with:

Item 3 – At the age of thirty-three the Divorced Person found herself taking her boys (by then, there were three) from her tiny house along the streets of suburban Chicago to collect her welfare cheque. In that area, at that time, she was the only white woman in the line.

The Divorced Person grew quickly tired of Chicago during those years, of seeing her breath whipped away by the winds from the lake. Eventually she sought the geographical cure, and moved to Florida. After a time she found an apartment near the Gulf, the building surrounded by miles of cinderblock bungalows with lawns of thick, springy grass. Her youngest son, her favourite, who was then starting college, had worked all summer and gave her enough money to make the move. She rented a pick-up, paid her outstanding bills and drove south with 100 dollars in her purse and nothing in her life that wasn't in the pick-up. She even brought her cat, Al, who slept on the passenger seat the entire journey. Al was a beautiful thick-haired Persian (male) that she had adopted from an animal shelter after his previous owner (also male) had maltreated him as a kitten. Al retained a deep residual suspicion of men, and would slink away if anyone other than her sons came into the house.

The first Floridian house the Divorced Person's pick-up pulled up alongside belonged to an Old Schoolfriend. Her Old Schoolfriend was separated from her husband, the split having come quite suddenly during one spring clean when the Old Schoolfriend discovered her attic to be housing a large supply of heroin. She had kicked her husband out of the house that same evening, notwithstanding his defence that he only sold the stuff and was absolutely fastidious in never sampling the goods. She allowed him to take the heroin with him, because she didn't want it in her attic.

Item 4 – We think we know people better than we do.

But the Old Schoolfriend didn't want the Divorced Person's cat staying with them, so Al was driven for a couple of hours to stay with a distant cousin of the Divorced Person over by Orlando. 'At least he'll have some mice nearby,' her youngest son had said. The cousin already had three cats, but it became quickly clear that they weren't going to adapt to the presence of a newcomer. When the Divorced Person's son went over to see how Al was getting on he found that he was being kept in the garage, for his own sake, and that he cowered in a corner as the son went to reassure him. When Al and the Divorced Person were finally reunited it took Al several days to calm down and be comfortable around her, days which nearly broke her heart. Her cousin said: 'What d'ya wanna bring a long-haired cat down to Florida for, anyway?'

Twenty-four years after she had left college to get married, and when her children were old enough to look after themselves a little better, the Divorced Person decided to go back to school to finish what she had started. She took part-time jobs – as a teaching aide, a babysitter, in a restaurant – to help pay the bills, and sometimes worked three jobs in one day.

She accepted the first job she was offered after she graduated, in sales, working mostly on the telephone, selling chemicals for industrial cleaning. But she hated the work and quickly realized that there was nothing worse than getting up every day to do a job you detested. Within a month she had decided to go back to college to study for a postgraduate degree in Counselling, even though this meant returning to the draining routine of working by day and studying by night.

The last time she saw her supervisor before she completed her second degree he told her that only seven per cent of Americans had a Master's degree. This made her change her mind about life. She decided that there was, after all, a reason for everything, and that it all, even the bad, eventually worked out for the best. She gave up making lists, and began to try and think positively. She would ask her friends, 'Did you know only seven per cent of Americans have Master's degrees? Isn't that incredible?'

The Divorced Person began working as a counsellor in the Emergency Room of her local hospital. Mostly, this involved listening to the stories of the people who passed through. She came to understand that if you think your story is something, you only have to listen to the person next to you, that people live remarkable lives, and suffer greatly. So she would listen carefully and not interrupt until they looked at her and with their eyes asked for help. Then she would try to find the things to say they needed to hear. Often, she would tell them in a soft voice that there was a reason for everything, that things would work out for the best.

She called the Emergency Room the Gateway, because for

her it was a gateway to all human behaviour. Pretty much anything could come through the door, and most things seemed to, at one time or another.

Here is one story from a single night at the hospital: the Divorced Person was counselling a woman who, just hours before, had become a widow, her husband having shot himself in the garage of their home and the doctors having failed to revive him. The widow explained that her husband, a dentist, had recently bought her a new car, a shiny black Mercedes. A week later he had spilled coffee in it, staining the leather on the passenger seat. The widow told the Divorced Person, her counsellor, how mad she had been, and how she had complained and shouted at him for his clumsiness, his stupidity. She showed the Divorced Person his suicide note which read, in its entirety: 'Enjoy your new car'.

This was the one time when the Divorced Person had not felt obliged to tell her client that everything worked out for the best. She hadn't really known what to say at all.

Dentists, she learned, had the highest rate of suicide for any profession in the US. She worried what this might say about her country.

When the Divorced Person was a child, long before she was old enough to dream of marriage, never mind divorce, her mother had said to her that she only had to open her mouth to blurt out some family secret or other. It was many years before she realized that there was no such thing as a family secret. As a mother she encouraged her children always to be open with her, and to share with her everything they thought or worried about. She wanted to be a good father and a good friend to them, as well as a good mother.

The experience of being a single mother, she liked to say, meant that she talked openly and freely with everyone, not just her children. In her self-sufficiency she grew smart and sassy. She developed a cutting wit, a greater analytical perspective. Her children liked this a lot, though single men seemed to find it uncomfortable. Her youngest son told her she was good company. She knew the Ex- would no longer like her. If he ever had.

She hadn't been so clever when they divorced. Already worrying about money, she had hired a cheap lawyer, who had been desperately ineffectual in the face of her then husband's (but only just) expensive one.

While her children were still children they moved between her place and their father's. As the Ex-'s wealth grew this became a movement between poles. By the time her youngest son was at school he was either the richest or poorest kid in his class depending on which parent he was staying with that week.

Her youngest son was six when they divorced. To compensate for their father's absence she put up posters of inspiring sportsmen around the house, so they would have positive male role models to look up to. Posters of Dwight Gooden – Dr. K. – before the revelations about his cocaine use; of Michael Jordan, then a young player on a weak Chicago Bulls side, in mid air, gold chains swinging as he slam-dunked a ball; posters of Bill Walton and Jimmy Connors. She let them choose their own pictures, as well. Her eldest son liked Kiss, and her middle son was a fan of Cheap Trick. She let them argue about it, so that they might discover for themselves that people would always live different lives. She took them to watch football games, and went along to the school to watch their first faltering efforts at baseball and basketball. She left small notes on their pillows with encouraging messages on, thanking them if they'd done something to help around the house, or just telling them she loved them. When they were very young she helped them to make lists of the things they wanted to achieve with their lives. When her two eldest had left home for college and her youngest was eighteen she found a list on the desk in the youngest's room. It read:

Some Things I Want to Accomplish

1.   *Learn how to speak a foreign language (French?)*
2.   *Be in business by myself at the age of 30*
3.   *Have a $100,000 in the bank by the time I am 32*
4.   *Be a millionaire by the age of 35*
5.   *Be able to play a musical instrument (piano?)*
6.   *Be married by the age of 35 with a child*
7.   *Be able to sing with the best of my ability*
8.   *Own a residence in New York, London and some place warm (French Riv?) by age 40*
9.   *Be more articulate, enunciating my words better*
10. *Obtain better posture*

After all her boys left home she spent many hours talking to them on the phone, speaking with at least one of them each night. Often, when they were out of work or on holiday they would come and stay with her for a few days or weeks. The eldest had taken a good job with a TV station and had moved to New York. The middle son moved to LA, and seemed to work in a different job every week. He, atavistically, was most like her own dad; a manic depressive. But back when the Divorced Person was a child, when her parents' marriage was the only example of marriage she had, and she had taken marriage for granted (indeed, when the sacredness of marriage had been repeatedly drummed into her, such being the benefits of a Catholic Education), mental illness was not something that was ever spoken of. These days her father, if he were still alive, would be given drugs to balance out the chemical swings that caused the mania and depression. Back then she had just known to watch for the times when she must keep out of his way.

The Divorced Person spent a lot of time talking on the phone. After the divorce she needed to create for herself a support system, a network of friends and family she could talk with and belong to for a while. Later, after she qualified as a counsellor, her role changed. Her friends, then, mostly rang her for support and advice. People she counselled at the hospital would call her at home if they needed more help. As it turned out she was extremely good at her job. Things tended to work out for the best.

She liked Florida, the laid-back low-rise look of it and the contrast with Chicago's tower blocks. She missed watching the July 4th fireworks which bloomed every year over the lake, but in return she had gained the pyrotechnics of sunset, which came every evening. In Florida she could sit outside on a deckchair in November and December to watch the Thanksgiving and Christmas parades without growing cold. There were parades of floats through the town (hundreds of floats put together by the Shriners, by local schools and companies and Scout groups and TV stations), then parades of boats bedecked with fairy lights, murmuring along the Intercoastal.

She liked the Highway – forty-one – peppered with endless malls and strip malls. She bought clothes for her sons, then later for her grandchildren too. Drove past neon signs advertising churches, palm readings. Stores which sold leather goods, books, pizzas, boats. Even the neon was calmer here in the South. In summer she swam in the Gulf, but she grew used to the higher temperatures, and found that she got chilly in the mild winters. If the water dropped beneath seventy she sneaked into the heated swimming pools of nearby hotels, where she talked happily with tourists from England and Germany. Her sons swam in the Gulf all year round. At Christmas she would tell them, 'You're crazy. There's a heated swimming pool just along the street.' Would listen to them reply, 'Mom, the Gulf is right *across* the street.' She shivered at the thought.

She never returned to Chicago. If anyone from there rang her she would ask them, 'You got any snow up there?' It didn't matter what time of the year it was.

When she had been in stable employment at the hospital for two years, the Divorced Person was able to set up her own private clinic. She rented an office in a downtown building, sharing with a lawyer friend. For much of the time she kept the clinic running she had just three pro bono clients, but she didn't mind this at all. When her youngest son was on the fringes of his high-school basketball team she told him, 'If you don't put anything in you won't get anything out.' The following season he had made the team. She told herself she was a terrific mother.

The Divorced Person's best friend worked as a Guardian, a nominated helper who took responsibility for the care of an old person no longer fully able to care for themselves. It was always a boom business in Florida. Most of the people the Divorced Person had met in this profession were in it for the money, which was plentiful and easy. They wore a pager. They gave permission for a leg to be amputated (or whatever). They cared over the phone. So the Divorced Person had known right from the start that there was something different about her Best Friend, long before they became friends, when she met her taking her ward for a slow walk through the park on a Saturday afternoon. It was simply unheard of. In fact, the Best Friend took her ward for a walk every day, usually pushing the wheelchair along the boardwalk in the evening to watch the sun set over the Gulf.

Like her, the Best Friend was divorced, and had faced similar financial struggles in the aftermath. Like her, the Best Friend was on less than amicable terms with her Ex-.

The Best Friend was, the Divorced Person liked to say, using her best imitation Southern-Belle accent, a gen-yu-ine Steel Magnolia. She had been raised in the Deep South, where nothing more had been expected of her in her home than to look pretty. The men would do the work. Prior to her divorce the Best Friend hadn't even known how to sew a button. These days she ran a small sideline in repairing her friends' cars, and had installed in her ward's bungalow garden a water sprinkler system with underground pipes. Frequently the Divorced Person wished she could do that.

But the Best Friend had less luck raising her children, and was not close to them. Her son and daughter grew up with her Ex-, and the bitterness she felt then developed into a deep distrust of youth in general which occasionally found itself expressed in frank (and sometimes vitriolic) criticism of the Divorced Person's sons. The Divorced Person learned to anticipate these outbursts and inured herself to them.

The Best Friend did shocked: 'You mean he didn't call you?' Appalled: 'They're so ungrateful.' And disbelieving: 'You bought him *that*?'

'She's part of the Fruit and Nut Society,' the Divorced Person's youngest son would say, after suffering many of these comments in his presence. 'That just about sums it up,' the Divorced Person would agree.

When one of her sons came to stay the Best Friend always commiserated with her about how terrible it must be to have her space invaded. This might have been true. You get used to living alone, unable to make the compromises of sharing. She saw it time and time again in the failed marriages of her friends and colleagues. But the Divorced Person had lived alone for only very short periods in her life. More often than not one or another of her sons was there with her. She didn't feel as though they had left. She had Al. And when she was alone she spent all her time talking on the phone to her friends and family, though never, not once, to the Ex-. No, her greater fear was that when her sons came home they wouldn't take her loneliness quite away. Sure, they were company, and good for hugs. They were good at being cooked for and looked after, good at being made content and appreciative. They could take you for days out, meals out. But they could not stay, and even while they did the Divorced Person went alone to her room each night. It was good to have people she loved in the house once more. But her room at night was still empty, and sometimes still she cried there, quietly, so as not to wake her sons.

The main difference between the Divorced Person and her Best Friend was this: after they had known each other for a couple of years they took a trip through Europe, a tour arranged by a company, which took them by luxury coach from country to country and from hotel to attraction. For the Divorced Person the highlight of the holiday was Prague, which seemed more fairytale than reality with its ancient spires and bridges and towers. For the Best Friend the highlight had been the location tour for *The Sound Of Music*.

It took a while after the divorce, but after that while the Divorced Person dated other guys, mostly great guys whom she stayed in touch with even after things didn't work out between them. They all seemed to suffer from the same problem as the Ex-, namely the inability to commit. If this was what it was. She knew this about each of them when she started seeing them, but wanted them anyway. She wondered what it would take for her to learn the lesson.

From time to time her Best Friend introduced her to men, and she came to spend some time with one of them, a quiet, slight man, who had been in Vietnam. He was painfully shy. If she visited him at his bungalow on the way back from the hospital they would sit in his garden, by the pool, while he slowly drank a beer. Sometimes he was so quiet she'd forget he was there and she'd start, suddenly surprised to be sitting alone in a strange garden. His house was mostly empty – a bedroom, a TV and stereo in the lounge. There was a stand-alone bookshelf, out of place in the corridor which ran through to a small kitchen. It contained a couple of books on the war, a manual on motorcycle maintenance, a handful of true-life accounts of crime. There was a *Playboy* magazine perpetually ditched in a waste bin beside the shelves.

Sometimes they ate out, because she preferred eating in restaurants. She hated cooking. If the Vietnam Veteran took

her out for a meal they would go to the same ribs place in a
strip mall by the highway, where they would sit in the same
leather-backed booth in the far corner and watch the other
customers. To her, they always seemed fat, obese, and she
wondered if she looked the same to them. She was a little
afraid of this, and convinced the Vietnam Veteran to accom-
pany her instead to an Italian restaurant she drove past on her
way to work. She thought she had an Italian background,
somewhere. She thought she was part Italian.

If the Divorced Person did eat at home it was always something she could share with Al. She sat on her sofa, holding
snacks in front of her and smiling as he waddled over, then
stretched, placing his forepaws high on the armrest, his back
feet still on the floor, stretched in an arc like a violin bow –
though a fat violin bow – one paw taking a swipe at her
shoulder, aiming for attention.

Her own apartment overflowed with her belongings. She
shopped in thrift stores, accumulating gradually. She bought
innumerable boxes of decorations for Easter, Halloween,
Thanksgiving and Christmas, then decorated liberally, wild-
ly, even if she was celebrating the festival alone. From Europe
she brought back two suitcases of souvenirs, mostly from
Prague. She brought puppets, carved leather masks, sculpted
bones, framed photographs, dolls in national dress, brass
bells and wax candles, and put them all on display in her
front room.

The Divorced Person's dishwasher was broken. Crockery
came out dirtier than it went in, with the remnants of food
dried across the plates like fish scales. But while she was waiting for someone to come and fix it the Divorced Person used
it anyway, because she couldn't afford a new one and
because she couldn't bring herself to do the washing up. She
scraped the plates clean as she emptied the machine. It
seemed to take forever.

When the Vietnam Veteran came round to her place he
slipped out onto the balcony where he hovered and watched

the sun set over the Gulf, or that small part of the Gulf she could see between the apartment blocks, that just happened to contain the part of the Gulf the sun set over. He lived alone all his life. When she called round to his place she found him out back, working in the garage or the garden. 'You doing some yard work?' she called out as she walked round from the front. She waited a long time for him to ask her out, properly ask her, but he never did.

This was the one thing the Divorced Person really regretted: the failure of relationships in her life.

For a while she believed that she should have no regrets. But she came to understand that this was naive and incompatible with human nature, or with her nature, at least. She saw too many people damaged as they left things behind without regret. They always went on to make the same mistakes over and over again. Instead she told her clients and her friends that the trick was to have regrets, then to face them down, if you were going to make anything from your life.

She faced her regret most days. It rose and fell with the tide, as if the moon were somehow to blame.

The Divorced Person quit her job at the hospital, not that she hadn't liked her work there, because she had, but eventually the pressures from some of her colleagues became too much to bear. She was asked to fill in for colleagues when they were away or sick, even though she was never away or sick herself. Eventually she became tired of giving up her days off, and told them no. After that it seemed as though there was always someone out to get her.

The nature of her fellow staff seemed to change in those later years, as well. It turned out that one of the doctors she knew at the hospital ran a sideline in prescribing drugs for fake patients, to build up a supply he could later sell. All of this came out much later, after she had left. The doctor had written hundreds of prescriptions for his wife, who knew nothing about any of it, nothing about the morphine or the methadone, and when they finally came to her house to ask about it she made protestations of innocence which were not widely believed.

The last patient the Divorced Person counselled was a woman who had been brought in while the police searched her flat. The woman had been unable to sleep because of the persistent cries of a child somewhere in the neighbourhood. She had complained to her landlord several times, but it appeared that there were no babies living within an even remotely audible distance. No one else complained about the noise. The day after she sat and comforted the woman the Divorced Person was told that the police had found the mummified corpse of an infant in a chest at the bottom of the woman's wardrobe. Date of death: approximately four years earlier. Cause of death: unknown. So the Divorced Person resigned, after a lengthy meeting with her boss in which she told him straight out all her grievances. She felt immediately better.

Even the bad works out for the good. And because she had once counselled, at three in the morning in the middle of her graveyard shift, a woman who had been brought in by the police after she was found wandering the streets, she was offered a job by the woman's husband, who ran the Jewish Family Center in the next town along the highway.

There is a reason for everything. At the Jewish Family Center, where she was the only *shiksa* in the entire clinic, her employers were delighted to find that she had plenty of experience working with adolescents. They felt it would be ideal preparation for her new job, where most of the clientele were geriatrics.

The change in job threw her out a little for a few days. The foods in her fridge were mismatched. When her eldest son phoned she sneezed down the line. 'Allergies, or something,' she said. 'Miserable.' He worried, because she never fell ill – a stint working in a school, then the years at the hospital had almost certainly exposed her to every kind of virus or bacteria you could mention. She imagined she had become immune to them all. Her eldest son telephoned the middle son, then unemployed in LA, and he had come to take care of her for a few days. He found her room piled high with clothes and linen and Al's playthings. But within a day of his arriving she tidied up and got on with things, and her cold left her.

The Divorced Person, who had accepted a pay rise when she moved jobs, spent some of her new money on weekly trips to a masseuse. Her masseuse, a calm and spiritual woman, would greet her each Thursday afternoon with an unlikely pep talk, a motivating 'Are you ready to relax? Are you ready for healing?' It seemed a strange way to make someone relax, but it seemed to help, so she never remarked on the strangeness.

Her Best Friend went on holiday to Honolulu and posted her back a coconut, the address painted in white on the shell.

The Divorced Person spent a lot of time on the beach. Some days in the roily blue-grey it was impossible to make out where the sky ended and the sea began. Some evenings, in the last light of the sun a brilliant green pulse would glow briefly over the Gulf, a quirk of refraction she saw three times in the first fourteen years she was there.

Nights she listened to the waves, the ratcheting chant of the cicadas and the persistent rapping of the rope against the flag pole on top of the beachside apartment block. Then she watched hospital dramas on cable.

Days when she wasn't working she watched the dolphins surface in pairs. Great blue herons standing stock still, like garden ornaments, pelicans diving for fish then swallowing them whole. Egrets which rose and fell with the tide. She realized that even now, sometimes, she could be afraid of making a living, of how you do this. She walked on the beach and wondered how she had grown so old, why she was happy, and she waited for her sons to build her the beach house which was the one thing she asked them for each Christmas.

Movie in Ten Scenes

On

I go on in to the flat, size things up. His wife's not around, but then I know that because I spent a careful two minutes ringing the doorbell, then another five peering through windows. God knows I'll be mortified if I get caught like this. Orson wasn't even sure if there was a wife, but a glance through the window into the lounge was confirmation enough. Even the wall lights have frills, for Chrissakes.

The key fits smoothly, and for some reason I'm surprised when the door opens and I walk in. It's an uncanny feeling walking into Somebody Else's Place, like walking around naked. Burglars must get to enjoy it. Perhaps elderly burglars become flashers. Not a thought to dwell on. I take my shoes off at the door, have a quick look inside, peer out through the windows.

I signal Ron the all clear and he gets out of the car. The street's empty. I put my shoes back on to go give him a hand with the body, which is freaking heavy. I have no idea who Ron is, except that Orson knows him. He's reliable, says Orson, very discreet.

He holds Alan beneath his arms, and hauls him from the back seat. I grab the legs. He's wearing shoes polished like beetles. Trousers a fraction too short, not a fashionable man. We carry him inside, where we have a choice of set-ups. In the armchair, newspaper across his chest, TV playing? Collapsed by an open fridge door, milk carton spilling out around him? Ron points out we don't know if he even drinks milk.

He could have been putting it away, I say. Maybe they have a cat. I point out the cat-flap, a murky U-shape low in the back door. Here, kitty kitty.

No point in speculating, he says. Armchair's a safer bet. Less grief.

You have to be sensitive about these things, after all. We put the TV on in the background. *Grandstand* plays, which seems right, Saturday afternoon a long eternity to die in. We put Alan in the chair, still in costume, as though he'd just got home and sat down. Looks convincing to me. I try and straighten up his head and it lolls back to the side. He's not rigorous yet. There's a chance we bruised him in lugging him around, but I can't bring myself to check, and then what would I do about it anyway?

Keys, says Ron. In his left pocket.

I was about to walk out with them and lock the door behind me. Ron's professionalism is beginning to disturb. Anyone would think he might have done this kind of thing before. He's just a little

too

proficient. His confidence is contagious, mind, and even I begin to think that we've gotten away with it scot-

free.

So Ron and I go to the pub. Where we undertake a serious and sustained steadying of nerves.

But maybe I should tell you what happened

before.

A few months back I bump into Orson in a pub. I've known him since art school, where I roomed with his brother. Orson was at college then, but dropped out to become a business-man, realizing money came easily to people like him. People trust him, which is unnerving, given his reliable unreliability.

The place I see him in is a swamp of carpet, crimson and blue, a morass which spreads up the front of the bar and halfway up the walls. Anything dropped into it – loose change, pint glasses, mobile phone – immediately disappears. No point or pleasure in looking. It's afternoon, and I've just come in for an early couple of drinks before I go out later. Orson's leaning against the bar with a glass of white wine, on the lookout for someone. I don't expect it to be me, and so I don't make an effort to hide. He sees me and waves me over, and I kick myself on the way. There's no ignoring the man though – he has this persistence which gets affecting after a while. After a while I even start paying attention. He's telling me he wants to make a film, and that he wants my input. He wants to do some kind of gangland feature, he says.

What the freak, I say, do you know about that?

He shrugs. I've been to the movies, he says. Anyway, I'm only going to make the film.

Right, I say. I tell him he should maybe be more original. Gangster movies been done, I say. You need something new.

That seems to make an impression. He goes away to think about this for a while, to come up with some ideas. I don't expect to hear any more on the subject. Next time I see him he'll have another project on. This is the way with Orson. ADHD, no follow through. All fine as long as he has something on the go. His brother was just the same, until he ran out of ideas. Went back to live with his mother and never came out of his room again. Orson refuses to talk about him, gets quite upset about it, so I always remember to ask.

After a couple of months I bump into him in a pub.

Nah, he says. I want to do a gangland feature. He starts talking about the shots he wants, so naturally I ask about the script. He looks askance, calculating a schedule.

How long will it take you to put one together? he says.

I give him an X-ray stare, trying to make eye contact with a girl two pubs away. He tries it for a minute then folds.

I'll pay, he says.

Couple weeks, I say. And mine's a pint. Thanks.

So I go back to my flat where I can't pay the rent, watch a few videos and bang out a short script. I just steal scenes from old gangster movies and tie them together. It's a blag, but then so's Orson. He doesn't know freak about films. He does have money though, enough for a vanity project like this one, and that money has to go somewhere, so as long as it goes somewhere near me I don't mind.

Five

months on from that and we're in production, which is to say a bunch of his mates are working on putting the thing together. We're standing on a south London back street hanging around until someone tells us what to do.

Two old mates of his – bouncers from some club, I think, are the PAs, that's Ron and Thor. The DP is some guy with movie experience. He's told me his name six times now and I still can't remember it. Miles? Don't know where he came from, and he doesn't act like a friend of Orson's, so I can only assume he's being paid, which means he's smart, at least, so I warm to him. Then there's Dylan, the sound guy, who seems all right, and Orson's girlfriend, Cheryl, who's doing make-up, mostly on herself. Then there's Kharli, a girl Orson is openly trying to shag. She's in charge of the vagaries of continuity. By my count we're short at least a production designer, and probably a few degrees of expertise in other areas too. I'm strictly moral support at this stage, by which I mean I expect things to go badly wrong, and wouldn't mind seeing the implosion.

We have two cameras – Orson's own digital camera, an object about the size and appearance of a cigarette lighter, and an old Arriflex. Dylan the sound guy has his own Nagra sound gear.

Alan, our lead, is a nervous bunny. Orson dug him out of some pub, he hasn't seen the light of day for a while. The camera's gonna eat him alive. He looks the part, though. An ageing gangster about to keel. Wrinkles like he sucked so hard on his cigarette his whole face collapsed. Even has a scar on his palm, wide and old, running right across, the result, he says, of a paper cut. Alan's in insurance. But he's desperate for this. More deluded, even, than Orson. My last chance, he keeps on saying. Keeps talking about Vinnie Jones. If Vinnie can do it, he says. Or: Vinnie's gone and done it. His voice is freaking fantastic – hoarse and whispered. Brando never smoked forty years just to get a part. He sweats like a sponge whenever he's about to go camera front, and somewhere among the chasms in his face mascara collects and clogs – there are pores there that haven't been air-permeable since the seventies. Cheryl the make-up lady is on strike, hands up. She wrings out her mascara brush.

S'all right, says Orson. Seediness, innit?

Alan pushes his matted hair across his forehead. It looks like a frond of brown seaweed – wet and ill.

We get going. Kharli flounces in front of the camera and wields the clapper-board. SCENE 5A, TAKE 1, she yells. The Arriflex whirs, until it starts to grind.

Can't you stop that BLOODY camera making that BLOODY sound, Orson asks the DP. He shouts when he swears, I think because swearing sounds wrong coming from him and he's self-conscious about this, so tries to add some emphasis, avoid sounding so bloody silly. It doesn't work, needless, but it's a little uncanny.

I could switch it off, suggests the DP, unfazed.

The sound guy shrugs. All I can hear is the camera, he says. They gather round and prod it, but the grinding clank isn't so malleably fixed.

We go to the pub.

Orson gets on his phone and half an hour later the guy from the camera shop joins us. We caught him just before he went off to do some sky-diving shoot. He does mid-air weddings, that kind of thing. Did a nude one, once, and when he

45

mentions that he offers copies of the video for a fiver, seems surprised when there are no takers. The camera's sitting on a pub table surrounded by a half dozen pint glasses, a wine glass and two spread packets of crisps, salt and vinegar. The DP lets it grind a little.

Film's not loaded properly, says the camera-rental-shop guy. He and the DP drag it over to a nearby empty table to sort it out. They sort it out no time.

Everyone packs up to go, downs pints. The camera-shop guy comes over to me, chiefly because I'm conspicuously inactive with chores. He looks thoughtful. Do you think they'll let me pack my parachute here? he asks.

Finding the camera-shop guy a place to pack his parachute is the least of our troubles. Permits, for example. Impossible to get hold of. We've adopted a hit-and-run approach to getting the required locations and there is undeniably something about our film-making which is reminiscent of a car crash. Or extras. Most scenes require a few, and we thought we'd just get whoever was at hand to fill in. No lines to learn, promises of exposure. You'd think people would *want* to be in a film – even a short. If you read the relevant press you'd think that was all people wanted, spent their entire lives waiting for the day. You'd only think that if you hadn't spent two hours on the street stopping passers-by and saying, wanna be in a film? Right up until you asked them they probably thought they did. But then they get all coy and self-conscious – I swear one woman giggled. I wasn't even asking for a date, I was serious.

Do I wanna be in a film? Is that a line? one girl asks.

Uh, maybe? I say.

No, she says.

And fair enough. She agrees to be an extra, though. That's how it goes. She gets to be a moll, and Cheryl does her hair up a little. Everything progresses remarkably well. After a while we go to the pub for a break, to get our

kicks.

When we get back we do the scene from *Armoured Car Robbery*. The scene in the restaurant from *Goodfellas*, so the DP can reverse zoom like he wants to. We do one or two other scenes from *Goodfellas*. Because there wasn't much in the video store when I went we do a whole bunch of scenes from Tarantino, which he certainly nicked from somewhere else anyway. We do scenes from *The Killing*. We do the gunfight from *Grosse Point Blank* except we replace the

7-Eleven

with a local Co-op. We have to pay for any merchandise we blow up. We smash a couple packets of crisps.

Save the best till last. The key scene is the demise of the elderly gangster, Alan. It's the scene where he suffers a heart attack. It's the scene from *The Godfather* with Brando and an orange, minus the orange. Orson doesn't know that. As far as he's concerned it's All My Own Work, by which I mean he thinks it's all his own work.

You see, he tells me as we're setting up. I could have had him shot. Being a gangster, that would be expected. But then he has a heart attack. See? It's so *true*.

He waves to Alan. Ready for your big moment, mate? he says.

I wanted Alan to be carrying a bag of groceries, and to drop them so that an orange rolled out and away for the camera to follow, but Orson wasn't keen. We want the Godfather, he says, not the BLOODY Grocer, so maybe he has seen it after all, or just got lucky. I don't want any BLOODY fruit in the film, he says.

Kharli's bored, letting Cheryl do her nails. Thor's been drinking steadily since this morning. Every twenty minutes or so there's a loud crunch as he folds down the can he's been drinking from, then a clatter as it lands inside the back of the DP's van, which by crew consent has become a rubbish bin.

He's no longer standing so much as rolling on the spot, like he's on a ship in a gale.

Orson wanders off to talk to Kharli about something, and seems to forget we're ready to go.

Behind his droopy lips Alan's tight-lipped. He's in turmoil with the pressure, standing off to one side. I notice he's wearing a different coat to the one he wore in the previous scene, but that's Kharli's job, not mine, so I keep quiet. I feel a real need to go to the pub.

There's the sound-speed, camera-speed dialogue. Orson finally gets concentration.

And . . . action. Oh, right, we're going.

Alan clutches his chest, tries to breathe. Doesn't fall like we instructed him to or we rehearsed, just bends over like he's out of breath and kind of folds downwards from there, putting his left hand on the pavement while he clutches his chest, and then rolls over. He plays it for all it's worth. He's good. Really very good. Even this high-pitched wheeze like air barely squeezing in and out of his lungs. Ron and Thor tweak the reflector boards so the light plays across his face.

Bloody prima donna, mutters the DP halfway through.

Blimey, says Orson, when it's over. Cut.

Nearly gave me a freaking heart attack, I think to say, but I'm a little

late.

The sound guy starts to applaud, but cuts off embarrassed after three claps. Bang bang bang oops. Alan holds his position, milking it, so we ignore him.

Eventually the DP, the sound guy and me decide we'd better go over to see if he's okay. I nudge him with my foot, but he just stays there lying curled up like a puddle. The sound guy leans over and fingers for a pulse.

Oh freak, he says. Alan's dead.

Now that's method, says the DP.

I go over to Orson, who's already looking in his notes for the next shot.

He's dead, I say.

Yeah, says Orson. Not bad.

He wonders what I'm on about, with a look which says, it was in the script, dumbass, and you *wrote* the freaking script. Of course he's freaking dead. Then something like comprehension dawns and he looks at me, then over at Alan, still in character. Beyond the call of his unwritten contract. The penny drops from a great enough height to dent his forehead between the eyes and empty out his middle.

He's dead? says Orson.

Orson panics. Blah blah blah and I'm shooting a freaking snuff movie? Without insurance? I have a BLOODY schedule to keep to. I have a BLOODY film to finish. The BLOODY BASTARD didn't tell me about his BLOODY heart, did he?

According to Orson there's no question of an ambulance or police, or even getting a doctor on set. That would lead to undue and adverse complications. He puts his mind to thinking.

Meantime for something to do we put the dead guy in the car. The seat goes back. If anyone asks, the star is catching some zzzs in his dressing room. Kharli starts crying and Cheryl goes over to comfort her.

He was very old, she says. All that smoking can't be good for you.

After a few minutes standing around, Orson looks at me and smiles, then at Thor and looks annoyed, then at Ron and smiles again. No problem, says Orson. Everything's going to be fine. The solution always presents itself. Just breathe deeply and count to ten. It's gonna be

fine.

I can't help but admire his confidence. I can't help but feel nervous about the way he looked at me. I get prepared to say no to whatever he suggests I do.

When we meet up at his flat later that night we plug the cigarette-lighter into the TV and watch the rushes. Orson's eyes are gleaming desperately, like a gambler nowhere near the end of a losing streak. He breathes out slow. Authenticity, he whispers.

That, he says, is bloody fantastic. He even forgets to shout.

They're gonna know, I suggest. When they see the film. Some doctor somewhere is gonna look at this and remember how he died and they're gonna say *wait a freaking minute* and they'll just *know* it's for real.

He thinks about this.

Nah, he says. It wasn't *that* good.

Then

I steer clear of Orson for a few weeks. Last time I saw him he's no longer on the film kick. He tells me he went to Alan's funeral, which I didn't know. Showing impressive sang-froid. Barefaced tells the widow there that Alan was great on set, that he seemed so healthy when we dropped him home. She tells him that some doctor told her that his acting out of a heart attack may have triggered something in his genetic memory, so that when he got home it happened for real. That's my Alan, she says, he always was that bit impression-able. Orson sympathizes. He tells me he made a speech at the service about how Alan had just discovered something he was good at, how he could have been great, how he could have been a contender, instead of dead, which is what he is.

I don't believe a word of it. The man is, after all, a mytho-maniac, a living cult of personality. For the sake of making an impressive impression there's not a single sly lie he wouldn't tell. I breathe deeply, count to ten. Orson tells me there's something he wants to talk to me about, some offer I can't refuse.

He offers to buy me a drink.

We go to the pub.

Dream #62
3/10/__

Hobbled by wealth and technology, no longer of practical use, lacking the physical means to claw himself from the resultant chemical pits of depression; decontextualized, his primeval hardness deprived of outlets, his aggression blunted and bent against himself, against trivialities. Crippled by modernity, by unemployment and benefits, by industrialization of the modes of production and thought, removed from the state of nature, bereft of Elysian simplicity and plunged into the complicit, the complicated and the paradoxical, his phobias have twisted and strained so that he fears neither hunger, nor fierce storms nor lions in the dark.

But he is afraid of stairs. Can't face them. Even kerbs leave him jittery. No buildings without ramps and elevators. No escalators. Definitely no ladders. His legs go weak as he approaches, seize up as he gets close, his fear is paralysing, anoesis-inducing. He can't watch *Potemkin* without looking shudderingly away from that sequence. His nightmares are laden with ziggurats, he feels their oppressive weight on his chest, stilling his breathing until he awakes and remembers to inhale.

He has no fear of heights. He lives on the nineteenth floor of a south London tower block, a crow's nest made accessible by elevators (except In Case Of Fire). His perch and retreat, his watchtower and sanctuary, his loft, a place he calls home. The air is thin but the views are striking. He rides the elevators up and down, timing the journey. Once, it took nearly twenty minutes.

One day in late summer the elevators die with a mechanical rattle, a slow whirring sigh. There has been no physical failure, nothing detectable, no isolated engineering fault; it is a demise of tiredness and despair. He was on the ground floor at the death, pushing the button to summon the lift. He pushed it, he killed it and sensed the silence convene uneasily around him like a vengeful spirit. He is severed from his home by two hundred feet, nineteen flights of stairs, almost twenty steps per flight. What is above is become a different sphere, a separate plane in forbidden skies.

This loss has shaken him, like a blow. His mind and body seem to hold, yet the damage is irremediable, like a window broken and held with tar paper. Nothing to do but kick it out and start again. For three days he hovers at the foot of the block, by the entrance, looking up. As close as he can get to home. He talks to the caretaker in his ground-floor flat, who shrugs, sympathizes and says, I don't know nothing about lifts. Someone'll have to see to that, I would say. But my stuff's up there, he complains. My books, my clothes.

Through this time he doesn't sleep. Leans back against concrete walls and shivers through cold dawns in the unquiet city, waiting in vain for repair, for restitution.

When no one arrives he deserts his post and moves in with a friend he never knew, sleeping forty-eight hours in a dreamless stretch, forever imprinting his shape on a sofa. His friend and his friend's Scandinavian wife are sympathetic to his plight. It must be terrible, they say repeatedly. It must be terrible. We can't imagine.

From his friend's phone, and later, with money he has begged for, from a phone box, he calls the Council Works Department. Where he is transferred between sub-departments. Placed on hold and forgotten. Accidentally hung up on. Told to write an official letter of complaint. His details are taken from him until he has no more details to give. Time seems to pass.

His friend tires of his presence, the sympathy gradually bled from the veins of his kindness. He is told that he should tackle his fears, just climb the fire escape. They require their sofa.

When he returns to the block, the caretaker's room is locked and the caretaker gone. The lift button clicks, but the mechanism does not stir and the doors remain shut. He contemplates prising them open and shinning up the lift cables. Tries the smooth doors, but can't get hold. Figures the climb would be in any case beyond him.

Other families in the block are managing by using the fire escape. They take up food to stranded geriatrics. Lean out of windows and shout joyfully to each other. Can you bring my cat up? Whose shopping is this? They've rigged a system of nets and pulleys to take things up and down the building. A flower pot is on its way up, a dog on the way down. They throw ropes across to each other as if they are workers on a quayside mooring a great liner. They see him down below and wave. Hey! they call to him. If you give us your keys, we'll send your stuff down! I don't want my stuff, he calls back. I want to go home. Get in the net! they say. We'll pull you up! It's like a comedy film from a more joyful age. They get as far as strapping a harness on him before the wind picks up and a net unfurls, releasing laundry like coloured kites into the sky. It whips about in the gusts. They stand silent for a moment, admiring the aerial display, then consensually help him from the harness. This is not a dream about falling.

For a day he lies on his back, arms spread, looking for all the world as though he is a star fallen from the tower and crucified on the concrete below. The tower sways towards him, holds up, dizzying, though he is not dizzied. He wills his apartment towards him. In the evening it starts to drizzle, and when he understands that the rain will persist he stands, waits for his blood to return, then abandons his pale silhouette on the ground to seek the shelter of the concrete Hall. The Hall is closed up, designed to be windowless, a mass of jutting cuboids, its walls are alleys which go nowhere. He finds a corner of shelter from where, craning his neck, he can see the window of his flat as it reflects the heavy clouds. A

wakeful alarm sounds in the distance and some pigeons startle up, fanning darkly against the sky, embellished suddenly
white as they pass against the drab tower.

Sensing that he has woken he understands that he has slept.
He kicks off newspaper and stretches. Listens for sounds that
aren't there. The activity in the block has lessened. There's
less shouting, less coming and going on the fire escape. The
pulleys are inert and lifeless, their ropes blow in the wind and
sound a skittering rap against the wall. Some of the families
seem to have moved out, gone to stay with friends perhaps,
tired of the stairs.

Time passes. The block is grown silent, a monolith of
grey, lightless in the evenings. He has been watching for
movement and is perplexed to have found none. The building is drained of people and no longer attached to life. It is
simplified, no longer anything other than itself, free to
imagine itself. He senses the truth but does not understand
how this has come about. Elsewhere the city continues, here
it has ceased, even the rats have hunkered down or cleared
out. Only his pains stir him from reverie and back to life. He
is somehow bloodied and scratched, as if he had been
attacked in his sleep and awoken knowing nothing. His fingers play idly with a gash on his ear. Ribs ache, bruises
bloom.

Nineteen days after the elevators failed even he is gone, the
alleys are free of his shadow. His cuts were not healing, in the
last days the kneaded fold of his ear swelled and oozed. His
skin darkened from the sun. He patrolled in search of food,
away from his building, attempting to keep it within sight but
needing to be near populated areas, their bins of discarded
food. Dirt deepened behind his nails. His hair snarled. He
roamed further, beyond known streets, and became lost,
uncaring of geography, no longer able to return. He grew
dazed and weakened by hunger, hallucinating. London
burned away in a fever, a fiery light settling in waves, rain-

bows curving and metamorphosing into rolling fields of corn, an endless steppe of gold. A tower block shimmered briefly in the centre of the field, looking somehow surprised to be there, until it realized its mistake, and was gone.

Molloy Dies

James Molloy, an academic at the close of his years, bent over the beginnings of his last work. He knew his death was near. Though he remained in reasonable physical health, his consciousness ebbed away. His mind and body receded from each other. Eventually they would separate. Soon, he would be too old for life.

Molloy cared nothing for his own impending death, and there was no one, he believed, who might mourn for him. He had withdrawn from the world long ago. He would simply be extinguished, and that would be the end. It did the living no good, he knew, to concern themselves with what would be left behind, or with what might come. He wished only to complete his final project, the rest was of no interest to him whatsoever. All his anxiety stemmed from nothing other than the work.

He lived alone, as he always had, in a house he had bought long ago, a little way out into the countryside. Up in the city he was still an emeritus at the university, but he had not seen anyone from there for many years, not since he retired here. He had used the time and freedom to continue writing articles and books, and to think. For the most part he avoided people. They had done nothing for him in his life.

Molloy's writing had, over the years, taken on a peculiar system. He approached all his work in the same way, tackling it in three clearly defined stages.

The first stage consisted of: 1. The determination of the subject; 2. The formulation of the hypothesis; 3. The assessment of the sources; 4. The accumulation of the evidence; 5. The verification of the facts; 6. The interpretation of the facts; 7.

The reinterpretation of the interpretation; 8. The composition of the argument and the counter argument; 9. The substantiation of the conclusion.

In the second stage Molloy pared down all his notes from the first stage until he was left with a block of writing in the form of a single paragraph, usually covering no more space than a single side of paper. Then he would put the rest aside and not look at it again.

In the final stage he would type his paragraph into his computer, then form the book around the paragraph, writing from memory. Until his memory began to fail him.

Molloy, now, was at the beginning of the final stage. He had set aside the sources and the evidence, spent a great deal of time weighing the material over in his mind, and had, finally, completed his paragraph. But for the first time in his long career he knew that something was terribly wrong with what he had done. He did not recognize what he had written.

It amounted to just half a page of neat blue handwriting. It was certainly his own, or an excellent forgery. Yet because he could not think of a reason why someone might wish to break into his house and leave work fabricated in his own hand, he accepted it for his own. Such, he understood, were the fallibilities of age. It had not always been this way.

His career as an academic had been glittering. In his prime he had held chairs at Oxford, Harvard and Florence. He had been a major contributor to an astonishing range of publications in fields as diverse as psychology, philosophy, biology and sociology. He had made his name when he was still very young with the publication of his doctoral thesis, *Blue*. Back then it had earned him an envied notoriety, though it was forgotten now. He had published other works since, and his name was presently better known, if it was still known at all, than his ideas ever had been.

Blue was a study of the colour blue, the result of six years of research during which time Molloy lived in isolation from all things blue. His central thesis was that abstinence could provide exemplary knowledge of its subject; indeed, that it was a necessary category of learning. For those six years he had lived alone in carefully decorated private accommodation. He accepted no visitors who wore blue clothing, nor any with blue eyes, unless they agreed to be blindfolded with black cloth. He wrote his notes in black ink on a white page. He watched television, but the tube had been altered so that it could not project blue, merely garish fantasies in green and red. His house was decorated with flowers of all colours, with one exception. He wrote essays on when blue ceased to be blue and became instead another colour. He wrote an entire chapter on a sunset he witnessed one evening, a flame of crimson and brass and gold – but he described the pyrotechnics only in terms of their blueness. He went outside only when the sky was covered to its horizons with cloud. Even then his route was carefully monitored by one of his research assistants from the university. He received funding from various governmental bodies – and in effect his study ended early, when this money ran out. He had always said he would need twenty years to get the barest understanding of blue.

In addition to the final financial setback, the study had many detractors. Academic competitors, some from his own department, argued that he could not possibly have completely shut out all blue from his life. When he closed his eyes, they said, he would see blue. He replied, that is not blue, that is merely what I think blue is. They said, blue is evident in the spectrum, and constantly visible, even if you do not know you are seeing it. He replied, but of course. They said, you cannot know that your blue is the same as ours. Blue does not even exist. He answered, it exists to speak of.

He did not feel in the slightest bit threatened by their criticisms of his work, because he was in a position to know more than they did. He met their angry taunts with genuine puzzlement. What was it they thought they knew about blue?

Though he never admitted it, there had been one question put to him that he had been unable to answer. At the time, his thesis almost collapsed, and he had been plunged into a deep depression. It was his niece, his sister's daughter, who had confounded him. She was seven years old, and visiting with her mother. She sat in a pretty red dress, and listened to the adults talk. She was extremely well behaved, a quiet young girl, perfectly polite and intelligent. After a while, her mother explained to her what Molloy was doing living in the house this way. She thought about what she was told for a short time and then asked, Uncle James, why did you choose blue? He stammered, and offered, feebly, that the colour itself was not important. He might just as well have chosen any colour. She was unimpressed. I, she said, would have chosen red. I think that would be much better.

He was haunted for a long time by the fear that she might have been right.

It was a similarly uneasy feeling that sickened him now. His skin prickled at the back of his neck beneath his shirt collar. His new work disturbed him. He did not understand it, could not remember writing it, and did not know what it was he thought he had been writing about. Yet it sat before him on the desk. He read the paragraph again.

From the very beginning the life of Francisco Baston Wallace had not been easy. Orphaned at the age of nought when his mother, Lorena Baston, died in painful childbirth, he was raised by a distant aunt until the day when his father, an English explorer, might return from a lengthy expedition deep into the Amazon jungle. Due to a serious accident, and the onset of temporary amnesia, this did not happen until six years later. Francisco's hopes, however, of being spirited away by his father to a life of exciting jungle adventures were quickly dashed. Though his remaining parent greeted him as his own, their relationship was never given the opportunity to foster and develop. In the end he knew his father for a single week – barely longer than he had known his mother. So Francisco grew up with no family of his own, and felt the loss constantly. He longed for the younger siblings he might have now, had things been otherwise. He wished he had been given the chance to look upon his mother's face, even just once. And above all he mourned his father, Ian Goodwin Wallace, whose destiny it had been to die, run down by a motorcycle in the narrow streets of Cartagena de Indias in Colombia, his blood splashed onto the brightly coloured plaster of the Spanish colonial façades.

This was, apparently, the entirety of his research. The culmination of months of labour. Molloy did not even believe in destiny. He believed that destiny was simply what happened. He despised the portentousness of the word.

And now, he did not know what he should do with what he had written. It was almost as though he were writing a story, or a novel. But this seemed unlikely in the extreme. Were these things, then, true? The real backgrounds of people he had some unfathomed interest in? There was a certain nagging familiarity to the lines, but no more. He understood that his memory might be deceiving him in some way. If this proved to be the case then it would be foolish to merely throw the page away. He might suddenly recall why – and what – he was writing. He was not, however, sure what he should do meanwhile. Perhaps he should start again, return to the sources. But he did not even know what those sources had been. He looked around, frustrated. Through his study door he witnessed the still of the house. Across the corridor the kitchen looked cold, uninviting.

Molloy wished he lived in a better house. He had made money, but used it badly. Poor financial judgement had drained what few savings he had otherwise, in his profligacy, managed to maintain. Royalties from earlier works had dried up. Only his professorial stipend allowed him to pay his costs. He retained a cleaner, who arrived daily, but otherwise he had few expenses. He no longer travelled, and his tastes were simple. There had been some material accumulation

over the years, but Molloy had consigned all items of no practical use, all objects of merely sentimental significance, to a
locked garden shed. Inside the house, the rooms were mostly
empty. Molloy owned just two chairs – one which tucked
beneath the kitchen table, and one beside his desk in the
study. Upstairs, he used only his bedroom and the bathroom.
The other rooms remained unfurnished.

He tried to remember when the cleaner had last visited.
Had she already been that day? Or not since yesterday? To
his annoyance, he found he could not say with any certainty.
The house seemed tidy. The surfaces were free of dust.
Perhaps she had already visited, without him noticing. She
usually bought groceries for him each morning, to save him
visiting the town. He would look in the fridge, later, to see if
it had been filled. Molloy thought he could detect the faint
scent of furniture polish from his table. On this evidence he
decided his cleaner had already been and gone, perhaps
when he was sleeping. The knowledge relaxed him somewhat. Yet he knew, too, that the internal tidiness of his house
belied deeper problems – dry rot in the outside walls, some
damp at the rear of the building. The air seemed to have a
staleness about it, the place was mostly cold. The warmth settled in pockets, and he slipped between them. He was old,
and wanted comfort, and found none here. His consolation
was that the discomfort would not last for long.

Because of this, and because the rest of the house held nothing for him, he remained at his seat in the study. There was
nothing else for it. He would have to continue with his book.
Angrily, he started up his computer, cursing its slowness.
When the screen finally lit with icons, he opened a fresh document and carefully typed in the paragraph. *From the very
beginning the life of Francisco Baston Wallace had not been easy.*
. . . He nursed his fingers constantly. He had learned to fear
the stiffness and the pain that gathered there. Today, however, the movements of his hands were precise, dexterous and
pain-free. He finished swiftly. Then he saved the document,

and read it once more. The words always took on new meanings on the screen, and he hoped they would suddenly become clear to him as he read. But they did not, and his mood darkened. It was the same mystery on screen as it had been on paper.

He reached to his pocket for a packet of cigarettes, but found it empty. Molloy, as a youth, had been overly concerned with his health, and had never smoked. It was a habit he developed very late in life, just two or three years ago, when he thought it could have little impact on his limited future. In recent weeks his dependency on cigarettes had grown. He felt almost as though the air around him were incomplete if it were not smoke-filled. Without nicotine he became uncomfortable, and began to panic if more than a few waking hours passed by without relief. Yet the diminution of his memory meant that he often found he had run out, and forgotten to buy more. Which meant, if the cleaner had already visited, that he would have to go out into the day.

Molloy sighed deeply. He did not relish his trips to town. These days he avoided people as he had once avoided a colour. Properties, or bearers of properties – Molloy did not differentiate. Leaving the computer, he collected his overcoat from the cloak cupboard, changed his slippers for shoes, took his walking stick from beside the door and exited. The air was chilly, but the sky clear, and the sun still in view. As he walked along the short garden path he adjusted his coat until it felt comfortable on him. He passed through the small gate, closed it behind him listening to the soft creak, then set out along the road that led up the hill towards the town.

As he climbed Molloy glanced disinterestedly at the blue sky. He didn't look for long enough to make out the flock of large birds as they circled over the town, beneath the high feathers of the cirrus clouds. Soon, he warmed up, and unbuttoned the top of his coat. His breathing grew heavy, and his heart rate quickened. But his mind was elsewhere. He trudged along the street, muttering to himself.

In fact, Molloy was arguing. He often found, when his thoughts drifted, that he would replay past conversations or old arguments. He heard the words of his interlocutors clearly, and replayed his lines in the exchange, sometimes changing what he had actually said for what he might have said, making covert improvements. History is only ever written by the victors. But he would unconsciously speak the words simultaneously as he imagined them, holding the entire conversation aloud. Only belatedly would he realize.

'You ass!' he exploded suddenly, then looked around in embarrassment. There was no one in sight who might have heard him. Relief flooded him, though he did not really care if anyone had heard. What did it matter what they thought? Not a thing, to him. The streets, in fact, were empty of people. It did not surprise him. The adults would be at work at this time, and the children at school.

As he reached the top of the hill Molloy saw the shadows of unusually large birds flickering across the road. Surprised, he peered upwards, but the light was bright and he could not see the birds themselves. He listened, but his ears detected nothing. All was silent. Not the flutter of feathers, nor the song of the creatures. His head turned back to the street and continued into town, passing by the first rows of houses.

Not far into the town there was a small corner shop which sold cigarettes and newspapers, some groceries besides. It suited him well to shop this way, allowing him to avoid the busier main street and the people there. He pushed at the door. A hidden bell tinkled brightly as he entered. Inside, the air was musty, and the room curiously dark.

For a moment he was not sure if the shop was even open, perhaps the door had merely been left unlocked by mistake. If there had been a sign in the window he hadn't seen it. But as his eyes adjusted to the low light he realized that someone was in fact standing behind the counter. It was a young girl. She was in her twenties, he thought, certainly no more than thirty. She seemed pretty, if a little bored. No doubt business was slow at this time of day. Despite his misanthropy, Molloy was elated to find himself on the edge of a conversation. It had been a long time since he had talked with anyone at all, and the prospect brought some of his old vigour flooding back. Unconsciously straightening as he did so, Molloy approached the counter and smiled. He was surprised how uncomfortable the sensation was, how his face protested the exercise. But he persisted. He remembered, now, how exhausting human relations were. She did not, however, return his smile.

Molloy was seized by a strange desire to flirt. He was aware he was too old for the girl, he knew, too, that sometimes this didn't matter. If she knew his stature as a thinker. Perhaps she would like that. Among his students, once, there had been women who thought that way. Girls who had lingered after class, or had visited his rooms, a certain look in their eyes. But back then he had been focused solely on his work, his rise to greatness. He had dismissed their attentions and their longings. And now it was too late. He would settle, at this moment, for the self-deceit of it, five minutes of forgetting the truth of the matter. He wondered what his will had become. How soft his brain must be to become concerned with these things. Instead he tried to look her straight in the eye, to see the truth of it, to see an old man reflected. It was too dark.

She stared back at him.

'Two packets, please,' he asked, pointing. He paid in coins, which he laid in a bright row on the wooden counter. He slipped the packs into his pocket and shuffled to the door. The girl did not speak, nor show any interest. He left, affecting confidence in his step, with a jaunty swing of his stick.

He was exhausted by the time he reached home, though the return walk was entirely downhill. He made some tea, and took a large mug with him back into the study. His computer screen still glowed, and he pressed a key to restore the document. But it did not read as he remembered it.

Such disingenuous reasoning persisted for several centuries, appearing in a variety of forms. The last and greatest of its propagators was Amin al-Umana (1196–1262). While professing adherence to the Zahiri school of absolute and literal interpretation of the law as revealed in the Qu'ran and Hadith, he yet sought to maintain that all revelations through prophets and lawgivers were revelations of a single Reality, and that neither should take precedence over the other. In his famous work, Al-insan al-kamil, he describes the sequence of prophets from Adam to Muhammad, and illustrates which of the Names of God was exemplified by each of them. Muhammad, the Seal of the Prophets, was naturally the most perfect of these prophetic manifestations. Al-Umana thus appears to pander to the existing structures of Priesthood, while he in fact offers a fundamental alteration of them. According to the second part of the work, there are also saints, who by ascesis and the miraculous possession of inner knowledge (ma'rifa) may aspire to the position of being mirrors in which the Light of God is reflected. Al-insan al-kamil is a double-edged knife. Prophets were unquestionably saints, but al-Umana insisted there were also saints who were not prophets, because they did not have the specific function of mediating the revelation of truth or of a law. The possessor of ma'rifa, like the ordinary unenlightened man, must still live within the limits of a law revealed by a prophet. As with the hierarchy of prophets, there was an equivalent, and similarly invisible ministry of saints who preserved the order of the world. For each age there was a qutb, or pole, standing at the head of the ministry. It is apparent from his later writings that Amin al-Umana thought of himself as being a qutb, and indeed as being the Seal or most perfect of them. For these theosophical writings he was executed, and his ideas died with him.

Yet Molloy knew nothing of Islamic theology. It was an area his research had never entered. He did not understand how he could have written this.

He thought, suddenly, that it might be the computer churning these words out of its circuitry, accessing recessed memories and bringing them to the fore. He fantasized, briefly, that the computer secretly longed to become an author, and that it was taking advantage of his weakness and poor memory, replacing his work with its own. Yet he checked the file structure, and found nothing untoward. He accessed the keystroke log, but it was blank, not working. And in the piece itself there were clues that he had more of a hand in the writing of it than he knew; the use of 'ascesis' and 'disingenuous', both favourites of his. The phrase 'a double-edged knife', which he overused habitually.

His head began to spin with confusion. The unerring rise of panic swirled in his chest. To calm himself he took a cigarette, struggling with the cellophane packaging. He leaned back in his chair and smoked. He felt he had to work hard to inhale the smoke, then push it from his lungs, as if breathing were a conscious act, no longer automatic. He forgot his tea, which grew cold in the cup. A tremendous weariness settled in his bones. Switching off the computer, Molloy went to bed. He slept without dreams.

It was early when he awoke. As he stretched he remembered his writing, and depression settled over him like a sheet. He did not wish to get up, if he was only to face the dilemma of his work. He felt quite stuck in a rut. He felt as though he might end up going round in circles for ever, if he didn't clear his mind now and decide on a straight course of action. Although his progress so far had been disappointing, Molloy began to consider taking a short break. He lay in bed and considered his options.

There was no one he could visit, nor anyone he would want to. He tried instead to think of places he had been, and liked. Places he might return to. Destinations for forgotten vacations. A vague memory of a childhood trip to the seaside came to him, but no details, no names accompanied it. Nothing that helped him now. He was finding it hard to bring to mind anything at all about the world beyond his immediate view. Perhaps his mind had not yet cleared from sleep.

And then he remembered.

Why, he had not seen his niece for years. Not since she was a child. His sister had died, he remembered now, and he had been unable, as a professional and as a single man, to raise the daughter. He had fully intended to keep in touch with her, of course, but somehow this had failed to happen. He realized he had been neglectful. Now that his mind was no longer focused on work, now that he was actively trying not to think of it, he had the chance to atone. As far as he knew, his niece was still alive. He believed she lived somewhere in the city, and he had contacts there from his past life who might know her, or know how to find her. Why, the poor girl, she must be worried about him, about his absence all this time. He must reassure her. He looked at his bedside clock. It was still only eight in the morning. He had plenty of time to walk to the station, and catch the nine o'clock train to the city. The idea pleased him greatly.

Molloy dressed. In his excitement he did not feel hunger, and ate nothing.

Although he had been woken by the light that morning, the day darkened as the hour of his train approached. Black clouds filled the sky in an early twilight. At eight thirty he left the house, carrying a bag of overnight things in case he decided to prolong his visit. He brought with him nothing that was connected to his writing. That could wait until his return. With exaggerated care he locked the door behind him and pocketed his keys.

He made his way down the hill towards the station. This time the route took him away from the town. It was so dark that Molloy was not able to see much more than the road he walked along, so he kept his eyes down and followed the verge. He used his stick to help him keep to the tarmac, and in this way made steady progress. After nearly twenty minutes he arrived at the station. He felt invigorated by the early-morning stroll, and was in an excellent mood. The ticket booth, naturally, was closed – except during the busy rush hours it remained unmanned these days – so Molloy progressed to the platform and stood calmly, awaiting his train. At one minute to nine a bell sounded, and the train moved slowly, almost silently into view, sliding to a halt alongside the platform's edge.

Curiously there were no guards on duty. No one who stepped from the train to blow the whistle, or ensure the train's doors had been closed, or even to open them and help the elderly man onto the train. Molloy was the only passenger waiting to board. He clicked open a door and with effort held it wide, took the two steps slowly, carefully, and then pulled the door shut behind him. It closed heavily. He then moved into the carriage, along the corridor and found a compartment. Sliding that door aside, he entered. And as the train pulled away, at one minute past nine, the dark clouds parted and cleared to reveal a pale blue sky. But Molloy, settling into his seat, did not notice.

The train had been underway for some time when Molloy noticed the absence of a conductor. He had waited patiently to buy his ticket, but so far no one had appeared. Molloy did not worry. He knew he could pay upon arrival if he needed to. On such an empty train, it could be no surprise. He allowed his thoughts to drift, but they turned back to his book, and darkened his mood. After a while he decided to stretch his legs. They had grown cold and uncomfortable. Recently he had developed slight circulatory problems, though nothing which taxed him seriously, and he knew how much worse things must be for many people of his age. He used his stick to lever himself to his feet, accustomed himself to the gentle rolling movement of the train, slid back the door to his compartment and then made his way along the corridor to the front of the carriage. A door blocked his way forward, and he found it was locked. The handle protested its turning, as if it had not been used for some time. Perhaps, he thought, he had boarded the front carriage, and only the engine lay ahead. He peered through the scratched glass, but it was smudged, barely translucent. He could make out nothing beyond. Disappointed, he walked instead to the rear of the carriage, noticing as he did that the other compartments were all empty. He had, it was clear, chosen a very quiet hour for travel.

But the situation was the same at the rear of the carriage – a sealed door with no egress. The glass here, though, was cleaner, and he peered through, taking his hand from his stick to shade his eyes. He could see the track as it appeared behind the train, curling away from him and out of sight around a corner. It was clear that he was not in the first carriage, as he had thought, but in the last. He was not concerned, and he had, after all, succeeded in stretching his legs a little. The sealed doors explained the conductor's failure to appear – he would have to wait until the next station to switch carriages. Molloy retired to his compartment, slid the door shut behind him and settled again beside the window, watching the steady line of trees beside the track, waiting for the signs of civilization to appear as the city came towards him.

He must have fallen asleep this way, for when he awoke the train was standing still. He had the distinct impression that he had been awoken by the stopping motion. Through the window he saw a platform, and the sight woke him fully. In a rush, he seized his bag and stick and stumbled from the compartment. In an instant he was on the platform, blinking, looking around for the exit, ready to push through the city crowds. But the platform was deserted. The only exit was a small passageway which ran past a counter, a blind pulled down over the window.

For a moment Molloy reeled. The familiarity was overwhelming, yet he did not know where he was. Terrified he had disembarked at the wrong stop, he made an effort to get back on the train, but when he turned round the track was empty. The train must have pulled silently away as soon as he had disembarked. He felt foolish, as if he had somehow failed, as if his age had finally rendered him incompetent. But the emotion was anger, and not panic. He was not afraid.

He began to walk, leaving the platform to find out where he was. His legs took him as if of their own accord, tramping a well-worn path. He was not in the city, certainly, or even in a town. A single road bordered by fields led up a hill. He adjusted his bag, evened his stride and settled into a rhythm with his stick, and in a few minutes he was back at his house, listening to the creak of the gate, then the metal rattle of his keys unlocking the front door. Pausing only to remove his coat, he returned to his study. Molloy felt suddenly curious about how he had left his work. The anxiety of time pressed upon him. His trip today had been a foolishness he could not afford. There was only the book to finish, nothing more. Yet he had managed to convince himself otherwise. He did not have time for this. He must return to his writing.

It began:

Another condition which effects a similar disjunction between knowing *and* sensing *is the processing error known as Capgras Delusion. Unlike Charles Bonnet Syndrome, what is at issue is not seeing what is not there, but failing to correctly recognize what is. The conscious brain acknowledges the familiarity, yet the emotional recognition is absent. Perhaps consciousness – itself teased out of emotional awareness – is now prior to another pre-conscious system of recognition, which we still retain. The delusion may well arise out of the disjunction between the two brain processes. As with Bonnet, the frequent coincidence with cognitive dysfunction can lead to disturbing results. And as with Bonnet again, in instances where the delusion is unaccompanied by cognitive dysfunction, one can suffer from the condition while knowing that what one so plainly experiences is patently absurd.*

Then, something that astonished him.

My own experience of such an aberration confirms much of what has been written over these last pages. I do not suffer from cognitive dysfunction, yet returned home one day to my two cats to find I did not recognize them. They looked familiar, and were the right colours, the right build. But the emotional 'click' of recognition was missing. Although I knew it to be unlikely, I considered the possibility that the cats had died, and that some kind neighbour had replaced them with similar creatures, so I would not feel so bad. I knew this was ridiculous, and the cats, for their part, acted as they always had done, treating me with their usual mixture of demand and disdain. I found much amusement in the situation, for I understood what was happening, but could not alter the feeling. I laughed often at the wonder of it. I rather enjoyed, too, demanding of my neighbours what they had done with my real cats. They did not seem to be entirely sure whether or not I was serious. Because they saw the same cats they did not know what I was talking about. I am quite sure they thought I was a little mad. In any case, within a few days I had accustomed myself again to the animals, and the emotional dissonance departed.

This was true. Molloy had experienced the delusion, once. But he was staggered to think he might have written about it, for the episode had taken place on a single occasion, many years before, and had never been repeated. He had not kept pets of any kind for over thirty years. Until he read the passage on his screen he had completely forgotten about the incident. What was more, there were certain stylistic flourishes in the text that were most untypical – never mind unscientific – of his writing, in particular the anecdotal intrusion of the author into the piece. He usually deplored such artifice. It struck him that perhaps this was a fragment of a work he had written in his youth, when his interests were more strongly biological. But if so, what was he doing with it now? Where had it come from? Molloy sighed. Clearly, this book was not going well. And he could not find the rest of it.

What was more, he had already run out of cigarettes, or misplaced the ones he had bought. He would need to return to the shop. The day's frustrations were beginning to take their toll on him. It had been a failure. He had begun it hoping to get away from the work, so that he might return with a fresh mind. But if anything the situation had worsened. He was finding it hard to think. Was it only that morning he had taken the train? It felt as though it had been weeks ago. The experience diminished within him. His book was certainly moving forward, but not in any way he understood. He longed to smoke, desperately, so he gathered again his coat and stick, and set off into town.

The day had turned misty while Molloy lingered inside. The world had become a blur of shapes. He saw outlines – of the fence, telegraph poles – but no more, no details. It was a dreary, monochrome walk. He did not find the mist too unpleasant, however, it was not as cold and wet as he had feared but warm and strangely enveloping. The furthest point of visibility was about halfway across the neighbouring fields. Beyond that everything faded into white.

It was the same with the buildings when he reached the town. They loomed up, square and dark, but he could not pick out any features, not even doors or windows. Their fronts seemed as smooth as oil. Though his footsteps echoed, the town was silent. He wondered suddenly how late it was, if the shop was even open. Perhaps it was already night, and the mist was lit only by street lamps, somewhere in the cloud above. He could not be sure. There was no point in turning back, though, not without trying first.

He almost walked past the corner shop. Only a simple shade over the window and door distinguished it in the street, and in the poor light he barely saw even that. Although there were no lights coming through the windows, the door pushed open when he tried it. It was as warm inside as it had been out.

Molloy half hoped to see the same girl who had served him previously. In the interim he had come to consider that she might have been having a bad day when he was last there, that something had been worrying her. If this were so he could hardly blame her for her rudeness. He had been intending to ask casually after her, and then to affect a concerned and worried aspect, to draw her into conversation. But his plans were in vain, for the store was empty. A single gas light on the left-hand wall lit the crowded room.

He waited a short while, but no one came. There was no bell on the counter, as he hoped, so he called, quietly at first, but then with increasing confidence.

'Hello? Hello? Hello! Hello!'

Behind the counter, the shelves were stacked with cigarettes. Molloy stood for a while, looking at them. He realized he had probably called by at an awkward hour. The place had a trusting feeling to it, and Molloy understood that the girl would not mind if he took the cigarettes and left payment on the counter. When he was next visiting he could explain that it had been him, in case there was any concern. He edged around behind the counter, picked up two packets, then carefully counted the exact change onto the wooden surface. He called once more, 'Hello?' and then shuffled to the door, pocketing the cigarettes. The mist welcomed him outside.

He had been disappointed to find that everyone had already gone to bed, though it was not too much of a surprise, for he knew it had been a long day. His hopes had been quite high that he might find some human solace at the end of it. But it was not meant to be. Sighing deeply, he walked home, lost in sad thoughts.

Behind him, the world ended, collapsing and unravelling into nothing. The void followed Molloy home at a gentle walking pace. As the man entered his gate and walked down his path the end of the world paused, settling to wait beside the gateposts.

It was dark – or darker, at least – by the time he reached his front door. Once inside, and shaking from the exertion, he went into the bathroom, leaving the door open. He looked into the mirror, widening his eyes and leaning forward. There were deep bags above his cheekbones, ugly and bruised. Focusing straight ahead he tilted his head around, seeing how his eyes looked when the light changed. For a few days now Molloy had been worried that they were losing their colour. They were not as dark as he believed they had once been. He began to mourn the loss of his deep brown irises. He tortured himself by imagining what he would look like when they turned paler still. Eventually, he feared, they would become translucent. For Molloy, this was a greater fear than even blindness. With each second the wraith returning Molloy's gaze seemed less and less familiar. He tried smiling at himself, and then pulling faces, until a genuine grin curled around his cheekbones, and the creases became smile lines. He saw that he looked old, terribly old. Suddenly tired, he returned to his bedroom and slept without dreaming.

When he awoke he felt confident and alert. Renewed, somehow. He decided to begin work at once. His determination stayed strong as he dressed, faltering only briefly when he could not find the door to his bathroom. But it did not matter. Today he would write. All his procrastination was over, he could feel it. At last his work could begin.

From his bedroom he made his way to the stairs. Somehow, though, he had taken a wrong turn, for when he reached for the top of the banisters, his touch met only the smooth cold surface of a plastered wall. Thoroughly confused, he tried to get his bearings. In turning round, back towards his room, he saw instead the door to his study, and through that his chair and desk, with his computer on. He was appalled at his memory – somehow he had come downstairs already, and instantly forgotten it. Shaken, he clutched the door frame. He found he did not need the support, and calmed. All was well, after all. A fading memory, nothing more. Simply the logical outcome of living. Molloy sat himself at his desk, and started his computer, which flickered instantly to life. His document was already on the screen, his title at the top. But the page was blank, as he had known it would be.

His book. He didn't hesitate, simply bent forward over the

keyboard, and continued his work. He knew what had been written, and what remained to write. He wrote:

On the face of it the punishment meted out to Sisyphus was a simple matter. He was by nature a perennial swindler, and was sentenced to a task which would occupy him always, leaving no time in which he might plot escape. What appals us about this punishment in particular is the apparent meaninglessness of his endeavour, the pointless and endless repetition of an inane activity. Yet to assume that is to assume that the rock and the hill also have no meaning, and this is far from clear. If he gets the rock to the top of the hill, perhaps he will build something. A home, perhaps. His situation is analogous to our own in the universe; hence the resonance, hence the durability of the myth. Camus argued, of course, that it was the labour itself which had meaning. In any case, it is a monotonous, physical labour that is precisely the kind that leaves his mind free to wander. Something is clearly wrong here. If anything, Sisyphus' imagination will be working overtime. Yet the splendid machination of the Gods in devising the punishment – the infernal machine, as Cocteau termed it – cannot be at fault. The Gods may be fallible, but a divine punishment is necessarily perfect, though it may be reprieved. Let us be allowed, then, to posit a hypothesis. An alternative account of the myth, one which takes into account something which has been lacking in the story so far, an idea of what is going on inside the mind of the hero. A psychological interpretation. It begins like this: 'Let us say that the Gods have cursed Sisyphus doubly. With the Task, firstly, but also with modernity. He is afraid of change, yet assailed by it. He cannot but see that everything around him is changing, that nothing stays the same. He is terrified of the future. His rolling the rock up the hill is directly equivalent to our lives – it is a routine in which he can feel safe. It gives him meaning. Without reference, there is no identity. It is predictability. He chooses it. This way, he doesn't have to think – he's trying to escape thought. He fears that if he thinks about it, he will go mad. On the part of the Gods, it is an act of genius to allow him to inflict his own punishment on himself so desperately. They are patient. They will wait until the day when Sisyphus realizes what is happening, when he sees how he has been manipulated. The scales of fear will fall from his eyes as they widen in horror. Until that moment the Gods will wait in the audience in this theatre of their cruelty, and will watch, even though the show might last an eternity. The only alternative is death, and death is no punishment.

This was not the beginning, but it was a part. The rest would follow, in time. Molloy felt a glow of pleasure, of deep satisfaction. He knew he was making good progress. After all the false starts his book, his last book, was underway, and the end was only a matter of time away. He continued to type, a steady stream of words issuing from his fingertips, the manuscript swelling, line by line.

A little later, he took a short break from writing. It was not because he was tired, nor were his eyes weary from the screen, but simply habit. He stood and stretched.

He thought he might go outside for a breath of fresh air, but could not find the door. A surge of confusion washed over him, and he looked around, seeing nothing. This could not be simply due to his memory. He could no longer find his way around his house. He wondered, vaguely, if he had had a stroke. What should he do? Perhaps he should lie down on his bed, to rest. If he were sick he was sure someone would come looking for him. Someone would come to help. But the stairs were not where he expected. Something was wrong with the rooms. He was in no pain, however, and after a while he realized he could not be having a stroke at all. He could move around quite easily, though he was not getting anywhere. With his eyes squinting, he walked with his arms wide and outstretched, his palms forward. He found a wall, and followed it along until he reached one of the windows which looked out onto the front garden. He knew the window only by touch, because every time he tried to look at it his gaze slipped to the floor. He could not make it out, however he tried to look. He drew on his reserves of discipline. By concentrating extremely hard he finally managed to establish the shape of a window, though it was not entirely as he remembered. Gone were the tattered and fading yellow curtains, and the cracked pane. Instead, the glass was perfectly quartered, and framed by neat sash curtains. They looked like the windows of a dolls' house, or the illustrations in a picture book. Through the window there was nothing except a soft white mist. Seeing that the visibility outside was so poor, Molloy's desire to leave the house faded for the day. He did not look through the windows again.

He found himself back in his study, just the chair before him, then the table, with his computer sitting on it. Finding nothing else to do, he sat down on the chair. He began to re-read what he had written, so he could continue where he had left off. Only a single sentence remained, but Molloy thought nothing of that. He wanted only to know if it was written in a language he could understand. He wanted to know what he would write after it. He squinted at the screen, struggling to recognize it, to understand what it meant, to decipher its mysteries and bring it back into his power. Only by regaining control over the words could he ever finish. But he had begun, and he knew now that he would not leave until he had won, until the work was completed. He stayed this way, just an old man bent over the beginnings of his last work, and nothing else in the world besides.

Hope

She went with him because when they were introduced he met her eyes and did not let his gaze slip so as
to stare at her breasts. Much later he admitted that he
looked at women's faces because he was fascinated
with them and tried to imagine what each individual
expression would be like when stretched in orgasm.
This kind of misunderstanding is always going to
occur, she reflected. She might as well get used to it, go
along with it, what else was there to do? Somewhere
along the line there was always the chance that things
might just get a little better.

Jack

Jack used to look in the hallway mirror on his way out and sometimes when he did, it was just that familiar face, himself, and the reassuring feeling he got from seeing it, even if he was getting a bit older and he couldn't help but notice, briefly annoyed, that there were white hairs breeding at the sides. But sometimes when he looked he experienced this shock of not recognizing the reflected face at all, it seemed to belong to a guy with a desperate look in his eyes, a shifty-looking guy who was anxiously searching for something that wasn't there. And this guy had different hair from him, the cut less good, making him look like a jerk, and he'd find himself reaching up and smoothing it down to try and get it to match with how he thought it should look, but then the guy in the mirror looked even more desperate and sad and he'd give up and let his hands fall to his sides. Then he'd set his jaw into a squarer shape and will the face in front of him into something better, something that looked more like a man – attractive, something like resolution in the expression – and slowly he'd begin to see it and he'd think, yeah, there I am, that's who I am. As though he'd forget, if he couldn't see. As though the image came first and everything followed on from that. And he'd do this maybe once or twice a day.

However wrong it all went, he would always retain the incredible memory of how she had reached for him the first night they were together, how just every part of her body seemed to be crying out for him, and how no one had reached for him in quite that way again or probably ever would. Or how after they were married she'd lie beside him curled up in his arms and she'd murmur all these things about her life which had obviously been bothering her for some time. About how when she started school there was something wrong with her ears and she couldn't stand loud noises so that every time the bell went – which was several times a day – she'd cry, and this was before the thing with her ears was diagnosed, so all the teachers thought she was not really ready for school and would send notes home to her parents advising them to take her to a child psychiatrist. Or about how she started having sex with her first boyfriend when she was fourteen and how one time they were so frenetic with desire that she broke her arm halfway through, stuff like that, and every time she told him something he felt like an old piece of her was gathered up from wherever it had been cast aside, was packaged up and delivered direct to him for storage and if he could just keep hold of all these things at the same time then he could know her as well as anyone might, and she'd always be there and he could tend to her using these scraps of information about her life, papering over the cracks.

But that was about the time too when he began to get the dreams. The first had been a dream of an old woman sitting in the darkness in a rocking chair, though not rocking, picking holes in her shawl. And there had been something thoroughly disturbing about it, something terribly frightening about the old woman or what she represented and for days he hadn't been able to lose this vision from his mind she cropped up when he was at work and even when he was sitting at home with his wife just watching TV. Then the old woman started to appear in his dreams more and more often and sometimes she was accompanied by another old woman who would stand behind the chair and would look directly at him, where he was seeing his dream from, with a look expressing a pure kind of disgust, and would just talk to him in a low voice the words out of his hearing but he'd be terrified by this and he'd try and run away from them but his legs would never work and he could never escape and he couldn't even tear his gaze away, the words would slide along his bare shoulders and neck trying to crawl towards his ears, or worse, he'd actually find himself leaning forward to try and hear what was being said and then the woman in the chair would lean forward too and they'd get so close they should have been touching and he'd freeze in horror. He'd never been so frightened in his life and he couldn't work out why it was all happening he tried to think if he'd somehow done something terrible when he was young and had managed to forget about it since, if he'd killed any old ladies, but there was nothing he could dredge up that seemed to explain it.

So in order to build up enough courage to face sleep he used to drink a lot after work, and then sometimes before work as well, until he was drinking pretty much all the time, even at work, and then he'd begin to have visions of the old lady in her rocking chair even in the middle of the day, and once his boss came into his office to find him crazily flapping his arms around trying to propel something away, and was almost overpowered by the whisky stench. The almost immediate result of which was that he lost his job, causing a complicated set of emotional responses – though essentially a shattering loss of self-esteem and the severe paranoia which grew out of it – and developed controlling tendencies over those few things left in his life.

And though he mostly quit drinking and the nightmares came less frequently and though he got another job driving minicabs the impetus of collapse couldn't be stalled and had settled his mind into certain channels of behaviour which tended towards the psychotic, and most of his time out in the minicab was spent trailing his wife around town, following her on her lunch breaks and so on. So as to avoid her recognizing him he wore a fake bushy moustache for disguise and drove one of the company's cars. One day, though, having settled into the routine, he wore the moustache home – she didn't mention it and he didn't notice until they started eating dinner together and he reached up to brush a scrap from the side of his mouth, at which point he froze and she caught his eyes with a baffled look – and he realized that the disguise probably wouldn't stand up any more. As a compromise position he wound up having a cab driver friend of his trail her whenever she left work.

Except that knowing wasn't enough, he needed her to know that he knew, he needed her to understand the control he could exercise over her life. And he needed this precisely because he knew that whatever control he might once have had was slipping. So she discovered the extent of his obsessive activity in the middle of one of his interrogation sessions when he was quizzing her at length about the exact route she'd taken on a trip to see a friend (though one of his friends, it turned out) and he was correcting her as she went along.

No you didn't he said.

What do you mean? she asked.

You didn't go that way he said.

What do you mean? she asked.

You're a liar he said.

He never, however, mentioned that he had her car bugged too, and would listen in to her talking to her friends about him. All of this thinking that she was having an affair, which of course she was, with that supposed close friend of his, and he was powerless to do anything about it except drive her further into it, with increasing and aggregating intent.

Somehow the worst thing about all of it was to do with the fact that he'd stolen her in the first place from his own older brother (they'd met at the wedding, and two weeks later she'd decided that she'd perhaps made a mistake), and now that she was being stolen from him it made him feel that his whole place in the scheme of things had been fundamentally devalued, particularly with respect to his brother. She stayed with him a while, much longer than her friends really expected her to, but that was mostly for the sake of their son and not for him, and then eventually the two of them got in the car and drove off and the last thing he intercepted on his bugging device was her saying to their son, who would have been five then, no, six, saying to him *we'll be safe now, sweetheart.*

But all that was a long time ago. People change. He'd even forgotten the old women who used to terrify him in his dreams so often. And now there was the grey-haired guy in the mirror who was taking longer each day to beat into shape. Getting old was fine with him as long as he didn't have to think about it, as long as he felt like he was well and had enough energy for everything he wanted to do. It was only when he was going down with the beginnings of an illness, or when he felt exhausted for no good reason, that he began to think properly about it and then he'd get scared. The way it mostly manifested itself now was sometimes when he got up in the middle of the night he'd find his legs would shake and his arms would have a buzzing weightlessness to them and he'd feel entirely old and somehow just *thin*, as though he was hardly even there, as though his consciousness might somehow sweat right out of his body and slip away, evaporate, leaving whatever was left to collapse a pathetic skeleton in the hall. It was such a crushing and overpowering reminder

of his mortality that he'd barely manage to take himself
to the toilet and when he was there he'd flip down the
seat and sit down to piss and sometimes he'd moan to
himself at the suffering. Then later, back in bed, his heart
would be beating so hard it felt like his fragile body
couldn't hold it in. So he'd just cling on to the feeling of
relief that he didn't have to do anything except lie there
for a few hours, that maybe things would be normal
again in the morning. And he'd worry that he'd never
have sex again because his body sure as hell didn't feel
like it could manage anything like that. That maybe his
time was up. And those were the nights that he was glad
he was sleeping alone and that no one could see him in
this state.

When he was feeling old in this way it would occur to
him, sometimes, that this must be how his parents felt
all the time, just old and exhausted and vulnerable, and
this was an important realization for him, because until
then he'd watched them wither up and turn into wrinkled caricatures of themselves and he'd never really
thought about what it was. But the thought of his mother feeling like that was almost too much for him to bear
and it would leave him terribly depressed and exacer-
bate the familiar and disgusting powerlessness which he
had come to recognize as the defining element in his life.

Both his parents, though his mother especially, were
Christians, and were always encouraging him to pray,
right through his life, even though he said they should
have stopped talking to him that way when he was a
kid, that he was way old enough to make that kind of
decision for himself and that frankly it was incredibly
patronizing. Plus he felt that the unspoken corollary
here was: *why can't you be more like your brother*, just the
thought of which was enough to make him shudder. But
though he felt an incredible anger seething through him
whenever his parents got on this tack, a fury which

brought him close to screaming, he also felt guilty about letting them down in this way, so he did actually try and pray a couple of times, despite knowing that it would feel weird and contrived. Which it did. Still weirder though was the fact that whenever he was genuinely worried about his parents, for whatever reason, it felt completely and utterly natural to pray for them and somehow reassuring too. And if the specific things he prayed for didn't work out, he would actually think that maybe it was *his* fault, for not having enough faith. This even though he had no faith, not a mustard seed's worth, that he didn't really believe for a moment that there was Something or Someone out there to whom his lack of faith would matter, which just goes to show.

Even after he was better, long after his wife left him, he didn't feel able to have another relationship for a number of years. And this wasn't just because of the overwhelming pain that lingered from the strangeness of how things had gone, a pain that settled in his chest and cracked his heart open every morning – that pain stayed for the rest of his life without growing old, but the surprising thing he found was that you can live with pain, that it becomes familiar and strangely comforting, even as it kills you – no, it seemed to him to be more closely related to the depression and the fact that he lost for a long time any real interest in sex, that he found himself unable to get an erection – an impotence which lasted a few years – and he'd make do with a kind of limp masturbation, which was pretty much all he wanted. But it was also a case of conditioning, how he had somehow come to associate the act of sex with a profound sadness, and on those few occasions during that time when he met a woman, or nearly got together with an old friend, they'd get about as far as undressed and in bed and he would start to cry, or even if he didn't actually cry his face would swim over with so much sorrow that the woman would stop what she was doing and maybe even start crying herself, as happened once. So mostly he avoided those situations, feeling he had enough sadnesses in his life, but there were still nights, even then, when he got fed up at sleeping alone all the time.

His problem, he was beginning to think, was that he just couldn't seem to straighten things down in front of him, couldn't get it all laid out so it was an easy walk, everything kept coming up in mountains, sending him off in other directions. Even when the future came up flat all by itself he'd stare at it long enough to identify the little ridges and then he'd watch in horror as they reared up into cliffs.

And then when he was about to give up on ever finding a downhill run any time again he met a Puerto Rican woman whom he'd noticed hanging around the bar he used to drink at those days. He found this woman to be startlingly attractive and funny and they used to talk about nothing half the night in the bar, cracking each other up, until one night she made it clear that she liked him too and they got together. They turned out to be entirely compatible in all the best ways, though he couldn't quite believe it because everything was suddenly so easy and so much fun and it felt like this was maybe how things should have been all along, but then, he figured, better that it came along late than never.

And the thing about this relationship was that it was so great, so incredibly great, and the sex was really unbelievably great – she used to come over to him when he was sitting in his chair and do this dance and she could move her hips like nothing he'd ever seen, he wondered if it was a Latin American thing maybe, and then she'd slowly lower herself onto him and she'd keep moving her hips in the same way and God it was . . . – so the sex, yeah, was something else, and it put all his memories of impotence way to the back of his mind, but the thing about it all was that he couldn't get used to the fact that it was going so well, he couldn't quite bring himself to believe it, and the feeling lingered in his chest that it was all going to go wrong and he was just killing time as though there were a surfeit of it, which there no longer was, that he was just waiting around for everything to fuck up.

Bum Rules

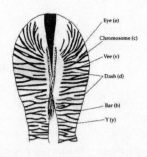

The door to the Chicken Shed is locked again and there's no sign of Dr De'ath. It's been this way for three weeks. Lately I've been coming past every day to see what's going on, and nothing ever is. It's not, to be honest, anything to do with me. But I feel a bit responsible, because I hap-pened to be going past when the chickens arrived, and got recruited by De'ath into getting them tagged and settled in to their new accommodation. We marked them with twists of coloured wire around their legs, a different colour for every bird. Foolproof, and easier than thinking up names for them all.

So inside the Chicken Shed there are indeed chickens. The shed, though, is anything but – it's a climate-controlled ani-mal management centre, the one genuinely high-tech compo-nent of the Zoology Department, an installation the size of a small warehouse. Pretty luxurious. And not only that but the inmates get to be part of a major academic investigation into pecking order. These are happy chickens we're talking about here.

There's great competition each year over who gets access to run a project in the shed. Last year it was monkeys, so it was known as the Monkey House (or screech city, to anyone who had an office in the same wing). This year seems to me like a wasted opportunity to call it the Chicken Wing, but apparently I'm the only one who thinks that way.

Things are heating up over next year's allotment. It looked a shoo-in for Professor Tuttle and his tortoises, because he's been waiting for years and his tortoises clearly need more room. But then a couple of his reptile colleagues jumped in with an audacious bid to work with Komodo dragons. Apparently they can get hold of a pair from a closing-down sale at some zoo.

There's no real chance I'll ever get a look in, because I work with zebras, and good as the facilities are the department would never envisage importing a herd for me to study. Though quite why anyone would want to study here when they can get funded holidays abroad to work on their animals is a mystery to me. I think it's all a question of departmental politics, not wanting to stray too far from the fray, in case you're overlooked for one of the top posts. In fact the only person who's never really here is the Head of Department, Professor Ayer. He's largely media-occupied, very much into fund-raising and *laissez-faire* management. De'ath's second in authority, but now there's no sign of him and it feels like we're a bit of a leaderless institution, which is making me nervous.

Also making me nervous these days is Sadie Macmillan, who works in the next office. She's the bright young thing in entomology around here. I've been incubating a crush on her for several weeks, and can't keep it cocooned for much longer. But I'm just a little intimidated by the certain fact that she is a good deal smarter than me, highly work-orientated, and way too pretty.

She's already in. Her office is lined with brand-new incubation tanks half-filled with earth, in which are gestating a few thousand maggots. I call by for coffee. She has her own coffee-maker, though it's been pushed into the corner to make room for the tanks. There's an open packet of biscuits there too, I notice.

'Hey, Sadie.'

'Hey. Any sign of De'ath today?'

'Nah. Locked again.'

'He probably isn't even in there.'

'Maybe. I dunno, though. He likes privacy.'

'Of course the chickens may be starving.'

I grin. I know something about the shed she doesn't.

'Automatic feeder. De'ath had it installed.'

'Uh-huh. Then unless he's trained them to clean up after themselves they'll be knee-deep in their own shit.'

'Do chickens *have* knees?'

'You're running a little late today, aren't you?' she says pointedly.

I head next door. In all the months we've been neighbours here and I've been calling by to visit she's never once offered me coffee.

I have the coldest office in the whole building. The radiators don't work and the only heat comes off my computer. It's also the furthest office from the coffee machine. On the shelf beside my computer I have a fluffy zebra toy called Spot which my sister bought for me, and a card a colleague gave me for my last birthday with a joke on it about a zebra crossing a road.

I sit and look at zebra bums until I go blind. Four hours every morning and five or six on an afternoon, depending. Some days when I go home all I can see is stripes. I think I've lost the ability to track vertically. There's an old joke about a leopard who goes to the vet complaining he sees spots in front of his eyes when he looks at his wife. Well that's perfectly natural, says the vet. After all, you're a leopard, you have spots. Yeah right, says the leopard, but my wife's a zebra.

At half-time I go to the canteen for some sandwiches. I'd probably sit with someone I knew if I could see anything apart from zebra stripes in front of my eyes. I sit and chew and blink for half an hour, then go back to work.

At the end of the day I head out down the corridors, trainers squeaking along the linoleum. From Professor Tuttle's area I can hear the gentle zlak zlak of mating tortoises. He's been studying the same tortoises since he was an undergraduate, fifty years ago. They're ageing well, and will probably outlive him. On the way out, just on the off chance, I call by the Chicken Shed, but the doors are locked.

Outside it's raining. The concrete of the Zoology block looks slick and stained. It's an ugly building. Always best viewed from inside.

I have a thing about rain, though. At the moment it's the one thing that stops me getting down, so I take off for a walk across campus. It's completely deserted. The wind howls through the bare poplars that line the concrete plaza. From the library's tiny windows you can see all these little student faces peering, wondering if the weather will let up so they can go home. I lift up my face to the showers, and take a deep breath, getting a mouthful of heavy drizzle. It's fantastic.

Blue is strongest subject. Subject is dominant, largely unchallenged. Hierarchical feeding pattern is demonstrably established from above. Groups A (Blue, Green, Red, Yellow, White) and B (Brown, Silver, Purple, Black, Orange) showing complementary results, equivalent to past studies. Initial segregation commences tomorrow.

I have dismissed my assistant.

I got into zebras by a circuitous route. My first degree was in art history. I wasn't very good at it, but you could hang around galleries all day and be thought dedicated, which was good enough for me. But I got involved with a class-mate, an Italian girl called Gloria, and after we finished the course I decided to go back to Rome with her. She was great – beautiful and wealthy (her student flat in London was a penthouse overlooking the Thames), and subsequently a blast to be with. I didn't pick up that she was a heroin addict until later.

Love really does affect the eyesight. And I didn't pick up about where the money came from until I had to go and meet her family. The circumstances for the meeting weren't ideal. Gloria had just got pregnant, and she decided it was my responsibility to let her father know.

They have a great house. Unbelievable place, really. Big mansion out in the nicer suburbs with a small jungle for a garden. I stood in the entrance hall, tapping my feet on the marble slabs, admiring the paintings. Trying not to look at the staircase, which was so wide and white and curved it was actually hurting my eyes. Then finally it strikes me. Her Dad is some kind of lawyer. In Italy. Even the best lawyers couldn't live somewhere like this. So standing by the optical assault that is the stairs I come to understand that I'm about to tell a probably-senior Mafia figure that I've impregnated his daughter. In imperfect Italian. A butler appears at the top of the stairs, beckons me upwards, and shielding my gaze I walk slowly up, suddenly unable to remember even a word of the language except *ciao*, and I get a palindrome stuck in my brain, playing itself forwards and back, backwards and forwards. It goes like this: *Satan oscillate my metallic sonatas*. Or backwards: *Satan oscillate my metallic sonatas*.

The next three years I spend out in Africa, working on a small farm in Kenya. It seems the thing to do. I get a job as an observer, camping out by myself at a hide overlooking a watering hole. It takes a long while before I feel safe, even before you consider the wildlife. I wasn't used to animals. Never quite got around my mother's cats, never mind having a pride of lions on the doorstep. But I get used to it, and after that I stay out in the isolation for as long as I can – for weeks at a time, forgetting how to talk to people. The only humans I meet are these tall tribesmen dressed in red who bring their goats down to the water, and are curious about me. They spend a day watching what I do, until they figure out there isn't much to see, and clear off. I consider whether

I'm supposed to include the goats in my report and decide against it.

Days are hot, nights are freezing, and I just curl up by the viewing window, fully dressed inside my thermal sleeping bag. The animals come and go. Some days I'm lucky if I get a solitary warthog. Others they turn up in streams – elephants, giraffes, hippos, wildebeest, buffalo, gazelles and leopards and you just have to gawk and admire, and wish you had someone there you could share it with.

A few weeks in, however, and I found I kept getting thirsty – even though I knew I was drinking enough – and bursting into tears at odd moments. I finally work out that I'm not sick, I just miss the rain. So that's all I do. I stay out in my hide, report on the animals that turn up, and wait for the rains, as if they'll wash me clean. I tried explaining this to Sadie once, but she was having none of it.

'Don't be ridiculous,' she said. 'No one *actually* just waits for rain. You're just trying to sound dramatic.'

She may be right, she usually is, but it felt that way at the time.

Eventually I meet an elderly zoologist called Hussey who's working on patterns of Grevy Zebra movement, and end up helping him with his research. It turns out he's one half of Hussey-Goldberg – of Hussey-Goldberg Method fame, which is some kind of arcane system for identifying individual zebras. And through him I get a place on his study, which a couple of years later leads to the graduate place here at the university.

A few notes re: the Hussey-Goldberg method. I remember my father telling me, when I was young, that if I ever wanted to know someone, I should just look them in the eye. You can see everything you need there – if they're lying to you, if they want something from you, if they're even listening to you. That has turned out to be a useful piece of advice for people, but it's completely obsolete with respect to zebras. For a start, according to Hussey-Goldberg, you're looking at the wrong end.

What you do is take photos of zebra bums, lots of them. As many as you can of the particular herd you're sampling. And then you go out and do the same every day for a couple of weeks. After that you spend several months back in an office analysing each photo, according to the rules.

You write in the sex (not always obvious: some males will appear to have five legs, while others will withdraw their fifth member right into the body, sumo-like). If they're female you write in whether they're pregnant (again not obvious: if they've drunk enough water even the average zebra looks like a barrel with legs. The tip here is to watch for labial swelling). You note down whether there's any unusual scarring. Then you record the stripes as they present down the rear right leg. *Bar vee y vee bar chromosome y chromosome*, say. Someday someone will invent a machine that can read a zebra like a barcode. Until then, I have employment.

When you're done reading the bums you let the computer whir on for about a day, running the equations, eliminating doubles, and out pop the results. Zebra numbers to a high degree of accuracy, according to Capture-Mark-Recapture (CMR) statistical models. You can track individuals, if you're on the Behavioural side. You can draw patterns, if you're into the macro elements. It's a breakthrough in zebra herd study. And it's a whole world of work.

Of course no one here refers to it as the Hussey-Goldberg method. We just call it striping. I reckon I have just about nine thousand more bums to stripe over the next few months. Mornings I stripe. Afternoons I stripe.

On the way out of work the next day I call by the Chicken Shed but the doors are locked. I haven't even seen Sadie for a couple of days and I leave feeling anxious and depressed.

Yesterday 8 p.m. Blue segregated. Yellow is shedding, even prior to climate change. Green is dejected, openly bullied by Red. Original patterns have reasserted themselves in approximately 13 hours against test conditions of four. Stage Two of environmental changes

underway, increasing humidity, night-time temperature fluctua-
tions, reduced light, white noise bursts. Some disorientation.
Reduced feed.

A few days later and my conscientious striping is interrupted
by a circular email from Professor Ayer inquiring if any students happen to know the location of Dr De'ath, or are wandering around with a set of spare keys for the Chicken Shed
in their pockets. It's reassuring to know I'm not the only one
who's worried.

I go over to the Chicken Shed but the doors are locked. I try
putting my ear to the door but it's pretty well insulated and I
can't hear a thing. I hang around for a few minutes to see if
anyone's going to turn up, but no one does, and I get bored.

On the way back to my office I bump into Sadie in the
corridor.

'Hey,' I say without thinking, 'I've missed you – where
have you been?'

'Really?' she says. She looks at me, a little puzzled.

'Yeah, I thought you'd gone the same way as De'ath.'

'Which is?'

'A complete mystery.'

'Right. Anyway, I've . . .'

'Wanna go for a walk?'

'What?'

'A walk. You know. Hey, have you ever seen the upper
floor?'

'Um. No. Actually I haven't.'

She tilts her head at me, weighing things up. I am slightly
thrown by the fact she's actually considering the suggestion.
I think she's genuinely trying to accommodate me. She looks
at her watch with a frown.

'Fifteen minutes,' she says.

'Great!' I say. I feel slightly nauseous.

We climb the stairs, without much to say. The lift no longer
runs this far. The upper floors used to belong to Ashville Life

Sciences, a company with Zoology Department links which ran animal testing projects. It's a bit disturbing, because that's where the Department got a lot of funding from, and hence where much of my money comes from. At least I like to think I'm putting it to good use. A zebra saved for every rabbit poisoned. They closed down last year and shipped out to some secure countryside location after the protests got too heated. All that's left is a battery of empty offices and cages. But there's a great view.

'That's a great view,' Sadie says.

We stand and admire it a while, pressing our foreheads against the glass. You can see out across to town. The campus beneath us is butterfly shaped, and we're out at the tip of one wing. I'm just working up to ask her out.

'Listen,' she gets in first. 'I gotta go. Everything's hatching this week.'

'S'okay.'

'Call by and watch, if you want. It's pretty exciting.'

'Uh, right. Thanks.'

And she's gone. We've finally bonded. I get a tear in my eye, but blink it away before it affects my eyesight. I bound down the stairs. Outside it's not raining, but I have this sudden burst of energy and go for a walk anyway.

Blue restored to group A 23–15 hours. Subject's bulk is turning finally to a disadvantage. Subjects are all shedding, and the weightier, more heavily feathered, are suffering most. Patterns slow to realign, yet there is a measurable resistance to levelling. Green is emerging to fill the power vacuum. Subjects are listless. Stage Four of the environmental shifts is underway. How many are required?

Yellow has made repeated attempts at flight. Subject segregated, denied light.

Back in Kenya I lived for a short while with a tribe. Those guys who came to visit me out at the hide came back one day with a present of some goat for me to eat, and invited me back to their village. I hung around for a couple of weeks, eating goat and giving the children something to laugh at. It was a bit disorientating suddenly being back among people, but I settled in.

At the end of my time there they sent me to see the shaman. He lives in a large hut at the edge of the village, and keeps to himself, unless he's being consulted by the villagers.

'What's his name?' I ask before I go see him.

I get a worried response. They look fearful and shake their fingers at me.

He seemed pleased to see me, anyway. In the end I never ask his name.

In welcome he gave me something to eat – a blob of paste wrapped in a local leaf. I was too polite to ask what. Experience since has taught me that it was almost certain to include some ground intestine, he's a big fan of that. Then he went into a bit of a comedy routine – jokes and laughter and dancing – and I was confused, so I just smiled politely and laughed along with him. Then splurge, he just melts away in front of my eyes until there's nothing left but his hands. I can't feel my legs, and when I try and move my arms horrible things start to happen, so I sit still. Turns out he was just waiting for the hallucinogens to kick in, and when they do, I spend the night completely unable to see anything except mad colours, and his big hands, playing around with the shapes in the air. I couldn't see straight for a week.

After that though we were pretty good buddies. And one day when I'm holed up in my hide suffering from long consecutive weeks of drought, a warrior from the tribe walks the twelve miles or so from the village over to collect me, then leads me back to the shaman. Who wants to take me out for a hike. He gathers up some of the shamanic gear from his hut and we head out at a brisk pace. These guys can really walk.

'What's going on?' I say

He points at the sky. It's clear, formed in blues I never knew the names for.

'Time for rain,' he says.

I check the sky again.

'But there isn't any rain,' I say.

'Ha ha!' He laughs. 'I will bring the rain.'

'Okay,' I say.

We search out a ridge of reddish earth to stand on, indistinguishable from the thousands of other red ridges across the plain. He looks around until he finds his spot. We crouch into the African sitting position. He takes a small drawstring bag from his belt, and rifles inside, coming out with a handful of polished grey pebbles. He shakes them and casts them on the ground like dice. He plays around a little with the pattern of their fall and drizzles snatches of sand over them. I glance up, and see that the sky is still a stubborn blue. He looks up too and stares directly at the sun, which is heading over west. He starts muttering words – I can't even catch what language he's speaking in.

In two minutes the sky goes the colour of wet slate. In five I realize that there seems to be a covering of formless cloud coalescing over us. The light goes dark and the thunder begins its warm up for a big entrance. A minute later and it's pissing it down.

It's like a dark ocean is falling out of the sky. The plain around us has completely disappeared. Squalls scream in like artillery fire. The noise is incredible. The ground starts to dissolve and run away with the weight of water. The drops are so big or fast that they really hurt.

I'm staggered. I stand up in the liquid blizzard. I'm already soaked through. My friend is still crouched and he appears to be completely dry, though that has to be some kind of optical illusion, like the rain's getting in my eyes and affecting my sight. He collects up his pocket monsoon rocks and comes over. He looks quietly smug.

'What the hell did you say?' I shout.

Some of the smugness leaves his face.

'No idea,' he admits.

We slog back to the village through thickening mud. The rain lasts five days. It's fantastic.

Perfect equality attainable. Only required are minor changes to the environmental conditions. There will be a levelling. Segregation has ended, but individual dominance has been expunged. Subject's coloured tags have become irrelevant markers. Subjects seem to sense their future. Subjects gather together in a single group. Subjects have ceased to eat. Shedding has reached critical levels. Recurrent shivering is observable in each subject. There is clearly some suffering. It will soon be eliminated.

Today the smell finally became officially unbearable. Our long-absent Department Head turned up early this morning wearing nose-clips, dragging Mr Warren the building manager with him. Warren pulled the master key from his pocket, attached by a long chain to his belt, and held it out between his finger and thumb as though it were a sacred relic. Professor Ayer nodded, and Warren carefully inserted the key. Only to find that sometime in the preceding weeks De'ath had apparently changed the locks.

There followed a short, heartfelt debate about whether the door should be broken down, an idea to which Warren was quite resistant, the fittings being his responsibility and the faculty staff an entirely secondary concern. He was only convinced when Professor Ayer threatened to make it a Health and Safety issue. They negotiated over who would pay for it (the Department), then Warren went off for a sledgehammer. By the time he came back most of the faculty were in and congregating around.

'Do you think the chickens have eaten him?' says Sadie, sidling up, 'Or he's eaten them?'

I give her a grin but she's looking past me at the commotion.

'Please stand back,' says Warren.

He gives the door a huge thump and the hammer bounces off, jarring his hands. He looks unhappy. But Ayer is affecting not to notice, so he sighs and tries again. An expectant atmosphere builds up among the audience. Eventually the door cracks inwards at the middle and starts to give. We applaud generously. A couple more thumps and then he uses the long handle to lever the doors apart.

We crowd round the broken entrance and peer in. The first thing we get a glimpse of is the smell, close-up, and everyone backs away sharpish. Professor Ayer steps into the breach. He takes three extra pairs of nose-clips from his jacket pocket and gives one to Warren. Instinctively the more senior, and wiser, fellows melt to the back of the crowd.

'Volunteers. You two,' he says, pointing at me and Sadie, giving his fingers such a sharp snap I wince, thinking he's broken the bone. But he seems fine.

'Ow,' I say, as the nose-clip bites. Sadie gives me a push forwards, and we go on in.

The main light isn't working. It takes a few moments to adjust to the relative darkness. There's no sign of De'ath. The main office is empty, though his notebooks are sitting open on the desk. I bend over to have a look, see when the last entry was, but it's too dark and I can't make out any dates. Ayer reaches in past me to gather them up, and folds them neatly under his arm. His research, he explains, will have to be kept in a safe place until he returns. In the corner there's a computer on with a screensaver playing. Several cartoon chickens endlessly running a race.

We go on to the viewing area, and glass crunches beneath our feet. The viewing screen is smashed through, inwards. There's a low glow emanating from the environmental controls. The thermostatic controls are turned up high, but something in the heating system must have given, because though it's warm, it's not sweltering. Just vaguely tropical. Better than my office, anyway.

There are no chickens in the main area of the shed. There is nothing which looks or sounds anything like a chicken. There is definitely some kind of a sound, maybe just the humming of the electronics, and maybe not. Despite the smell – which the nose-clips ameliorate but don't abate – the sound is somehow making me hungry. Against the near wall the automatic feeder seems to have clogged up with uneaten grain. Leading away into the warehouse-space there's a carpet of feathers, in browns and oranges, ruffling a little with the air. In the middle there is a large mound, like an unlit bonfire. We squint over at it in the half-dark.

'Where are the lights?' Ayer snaps, in a voice which suggests that one of us should find them imminently.

I go back over to poke around at the switches on the control panel until the upper spots come on.

'Is that it?' I call.

There's no reply. Clearly they are impressed with something. I wander back over to see what it is.

I nudge Sadie to step aside and let me have a look. She doesn't protest, just keeps staring forward. The mound is fully lit. When your eyes adjust to the bright light you can see every little detail. It is a putrid, decaying pile of chicken flesh, and it is moving. It's disgusting, like someone just threw up an abattoir. It shines, glistening white and red. It turns over on itself, boiling up from its peak. Tiny flies flit around everywhere above it. It's actually affecting my eyesight. As we're looking a part of the pile falls away and a gooey liquid oozes out the hole. For a second there's a flicker as something writhes out of the wound and then darts back in. It looked like one half of a maggot, except way, way too big, surely too big.

I turn away to go and vomit in the corner, only remembering to pull the nose-clips off when I start to choke. The sudden return of the full force of the smell makes me heave again. My stomach just keeps contracting, even though all the breakfast coffee is already spewed out. Finally, I get it under control.

'What the *hell* is *that*?' Warren is asking.

'That, apparently, is the chickens,' says Ayer.

But not any more it isn't. The brightly coloured chickens of Dr De'ath are no more.

'Nah,' says Sadie, 'those are maggots.' She is genuinely fascinated. Can't tear her gaze away.

'Aren't they beautiful?' she says.

I exchange a green and worried look with Ayer. There is such a thing as too much enthusiasm, after all. I spit, wipe my mouth with my sleeve and reattach my nose-clips. Relief. Unable to help myself I look back at the mound, its wriggling skin. Surely it can't all be maggots? There must be thousands. You can pick out some of the bigger ones, and they look enormous, fat and round like white grapes.

'Where the hell do they all come from?' I ask. 'I thought this place was sealed, like hermetically?'

And then my stomach lurches again and I shudder, wishing I could take the words back, wishing the thought hadn't even come to mind, because Sadie's taken a deep breath and is going to tell us all about it.

A low-key departmental memo the following week has three minor announcements. The retirement, for family reasons, of Dr De'ath. The opening of a Maggot Farm, the latest research project to be run in the department's showcase laboratory. The subsequent promotion of one Sadie Macmillan.

Sadie has softened, these last days. And two nights after her promotion we writhe in a bed, soft like earth, white flesh on white flesh, open mouth on open mouth, turning over blindly, something hatching in us. Outside it rains as though that were all it had ever done, as though nothing else were even possible.

Dream #36b
21/07/__

I'm in a bike race – mountain bikes, though the one I'm riding is actually my old bike from a few years ago, a battered racer, serviceable enough, it was stolen in the end, I was fond of it once – and we're riding in pairs. I'm not sure where the other riders are, I think they're travelling an alternate route to the same destination, or perhaps it's a time trial and we won't see them, won't even know if we've won until the end of the day. The region we're cycling through is rough moor – cut through by a jagged track of sand and stone. It's very familiar – an amalgamation, somehow, of both of the areas I spent my childhood in. Except that I know for sure that we're racing across China – west to east in an afternoon, in fact.

My partner, I mean the one I'm riding with, is my mother – I'm quite sure, though I'm only aware of her bike, perhaps her voice too. I couldn't tell you if she looks like my mother or not. We take turns at leading, but I have some problem with my legs and every time I freewheel to the front I don't then have the strength to push down on the pedals and accelerate or even keep the speed going. It's an unpleasant feeling. I can only overtake, in fact, when we're going downhill, when I recklessly let the brakes alone and slide through the gravel to make up for time lost on the flats. It carries on like this. It's kinda fun, really, as long as I don't have to pedal.

Except it's not just a bike race. There's something we have to do on the way, some task that has to be accomplished. Today it's that we have to hand in at the finish the largest bird we can catch. Our plan is to get close to the finish line and catch one there, so we don't have to carry it too far. For some reason we're not really too worried about getting a really big bird. No turkeys or eagles or anything. A medium-sized one will do nicely.

So we reach the lip of a hill with the finishing line beneath us in a small green valley. A rider or two – and perhaps a marshal – is hanging around below.

I pick up a bird from the side of the road, reasonably big, other people will do better, but it's brown and feathery and some kind of a duck/raven hybrid. With the duck dominant. You can imagine, yes. I can't explain it any better than that. Anyway, as I pick it up a peregrine falcon flies up from the heather and into the sky, it's beautiful to see it, but there's no way I'll catch that, so I let it go, maybe someone else will bag it. So I'm holding this bird in both hands from either side, its legs between my fingers its wings neat and safe beneath my palms, and I ask my mother, 'Do I have to kill it? Do I just wring its neck?'

My mother seems to know what to do, and reaches over to hold the bird's neck. She presses hard at the base of the neck on the left and pushes over and there's a shuddering crack. The bird goes limp, but it's not dead, I can see its eyes, and it's a bit upset, understandably enough. My mother was a little too perfunctory with the manoeuvre, and I have to finish it off by repeating the action, I press down with as much force as I can and push across and I can feel the bone beneath my thumb and it's not moving, and time's passing. It feels like it's not going to go, and I feel bad about it, guilty. I don't know if the bird's in actual pain, I don't know if it can feel it, but I know that it wants the end, now, and I can't provide it. It's just not breaking. Only as I wake does the pressure release and there's an overwhelming feeling of relief that the neck finally gave.

New Orleans Blues

The first time it happens it's like this. I wake up in an unfamiliar hotel room, unable to remember the events leading up to my being there. At the time it didn't seem like too big a deal. I just assumed I'd been drinking. These things happen, after all.

It's a nice room. There are twin beds – the other one is untouched. A big TV in a cabinet, with a posted list of acronymed cable TV stations, none of which I recognize. A bathroom full of free samples. I pad around in the complimentary dressing gown and try and remember what happened. No go. Out the window there's a view of balconies, heaped with flowers. When I get dressed I find a fold of dollars in my trouser pocket. I guess that should have been a pretty big clue, but it didn't register at the time. I just knew I was late for work. I got my things together, noticing how light I was travelling, flipped over the Please Do Not Disturb sign and took the lift down to reception.

'Hi,' I said. 'I'm not sure how I got here, but I have to check out.'

'Room number please,' the receptionist asks. Ah, an American, I remember thinking.

'Uh, 524, I think.'

She taps in the computer, switching on an automatic smile not quite like the real thing. 'Mr Henry?' I nod, relieved. At least it was my hotel room. 'There'll be no problem. Your bill is paid in full. Have you used the mini-bar?' I shake my head, hopeful. 'Check-out time is twelve. Do feel free to stay until then. It's been a pleasure having you here.'

I set off out. Then remembering, say, 'Can I get a taxi?'

'The doorman will call one for you. Where are you travelling to?'

'Cowley area.' Blank. 'Oxford?' The smile stays, mechanical and bright, but her eyes are waiting. 'Uh, England?'

'Oh. You mean the airport. No problem at all, it's about twenty minutes.' And she's thinking: crazy tourist.

And I'm thinking: the airport? What the hell did I drink?

Outside it's warm. Bright sun, humid air. Exactly unlike England, even on a good day. There's a distinct smell in the air, but it's nothing I recognize. The doorman too is American – 'Where are you heading today, sir?' he says. Ever so slowly I'm beginning to suspect I'm in America and I have no idea how I got there. It's a bit embarrassing, really.

The doorman whistles a taxi over from the far side of the street. It's a black car that looks like it belongs in a funeral parade. A battered driver-door logo reads *New Orleans Cab Company*. I shrug it off, taxi to the airport and get myself on the first flight home, knowing that if I'm lucky I'll only miss the one day of work. A long flight, a short train ride and a brief bus journey later I get back to my flat. It's around 4 a.m. I take myself to bed for a couple of hours, planning to get to work early, and sleep soundly with my dreams all confused from the travel.

And then a few hours later I wake up in New Orleans. In the same hotel. The same room. The same bed.

'Welcome back, Mr Henry,' said the receptionist, professionally ignoring my stupefaction. 'Will you be with us long this time?'

Clearly there was some kind of a problem here.

For the second time in two days I get my stuff together, count up the dollars and shell out for a taxi ride and a plane ticket, and make a dazed Atlantic crossing. Then the train, the bus, and home. Having practised the run previously, I arrive in good time, it's barely 2 a.m.

'And where were you last night?' asks Jenny when I get in.

She's been waiting up for me. I'm exhausted from two days of long-distance travel, but I feel some sort of an explanation is owed, so I do the best I can.

Jenny isn't too impressed.

'You went to New Orleans? Why didn't you take me?' She's wanted to go there ever since she saw Dennis Quaid in *The Big Easy*. I try to explain but she's not interested. 'You went to New Orleans,' she repeats, sadly.

Lately I've been getting to know New Orleans pretty well. The hotel seems to be well located, on the edge of the French Quarter, one of the safer streets. There's a pool on the top floor, a gift shop and a terrace for sunbathing with a roofy view over the Quarter. It's a nice hotel. *Gateway to New Orleans*, a brochure in the lobby reads. Or maybe, come to think of it: *Getaway to New Orleans*.

Even before this things with Jenny had been a little strained. It started a couple of weeks ago with a conversation I knew I should never have got into. All the warning signs were there.

'Are you happy?' she asked.

And of course I was happy. And I would have told her so. But I did have something on my mind and figured she might want me to share it with her. Admittedly, I may have misread her tone a little when I answered.

'I'm fine,' I told her. 'I've just been feeling a bit strange lately.' It was true. I had.

'What?' she asked, sharp as a kitchen knife.

By then I'd realized my mistake. This wasn't a time for sharing. But it was too late to backtrack, I'd already said it, and she was determined to get out of me what exactly was wrong and she bullied me about it until eventually I said: 'Well, I just feel like something's missing from my life.'

She hit the roof. I managed to talk her round a bit but

she's been very sarcastic since. So when I got back from New Orleans the second time, we had quite a bit to talk about. I didn't even get to sleep before I had to head off to work.

My boss, Steve, doesn't seem to mind that I skipped a couple of days. 'We were quiet anyway,' he says. 'But we've a big order in now. Don't plan on going anywhere for a while.'

'Okay, Steve,' I say.

I do a twelve-hour shift, partly to make up for the lost hours. I get so tired by the end that Phil, a co-worker of mine, has to come and pull me off the machine.

'Hey,' he says. 'Time to go home. It'll still be here tomorrow.'

I try to avoid thinking about what might happen if I wake up in New Orleans again. So having gone two days without sleep I get back home and find a note from Jenny to say she's gone out to get us some dinner. I collapse on the sofa, zap the TV and fall asleep in front of some athletics event.

For three days straight I wake up in my own bed. Jenny calms down a little. And just as I'm beginning to rationalize it to myself – someone's playing a practical joke on me, or spiking my tea with hallucinogens – just as everything is returning to normal, I wake up in New Orleans. And I wake up crying, even before I realize where I am.

Lately I've begun to feel like something's missing from my life.

It seems to grow stronger as the days go on. Some days when I wake there's a cramping pain in my chest which takes a while to go. And I feel uneasy, as though I've forgotten something important. But there's nothing, really nothing. I've been through it. The worst days are the ones when I dream I wake up at home, but then minutes later wake up for real, in New Orleans.

Oh shit, I think, when I wake. That's what I hate the most. Waking up, and things being so bad I have to swear. Some weeks it's like this every day.

It's not entirely predictable, but it works out that I end up in New Orleans about three days in every two weeks. I've tried to find a pattern, but there's nothing I can work out. I don't even get a feeling of foreboding. It's like the very moment I awake I instantly transport there.

I tell Steve I've been ill, apologize for the days off. He looks at me with no small degree of suspicion.

But he seems easier about things than Jenny. It's like she didn't even listen to my explanation. So I find myself lying to her, providing reasons in advance why I might not be around for a while.

'I may be heading out with Phil,' I say. 'Might be out late.' Or: 'I'll be off to work before you wake tomorrow.'

Jenny just takes it in silently. She can be pretty heartless at times. Or maybe she's just noticed that my tan is gradually getting better.

My tan's better because I'd realized by this time that while I'd seen a good deal of New Orleans airport and the drive there, it's nothing to write home about. And once I'd worked out the plane schedules I found I often had an hour or two of time free in the morning after I woke before I had to get a taxi. So then one day I figure: what's the rush? I decide to get a later flight back, have a look around. I wander round the Quarter. It turns out the smell I noticed when I first arrived is pretty much everywhere. Sometimes I think it's the river, the Mississippi, and sometimes I think it's just the town. The heat has been hard to get used to. I'm often looking for a place to sit in the shade. Where from somewhere, there's music playing. There always is, here. I can hear Louis Armstrong singing jazz, voice like a happy hyena, asking if I know what it's like to miss New Orleans.

I get to know the area around my hotel pretty well this way. One day I end up at one of the touristy occult shops. There's a window display consisting of a coffin filled with skulls and rubber snakes. A big sign advertises:

WHO DO
VOODOO?
WE DO

The note just beneath it reads 'The Voodoo Priest is IN'

And I figure: why not? The shop's packed with voodoo mer-chandise, and a handful of tourists weighing up whether to invest in shrunken-head key-rings or pocket-sized books of spooky voodoo stories. Behind the counter there's a curtain of beads concealing the back of the shop. It looks dark and smoky through there. The guy behind the counter takes one look at me.

'You should see the Priest,' he says.

'Okay,' I say. 'I'll see the Priest.'

'Fifteen bucks,' he says, looking down at a notepad. 'Up front.'

I'm not even sure the money's mine, so I don't feel too bad about spending it. He takes the dollars and tells me to wait, then he goes out the back of the shop, returning in a minute to point me the way.

I push through the beads. A wrinkled old woman sitting in a wicker chair nods me towards a door. It feels exciting. It feels like I've found something. Except when I go in it's not the voodoo shrine I was expecting, just a simple room, with an office desk and two chairs. The chair on the far side of the desk occupied by a black guy in jeans and T-shirt. No feath-ers, no skulls. He's rocking back and forward casually on his chair, using his foot to push against the edge of the desk.

'Where y'at?' he says.

'Uh, are you the priest?'

'Whatever you say, man.'

I almost want to ask if I can see his qualifications.

'You are the priest, right?'

'Man,' he says intently, 'whatever you say.' Okay.

'Just tell me what your troubles are and I'll fix them,' he says.

112

'I keep waking up in New Orleans,' I say. He looks up in surprise and his foot slips from the table, the chair coming forward with a thump.

'No shit, man,' he says. 'That's seriously weird. *Exactly* the same thing's happening to me.'

'Wait,' I say. 'What?'

'Oh yeah,' he says. 'It don't matter what. I wake up in New Orleans *every day*. I don't understand it.'

There's something here. Some communication thing I'm not getting.

'And you're from?' I ask, my heart sinking like it had a concrete overcoat.

A carnival smile parades across his face, one side to the other. 'New Orleans, man.' He has the deepest laugh, slow and rich, coming up like bubbles in hot mud.

I get up to go.

'Hey wait,' he says, still chuckling. 'I'm sorry. Listen, you paid your money, you better tell me what's going on with you. Most people come in here, they just want their fortunes told, you know? It's like they didn't even *see* all the card readers out on the street. I mean what's going on with that? I'm *Doctor Lézarde*. This ain't no tourist shit in here, you know.'

I explain what's been going on. He beckons me to lean forward.

'Now breathe out slow,' he says.

I take a deep breath. I feel a lot better for it. But he just darts his head forward and takes a good drag on my breath. He grins.

'Just checking you're not stuck on the bourbon.'

'That's really not my problem.'

'If you say so. But most everyone who comes in here has been, you know what I'm saying?'

He weighs things up for a while. He tilts his head to one side as though he's listening for something.

'You're trying to live in two places at once,' he says.

'I'm trying to live in *one*. And it's not here. I'm really not trying to be here at all.'

'Well you sure as hell are here. I can see you.'

'Well, yes.'

'You don't understand. You're here. And you keep coming back here, even though you try and stay away. You can't live in two places at once – and when you go, part of you is clearly staying here. And after a while it just drags you back. It's basic physics, man. Matter and bodies.'

'But I'd never even been here before – how could part of me get here in the first place? I didn't *lose* any bits of myself recently, nothing that could have actually got shipped out here, I'd notice that kind of thing.'

'Then probably it's something external to you.'

'I thought you said it was part of me?'

He looks at me as though I'm crazy. 'Do you have *any* idea what you're made of?' he asks.

I let that one go.

'Listen,' he says. 'This is all mojo. Good voodoo, bad voodoo, doesn't matter. Just mojo. And you've got problems. You should really find what you're missing.'

'And if I can't?'

He shrugs. 'We can always cut it out.'

'Cut *what* out?'

'What you're missing. Doesn't matter. Here.'

From a drawer in the desk he produces a small leather case. He lifts the lid and takes out a small silver knife. There's a thin red ribbon tied around the handle. As he hands it to me there's a sort of shimmer as though the knife's passing through some kind of a barrier across the room, I can almost see it *ripple*. I take the knife. I put my other hand out to touch this barrier but I can't make my arm move forward.

And then I get an overpowering feeling that the rest of the room beyond this boundary is just a visual illusion, that the room stops just in front of me, that I'm looking at a projection on a wall, an ultra-real TV screen. Suddenly I can actually see the line around the edge of this wall, I can see where my reality stops and this projection, or whatever it is, starts. I can see the *seams*. And as soon as I see that, I can see that the jeans and T-shirt of the guy are just what I want to see. If I catch him out of the corner of my eye, what he's actually wearing is: a long white robe, a set of what look to be costume-shop wings on his back. His head glows with a penumbra, like there's a light-bulb immediately behind him, eclipsed by the orb of his skull.

'Oh my God,' I say. There's patchwork quilt of divinity, sewn into the room. A fissure in reality.

Doctor Lézarde's looking a little nervous. He can see me stare. 'Uh oh,' he says. 'Uh, are you okay man?'

'Oh my *God*,' I say. I stand up and start backing away. I can't help it.

'Hey,' he says. 'Don't go. We were just sorting you out. Hey. Come back.'

But he doesn't come after me, he doesn't leave his side of the table. And I know this is because he can't, because his side of the table doesn't exist, because I'm projecting it. I started waking up in New Orleans and now I'm seeing *angels* or something, it's a completely natural progression, and there's no longer any doubt: I'm crazy.

But then standing sunbeaten and shocked back out on the street I think that if that's the case, then where did the knife I'm holding come from? I slide it up my sleeve. I don't think it would be too unusual here, walking round with a weapon on display, but I don't want to give anyone the wrong impression.

I collect my stuff from the hotel and head to see my old friend the airport.

I sit waiting for my flight to board, trying to work out what the hell's going on. A distracting shadow keeps falling over me. I look up. There's one guy who keeps walking right by in front of me. He's walking in a tight circle around the row of chairs I'm sitting on, like he's circling Jericho. And I'm getting more and more irritated. One time I look up just as he passes and he's carrying an ice cream. It's a neat trick because there aren't any ice-cream stalls around here and I swear he didn't take a break from his walk.

And I think, if he goes past one more time, *just one more time*, I'm going to hit him.

And then I realize how irritable I've been getting lately. After all, the guy's just walking, probably to calm himself down before the flight.

And then I realize how tired I'm feeling.

So I decide to give myself a break. This isn't easy stuff, I tell myself, I shouldn't sweat it. I leave the airport. I check back in at the hotel. I kill some time, because it's what I've got.

For a few days I do the tourist things. I take the St Charles Avenue tram. I catch the ferry over the muddy Mississippi to Algiers, and wander through garlanded suburbs. I go to hear some jazz at Preservation Hall. For a while it almost feels like fun.

But the dollars start to run out. This isn't because I'm not being careful. I'm living fairly cheaply. Mornings I buy an immense Po' Boy sandwich, which does me for breakfast and lunch both. It's more because I get mugged three times in three nights. Each time at gunpoint, in pretty central locations. Other tourists wandering by oblivious. A couple of locals probably perfectly aware but keeping well out of it. And each time I hand over my money, not wishing to get shot. It would have been four times in three days, because on my way home after the last time I was stopped again, and had to explain, after being bundled against a street wall by two men, that they were too late, that I'd already been done that evening. The thing was, they didn't seem at all surprised by this, and didn't even bother to check. Must happen a lot. I've been using the line ever since. Still, it shakes you up.

I leave the knife in the desk drawer in my room when I check out.

'Thanks for choosing us again, Mr Henry. We look forward to your company soon,' the receptionist says. Her smile isn't getting any more real. I smile back and I feel for a second that my smile is just as blank as hers is. I fly home.

Even though I obviously look exhausted when I get in – I looked in the mirror at the airport and my whole face is bruised with tiredness – Jenny doesn't ask what's wrong. She just stands there waiting for an explanation. She looks like she's been crying, a long time ago. I'm so tired I can barely shrug.

'So quite clearly,' she says, 'you think it's perfectly all right to disappear for three days without even phoning me.'

'I'm sorry. Really. I should have called.'

'I PHONED THE FUCKING POLICE!' she yells.

'I left you an address.'

'No you bloody well didn't. Don't you start lying to me.'

'I did. I told you. The hotel in New Orleans.'

Mentioning New Orleans wasn't a wise move. Her voice somehow narrows. Becomes so precise it begins to cut me up.

'Oh you were in *New Orleans* again. I see. But you didn't tell me you were going to *New Orleans*. Like last time.'

'I didn't *know* I was going.'

'How? How can you just *not know*? Are you a complete idiot?'

I let that one go by too.

'Listen,' I say. 'Listen. Can we do this later? I'm so tired. I have to go to work. I have to pay our rent.'

I've missed so many days at work the last month Phil does a double-take when he sees me, like he didn't recognize me the first time. Steve calls me in.

'You've been taking some more holiday time, then? It's traditional to arrange it in advance.' It seems like sarcasm's the in thing back home at the moment. Then he looks me up and down, sees how tired I am.

'Son,' he says. 'I can see you've got problems. And I'm not going to ask you what they are. I figure if you want to share it, you trust me enough just to talk to me. And you know I care, right? Whatever it is, if we can help, we'd like to. If you need some time off. I mean, more time off. Whatever.'

I'm tempted to confide in him, though my instinct to reciprocate his generosity is tempered by the feeling that if I did tell him what was going on I'd be out the door right now. They can't operate as a business if their employees are astral projecting 4,000 miles a night and having to long-haul it back home. The scheduling would be hell.

'Okay, Steve,' I say. 'I'll sort things out. I promise.'

I go home and try to work out what to do. There is one thing that comes to mind. If I'm only going to New Orleans when I sleep – or when I wake – then I just have to avoid falling asleep. Obviously this isn't sustainable in the long term, but it occurs to me that if I just stay awake long enough, if I just establish myself here at home, I might break the back of it.

There is something else. I wasn't going to mention this. I'm kind of embarrassed about it, to be honest. But I will: I tried this sleep deprivation knock before. I had it all planned. I bought the Pro-Plus. From a guy on the street a small wrap of cocaine. And pharmaceutically primed, went to the airport, prepared to go home and *stay awake* until I felt like I'd be pretty sure where I was waking up.

And then I fell asleep on the plane.

I start off with one good night's sleep, so as I'm properly rested. Of course, I wake up in New Orleans, but I don't regard that as too big a setback. I simply fly home.

I come back to find that Jenny has left. There's a note pinned to my pillow which reads: *It's not me who's leaving, it's you*. Kind of accusatory, really. Even though I explained things to her.

It works better the second time. I'm spaced out at work, but I keep my eyes open. I know that if I just will myself into being at home, I will stay. I just feel it.

I go two days at work and stay up the night between by drinking coffee and watching movies.

Steve's worried about me. He's worried about the work too. He comes over just before I start a print run and re-sets the colours, saving me from a big error. But I couldn't even see the colours. I'm feeling manic and looking deranged. Steve starts to ask me about some more work but he cuts off halfway through because he sees a sweat snap on my forehead. 'Never mind,' he says, 'I'll get Phil.'

I've been funnelling Steve my supply of free hotel soap, so he's giving me a bit of a break, but his lenience is not going to last for ever.

All the coffee is giving me the shakes. I shake at work, shiver when I get home. I'm just wondering, am I ever going to get any sleep?

I finally pass out on the sofa four days in. There are some strange dreams. In the only one I remember Jenny is Juliet and I'm Romeo and we're both about to kill ourselves. But I'm not just Romeo, I'm Jesus too, so I'm not just in love with her I have to *save* her as well. I sleep twenty hours and wake up with the dawn chorus on surround sound. But still on the sofa. Okay. Things look like shit in the mirror, but I go out, full of relief and confidence. I feel great. I go to buy a paper. A kind of bounce has worked its way into my stride – I'm on the moon. Next thing I'll be riding buggies and playing golf. I start making plans. I'll find out where Jenny's staying and give her a call, tell her I've worked things out. No more going to New Orleans, not unless we fly there together. I can show her round. It's a great feeling, thinking about these things.

But then in the shop I start to get nervous. There's a long queue, a whole bunch of people buying lottery tickets and it's taking too long. That old feeling just starts welling up inside – the feeling I'm missing something incredibly important.

I stagger home. The nausea is crushing, all I can feel. It really shakes my confidence. And when I get in all I can do is curl up on the sofa and wait for it to pass.

A few hours later I wake up in New Orleans. I could cry, really. I weigh up whether to call Jenny, get some help, but what am I going to say, 'Hi. I'm in New Orleans . . . '?

'Oh, won't you come back to New Orleans,' growls Louis Armstrong from the car stereo.

It's the same taxi as before, from the first day. The same car, black and the seats somehow slung back, bead necklaces draped thickly from the rearview mirror. It's a nice car.

'Last night I went to bed in England,' I tell the driver. 'Just woke up here.'

'Crazy, man,' he says, without interest. Like he's seen it all before. Like this is California or something. Like shit just happens.

'Oh, don't you come back to New Orleans.'

'Can you turn that off?'

'Man,' he explains, 'this is *jazz*. No.'

But when we get to the airport I break out in a sweat. I feel like I'm living out a curse, that I'm never going to get free of this cycle. Wake up, fly home. Go through it all again. I tell the driver to take me back to the hotel.

'Crazy man,' he sighs.

I take a long walk off a short evening. I set out determined to find my missing pieces, to look down every alleyway until I turn me up. I start by having a few drinks. After that I don't remember too much. Except that for some reason the town is filled with parrots. Everywhere, everywhere, parrots. Perched on people's shoulders, on balconies, in trees. Green parrots. Of course it may have been the drink.

At some point, in some bar or other, I get to thinking that maybe I'm not even going to recognize the part of me that's here. Maybe she's a waitress working at one of the bars or restaurants, maybe she's one of the velvet-skinned girls in loose summer dresses hanging round a terrace or sitting in a swinging chair up on a balcony. Or maybe it's something more complicated than that – maybe whatever it is, it's not

even here and it's just that here's where I have to start looking. Sometimes I get the feeling that what I'm doing is plot-
ting a course through possible worlds, and that I just have to
get it right, or as close as I can manage.

In the morning I wake up at the hotel. I'm not sure if it's
because I actually made it back last night or I just woke up
here the way I have been doing. But then I'm running out of
money and I can't bring myself to fly home because (a) it's a
nice day and (b) what's the point?

I walk up to the lake and find a short quay to dangle my
legs from. It's a big lake. One freak storm, one decent size
wave and it'll wash the whole city into the river. This town's
sinking and I think it'll take me with it. I can almost feel the
wave like nausea inside of me, it starts in my stomach and
swells up into my chest, cresting in a peak of pain that breaks
over my heart. And I know partly it's homesickness, that I'm
so tired of being here and I'm missing Jenny and our life
together. But it's also this hole that's grown inside me, and
the thing that hurts most about that is that I still don't have an
idea what it's all about. I just sit and dangle my legs, feeling
miserable. I stay there a long time. And it's while sitting up
there by the lake when I realize I can't live like this any more.

Back in my room I start to look around. I find the silver knife
in the desk drawer, sitting on top of a pad of hotel notepaper, as
though it were a letter-opener. Doctor Lézarde was right all
along. Something's missing, and I can't bear not knowing what.
But how do you cut out a hole? Isn't that just going to make a
bigger hole? And then what if there's nothing else that fits there?

I go to look for Doctor Lézarde. The sign on the shop door
has changed. Someone has taken a marker pen and written
over the letters so that it now reads:

WHO DO

VOODOO?

SHE DO

And it turns out the price has gone up to twenty dollars. It's all the money I have left. I pay up and wait my turn. I go through the beads past the old woman and she nods her head. It looks like she hasn't moved since last time I was here.

I look for the seams but the room is whole, the wall-to-wall TV isn't playing. The desk seems real. The chair seems real. The serious-looking woman behind the desk seems real. For some reason she reminds me of my mother.

'Where's Doctor Lézarde?'

'He ain't here no more,' she says. 'He had to go. Someone gave him some bad news one day. What*chew* want?'

'I want to see Doctor Lézarde.'

'Honey. You ain't too smart. I just told you he was gone. Don't you believe me? You can look around if you want, but there ain't no hiding places.' She waves to the empty room, challenging me.

Then she leans forward. 'But I can help you just fine,' she says. 'My name's Madame LaBohème.'

To be honest, Madame LaBohème is scaring the shit out of me.

'Come on, my little chicken,' she says. 'You tell me what's wrong.'

I slide the knife out of my sleeve and lay it on the table, pushing it towards her. But before I can offer a word of explanation she grabs it.

'Oh, he gave you *that*, did he? Well why didn't you just say so right away? That makes things a *whole* lot clearer. So what's your problem?'

'I don't know what to do with it.'

She laughs. 'You don't know how it works, honey? Well that's okay. Let me show you.'

She holds the knife up in her hand. She motions me to lift my shirt. I pull it up, then hold on to the arms of the chair.

'It *ain't* gonna hurt,' she says.

I take a gasp of breath. She runs the point of the blade down my chest, on the left side. Then she makes a horizontal move, just below my nipple, the lines intersecting over my heart. I didn't feel a thing but there's a thin cross of blood on my chest.

I breathe out, except I don't breathe. My chest's stuck.

Then I realize I can't move. She's paralysed me.

Madame LaBohème is laughing, and talking in a language I don't understand. It's like she's talking under her breath but the words are booming on out, like some darkened tongues. I know she does it just to scare me, but it really is scary. She seems to have gotten much bigger. I look for the line across the room, a sign that this isn't real. But it's hyper-real, like a dream I can't wake from. She runs her finger along the knife edge in appreciation of the sharpness. Then her eyes flash and she starts laughing again while I struggle to get free. But it's only my mind that's struggling – my body's locked down and inert.

Back goes the knife in her hand. It's like a scene from *Psycho*. The shadow on the wall. The quick cuts. Then she lunges brutally forward, plunges it right in my chest. I swear I feel my breastbone crack when the blade punches through. I look up from the silver handle protruding bluntly from my front. I try to take in a breath but still the muscles aren't working, it's like she's nailed my lungs to the straight wooden back of the chair. She leans so close I can see my surprised face reflected in her eyes. They shine with insanity. But then the delay's over and the pain starts. And oh, God, the *pain*. It's unbelievable, it's awful. It feels like my soul's rising out the wound, being pulled right out from my body, the cells tearing away, divided by the force.

And then I pass out.

I never wake up in New Orleans any more. The world's a smaller place. Whatever it was that was so important to me is gone. The pain's lessened with time, though sometimes it feels like my chest freezes, my insides icy and expanding and putting pressure on my bones and frame. There's a perfect two-inch-long scar just to the left of my sternum and when I'm sleeping with Jenny I often find her fingers dwelling there, stroking up and down the invisible line of it as though she'll rub it clean away.

So things are going along okay. I feel less than I was. But at least I'm in one piece. Every morning I do a quick tally to check. Some days I have Jenny do recounts, but mostly I come up complete. I can sense the hole, but it's not what it was, it doesn't drag me screaming in the night to Louisian-i-ay, it's somehow less a part of me. Truth is, I can get on with my life again. Only old-style jazz on the radio will make it twinge, or a breath of humid air from the river in summer. But no, I've put it all in the past now, put it behind me, and got on with living my life where I am.

Oh, but God I miss New Orleans.

It's All True

Here's a true story for you, if I can get it right first time (I couldn't bear to tell it more than the once). I want to tell it straight, with no repeats and no rehashing, no exaggeration, no lies. So here it is, truth or dare. How my sister got over the worst of her (first) depression:

It was another cold, chemical day, a day full of ordinary horror. She was at a train station, and train stations, like gun shops and the tops of tall buildings, are less than optimal locations for the suicidally inclined. A quick Bovary off the platform and you're paint, a Jackson Pollock over the commuters.

And suicide was a definite likelihood that afternoon. Her depression had been building for months, the growing desire to die overrunning her thoughts, and she caught somewhere between trying to suppress that desire, or fulfil it. She hadn't talked about it, not to me, not then. She had hidden the horror from us. As great and expanding as it was she kept it all inside. She had endured an unendurable suffering, and did not know how she had done so.

There had been then, she told me later, a *bad night* (but the bad nights are another story). In the early hours of that morning she had felt something trigger within her, her fantasies of dying mutating into something more powerful, passing beyond mere longing, beyond the idea of death as relief, release. I have heard it said that everything's creation contains within it the kernel of its own destruction, and perhaps this remains true for humans, too, our conscious lives. A chemical switch had been flipped, and every constituent cell of her body had started to long for its own end; they screamed to her, a billion individual entities bent on oblivion. Holism went right out the window. If her cells were lemmings they'd have leapt off the cliff of her being.

Such sufferings, though impossibly loud on the inside, are invisible, save for that look in her eyes, the smudged suggestion of tears on her cheeks. If you'd seen her crossing the station forecourt you'd have registered nothing more than a thin girl, wearing a coat too heavy for the season, her body a slippery expression of pure stumbling exhaustion. But you wouldn't have seen how she detached for a moment from her head. Watched herself move a step ahead of her, not feeling her steps. She does not know how she came to be at this station, or what it is that still puts this foreign foot forward, then the other. What it is that keeps her standing.

It helped that the station was quiet. It helped that the train was at the platform waiting, for she had known stations where the platform edges pulled with insistent gravity, where through-trains came screeching with promises of relief. So for want of alternatives she hauled herself on board, finding herself for a moment unable to breathe, assaulted by the thick stench of the smoking carriage. Reluctant to sit there (smoking kills; but slowly, too slowly) she tracked two carriages back, located an empty seat and collapsed in it, instinctively curling up against the window, eyes closed, affecting the symptoms of flu so as to ward off company. Desperate and alone, but still she could not bear anyone else, the weight of her own soul quite enough. Silently, she begs to be left alone, *begs*.

The train insistently sits. Twenty minutes after its supposed time of departure. Not even granting her the luxury of forward motion, the promise that at least she is going *somewhere*, that around the next bend things might somehow, somehow be better. Her desire to die seems strong enough to kill her, all by itself. It's pressing in, an urgent alarm, infinitely irritating, ringing in her ears. It's gonna make her head implode.

And then she feels someone sit beside her. Though the carriage must still be empty, though free seats still must beckon.

You fuck, she thinks. *You couldn't have sat somewhere else.* A brief, exhausted swell of anger, though merely an extension of self-hate, of her disgust for how she feels. She wills him – she is certain it is a man, his scent is sharp in her nose – to disappear. Or if he is to sit, to keep his distance, to shut up, to die quickly in the seat.

And then he touches her arm, quite lightly.

She remembered, months later, when she confided all this to me, the shock of it. How persecuted she felt. How had he dared? Hadn't he known that his touch alone could kill her?

She opens her eyes, ready to turn on him, re-energized with fury. She looks to her right. But the seat beside her, like the rest of the carriage, is entirely empty, with no sign that anyone has even passed by. The train too is moving, has pulled from the station without her noticing.

And then she realizes she does not feel it any more. The desire to die, so strong it had a weaving nausea patterned to its path.

It has been lifted up.

And she rides the train home, bewildered and a little numb, bereft of that terrible longing. Relief coming in like a midwife, something like the faintest precursor of *hope* being born in her heart.

There will be the cynics, of course. Scornfully seated in the back row, rolling their eyes at each other. *Angels*, you say? Oh please. The girl was mad. Well, she was upset, granted, but not mad. I've enough familiarity with depression to know that you become sensitive to certain things. Sensitive to the truth: to the brutality of the world, to the provisional nature of our lives, to all our failures, to our unremitting lack of love. So why not to other things too?

This next, though, is hard to tell. As many times as I have told it. I still pause before beginning. You will forgive me, I hope. You see, everything that has been given may be taken away. Or everything that has been *taken* may be returned unto you, heaven notwithstanding, no questions asked.

In the end she got five more years from it, my sister. Five years of unexpected and relatively blessed life. More than many people receive. But once such paths of depression have been scored into your mind they are never truly erased, no matter how much junk you throw at them. Once the pattern has imprinted itself.

So then five years later, driven once more unto desperation, she found in time her way to another train station, and this time the angels were not waiting for her, or were looking the other way as she eased herself quietly over the platform edge. She was pulverized there on the tracks, a freight train reducing her to rags as it hustled on through.

You will forgive me if that is as much as I can bear, for the moment. But already I know that it is not enough, not nearly enough. I didn't nail it down, I didn't get it right. I can feel the truth out there still, my stomach growling. So we shall come back to train stations (for in our beginnings are our ends). I find that I have skipped introductions. Instead of the story, then, or as well as it, allow me to offer to you a *true history* or two.

I will start – no false modesty, I am not shy – with myself. It was my first love, you see. When you fall for the truth, bam! You fall hard. You fall with your gut, as much as your heart. So it is with all loves, perhaps, you give yourself over to them. You look for them everywhere they might appear, you find the fragments and bind them together. You fall for it the way you fall for a beautiful girl (for truth is beauty, and vice versa). You would ruin yourself over it, if it came to that, because it is your first love, before you have learned to keep something of yourself back.

In every generation there has to be some fool who will say the truth as he sees it. I was a veracity vulture, a prepossessed prodigy, precocious punk kid. A pain in the neck. And if my grades did not reflect the perspicacity of my genius, then you may imagine that it was only because there were teachers to whom truth did not matter. Utterly unsympathetic and (t)ruthless individuals. Who were only interested, in their limited way, in *correct answers*. And you may also assume that our schooling system used too often the method of the multiple-choice test. True or false? I ticked false, every one. Do they think truth comes in boxes? That you can locate it with pencil marks? It's a miracle I emerged unscathed from these nurseries, from the Manichean, the class-ridden and the ghettoized. No, truth lives in the stomach, not the brain. I can feel it in me. Untruths fester, give me stomach ache.

I came to long for explanation, to know the truth of things. I am a little embarrassed by the lengths I have gone to, at times. I have spied on everyone I have known – rifled their drawers for letters, diaries, photographs, I have stolen their passwords, their post. If I could have read their minds I would have done so, without hesitation. And all, you must understand, without malice. I simply have not been able to abide things being hidden from me. I have wanted to understand, to know the beauty of explanations. I have wanted to see the whole picture.

My teachers, bearing what they knew of this in mind, tried to usher me into a career in science, one area where they felt my interest had been pricked. I was having none of it. I followed my meagre gut, hungry in its rumbling for truth, and it led me to, of all disciplines, history.

I hear the cynics at the back piping up again, the deconstructionists among them lifting their smug little heads and hands in protest. True history? Hubris, or what? In our relativist age . . . Who can really say what the truth is . . .? Or there next to them, the raised protestations of economists, those obsessive enumerators of human nature, which defies enumeration.

But *history*! History is lies – you synthesize and summarize, excise all that is clumsy, all that does not fit the plan.

You dismiss the junk DNA of our past (which will no doubt turn out not to be junk, after all). You choose what to keep, what to lose, you pare it all back to theory and evidence. Histories, you see, oppose. Histories contradict. A correct explanation of history will take as long as history, as a truly accurate map of land is of equal size to the land itself. And yet, and yet. Somewhere in the synthesis and the summary you can get close to truth. Somewhere among the lies it lingers. Or if not lies, then let us say stories. There is no history, only stories. And stories, it transpires, have manifold ways of aiming towards the truth. Some of which involve facts. Some of which do not. Stories are protective capsules, designed to contain truth. Though a warning – they may be misused. Ultimately they will contain what they contain. Caveat emptor.

Guilelessly, then, allow me to proceed with my history, my lies.

For though I have told you about my love, I have not yet mentioned where we met. I will have to go back to the beginning, or a little beyond.

In truth we never know our beginnings, but as far as I am concerned, it began with my great-grandfather. Who chose, no doubt imagining it a great wheeze, to sign up for King and Country. Let us skip the tiresome moments of training and fear and male bonding, and rejoin him a year or so later. The scene: the Somme, day one. The context, an early morning exchange of artillery, the opening salvo, even. He was sharded with shrapnel while he shaved (messy deaths, too, in our family), the first casualty of the battle, if not the war. Not even the time to take to the trenches, caught in the ignorance of his youth, his age. From obliviousness to oblivion in no time at all.

At home, though, he had sown a seed, which grew over the years into my grandfather. Who, in an act of almost loving filial imitation, managed a similar trick twenty-five years later.

Some nastiness involving a tank, the army has never been conclusively clear. It seems we have always found ways to die young. Our family tree has shot many shoots, but not retained much to show in the way of actual branches. There was no shade for my generation, no canopy. Yet amongst the panoply of premature death there have though been one or two (and I hope yet to number myself among them) who have gone a little against the grain.

My grandmother (not one to go to her grave with grace) resents her survival. The one member of my family who might actually have been happy to die young, she stays alive very much against her better judgement, and suffers terribly for her choice. A litany of mounting pain. But something in her clings to life, even as life tortures her. The old girl just can't help it. First the hips and the knees, then the eyes, the teeth – they all gave way. Composting, as we all do, though some of us have the good sense or fortune to be buried first. Her most recent complaint is aplastic anaemia (an attractively alliterative ailment). No blood cells, or very few. No red, no white (the cellar being bare). The inability to produce more, to restock. As for platelets, the minimum count, the required count, is 150 (some unit or other, much too complicated to explain). My grandmother had a count of 4 (rising to the heady heights of 25 after treatment). A number too low (way too low) to sanction serious operation. But an operation she has lately occasioned, after acquiring appendicitis. So they scrubbed up, cynicism notwithstanding. They pumped her full of platelets and did the job right away, crossing all available fingers, even her own, an orderly leaning over and plaiting the anaesthetized and arthritic appendages for her. To nobody but the doctors' great surprise, she survived.

'Never grow old,' she whispers into my ear every chance she gets. A veritable Peter Pan of infirmity. Pinching my ear to bring it closer to her mouth. A disturbing thing to hear, given our ancestral history. *Never grow old*. A recommendation – no, practically an *invitation* – to die young (for youth is beauty, perhaps). A sentence that circles subliminally, a submerged spur to suicide. I confess she is a somewhat nightmarish presence in my mind, my grandmother; she comes in like a lone horsewoman of the apocalypse with the promise of torments to come. But I was young then, and if I had understood how she suffered, how she could abide neither her age nor the accompanying agonies, I would have had a greater enthusiasm for euthanasia. Perhaps I would even have abetted her exit.

'How are you?' I would ask.

'Old,' she would say, with a sharp glance (suspicious of my ability to truly grasp the significance of it. I would not grasp it. *I would smile*, in fact, *and go on drinking tea*), and I can see now that this was all there was to it, for her. Condemned to near perpetual suffering and everything expressed in just that one word. *Never grow old*. But then there is so much we should not do that seems to come quite naturally to us.

She is a confused old bird, in any case.

'Get yourself a nice job in a bank, like your sister. Earn some money, and enjoy it while you can.'

My stomach aches.

But I'm getting distracted. Stories, they spread like butter, and I'm short on bread.

Moving on swiftly, we come to my parents. My father, lacking his own (and no doubt worn down by his mother), perhaps disappointed too to find no waiting war in which to waste his youth, found instead *truth*, a noble find, vitiated only by the place he found it, at the bottom of a bottle. Still, in vino veritas.

My mother was an American, now naturalized, a graduate of the Jack Kerouac School of Disembodied Poetry. Unlike myself, she is a terrible judge of character, which is how she came to marry my father. She suffers grief at the loss of her parents. Fear for her mother-in-law (fear of ending up like her mother-in-law). Horror at the suffering undergone by her husband, my father (which I shall come to presently). But she has repressed these fears, these griefs. She has painted a smile and a bright, inquisitive voice over them, and they in turn have nestled in an irritable bowel, which she grins and bears. Aside from that, she is content.

They did not die young, my parents, though in their own way they chose not to live. They retreated from everything that met them until there were just the two of them left (and then two more), living quietly and happy. They accepted all the lies you need to accept, in order to live peacefully. My mother firmly believes that the world is good, that things tend to work out for the best.

Though things, I have observed from cursory observation, tend to work out for the rich, privileged inhabitants of the West, rather than, say, for Zimbabwean AIDS orphans. It's probably coincidence.

Such was my upbringing, suspended in more bubbles of delusion than I have been able to burst. Believing we're good, believing we're liked. Believing even that people find us interesting, attractive. Believing that the terrible things that happen in the world have nothing to do with us, that we deserve all that we have, our health and our wealth, that it is neither *luck* nor *accident of birth* that has allowed us to live such tremendous lives. That, secretly, the sick and poor deserve what they have.

Really, how are we to survive?

They believed in ignorance, my parents, self-inflicted ignorance, chosen ignorance. They affected not to understand the world. The mention of a distant genocide in a newspaper headline would cause my father to grunt and move on, that far foreign land belonging to a distant world, distinct from the one he chose to live in. The darkness of our species being an absurd idea. His black alcoholic heart unrecognized by its bearer.

Until, a stroke. And then all of his secrets spewed out, spat from his mouth with a primal venom. All the bad things of his mind, all the things he thought he could keep locked hidden deep inside of him, that no one would ever know. That he has feared even existing. He tried to keep them in, strained for control, and still the words escaped him, terrible words. Terrible, terrible things about Jews, blacks, gays, children. About my mother, my sister; about me. And then he died, having at least passed, by some margin, the ancestral average. Perhaps, of course, they were not really his words. In any case, the propensity was clearly within him, as it is within us all. The truth will out. But those last, tortured months, they were a *revelation* – at last, my body said to me, here is something unalloyed. You have been starved for truth and now here, finally, here is something that satisfies. My great infatuation was spawned, and I would not settle for lies ever again.

I am not entirely ungrateful. They meant well, my parents. They wanted to give us good lives. They wanted to protect us from the perils of living, send us out into a better world than in fact existed, into a safe world which rewarded virtue. They had *good intentions*, which pave the road.

Which perhaps explains why we rebelled, my sister and I; why we abandoned their better world in favour of the real world. It explains why I fell in love with truth and why my sister felt herself to be driven far from home, why she went to Africa in the midst of a famine, saw the suffering and decided to take a part of it as her own, and found solace for her conscience by helping others. Until it all became too much. The years bore on her there, wore on her, the suffering, the hopelessness. They brought down upon her a deep depression which led her ultimately towards four psychiatrists, three hospitals, and two train stations, at the last of which . . .

She used to say, my sister, that the good thing, the one good thing about the illness, though it gave no comfort, was that you saw the world as it was. That something going wrong in the brain might actually be something going terrifyingly right. And her miraculous five-year extension brought with it a curious sadness, because it laid like blankets her old illusions over her again, and she felt their deceiving weight, their suffocating warmth.

No, I can't do it. I'm losing my grip on this story, I can feel it going from me. You want the truth? You can't handle the truth. Or at least, I'm not sure that I can. Shall I try again? If you wanted me to, I could *begin again*, I could start from scratch, and this time, if you wanted me to, I could embroider the story with some facts. What if I said that the train my sister faced was not a train? If I said it was not even my sister? That my grandmother had it right and my sister works in a bank. Would it make any difference? What, I lose marks with you for attempting to *humanize* my family?

Oh Jesus, leave me alone. Can't you see I'm doing my best? It's not easy, this. You aim for big things, true things. I had grand ambitions. You hope that the truth somehow creeps out. You hope that the listener has truth in their own heart, and knows how to recognize it when they hear it. Because you set out to tell the truth, and words cluster, they get in the way.

Because it's all true. Names have been changed, facts have been embellished (The Jack Kerouac School of Disembodied Poetry? My mother?). I have allowed one or two future hopes to creep into the telling. Events, yes, have been made up. I confess to it. But still, it was the only way to get such things across. If I were to try again from the beginning:

'And so I look out now at this darkening platform and . . . and . . .'

No, it is not enough. I am at a loss to say what this feeling is, what this sight before me means. Oh, my misshapen soul. So instead I tell you that once there was a train station, and comment banally that train stations, like the tops of tall buildings and gun shops, are less than optimal locations for the suicidally inclined.

I am repeating myself now, as I told myself I would not do, and with the story already told, too. Over, nearly over, the end in sight (a relief for you, no doubt). I feel that I have been condemned to know truth, yet be forever unable to tell you what it is. I know how it bends, like light by gravity. I know how truths, uncontained by mere logic, can contradict each other. How truth can be simple or complex, shredding sharpened razors. And here I am, throwing words at it, hoping the right ones will stick, and not just in my throat.

Here it is, this great inexpressible inside of me, imbuing in me a terrible desperation to see justice done, despite the sub-Tourettic tics of my speech, despite my effusion, my mania. I have done my best, I have tried to explain *my* terror and *my* fear and *my* life. I have given it my best shot, my best words. And I am distraught, because I look at it now and it seems like a blind stammering after the truth, I mean, not even *close*.

Dream #100
All night, every night

When you run, you run hunched over, fists up and swinging always inwards, head ducking forward behind your guard, like a boxer. Your back arched, as though the heavy pack were already there. You run five times a week, regardless of whether you feel like it, whether you want to. You always want to. You wear shorts, a hooded top, a woollen hat fitting tight to your shaven scalp. Running shoes without socks, shoes that fit tight as skin. You lope, idiosyncratic, almost stumbling, for miles without rest or break in your stride. You drag your feet, pound the pavement.

In the beginning you do not go outside for six months. You are too sick to care for anything outside you. You want only medicine. Across from your bed, or the sofa, a television plays, analgesic, and the screen blurs with your mind. You see moving pictures even when your eyes are closed. You do not sleep, but you have nightmares all the same. The television plays when it is switched off. And people die. Some of them, somewhere, are real. You do not know the others, and do not care. Your mind is a coal, fading in the fire.

Your plane lands in a sudden rush of speed and braking over the desert, into a purple dawn. A low crescent moon welcomes you, the military machines beneath – radar towers like minarets, tents, jeeps, tanks. You are all here now, your brothers, your officers, your friends. You would die for them, as they may die for you. You do not wonder who will be first to die. You wonder who will be first to kill. You cradle your rifle

137

and you step out onto the dusty landing strip and stand like a prophet on the edge of your promised land.

You are in a park, a wide expanse of grass, a periphery of trees. The summer air is super-heated. Endless, overlapping games of football and Frisbee play out in front of you. Some of the kids in a nearby game are good, and their accented shouts are harsh, eastern-European. They could be internationals, stars. Your friends suffer from the heat. You watched them, these last years, drink until their bellies filled out. Watched them breathe smoke, and yet it is they, not you, who play football in the park on Saturday afternoons, they who are in better shape than you.

After a year, or more, they do further tests. The tests are inconclusive, they prove nothing. Why do you need tests, you ask, when you can hardly walk? They have disowned you, pensioned you off, along with a few hundred others, maybe more. There is some talk about the effects of biological warfare. There is quieter talk, too, about reactions to injections, vaccines. Numbers build, even some evidence, somewhere. The army, finally, relents, grudging. Scared. Your doctor talks about experimental programmes of drugs, new chemicals which may help. You want none of it, want only life or death, not half-life.

When she leaves she leaves the ring on the dresser beside your bed, as though you might pick it up and wear it. She is not going to another man, she is going away from you, from this end to her dreams, so that she might keep them alive. She does not want to suffer, no more than she wants to see you suffering. Your lives, after all, are separate and there is nothing that binds her to you. Her presence meant little enough, anyway. She did not stop the sickness, she did not take it away. It simply is.

Fire burns in your stomach, an electric hum lives in your arms, your legs. Malarial shivers shake you. Your mouth is always dry, the taste bitter, familiar. Your stomach is an opening fist, angry and empty. Your ribs are fingers stealing the strength from your limbs. You shit blood, mucus, explosive. Your skin crawls, and your spine is a worm, tunnelling. Consistent REM sleep is beyond you, and when you dream you dream in deaths – car crashes, trains derailed in flames, people dying. Buildings on fire. This time will not be bracketed, it can never be as if in parentheses.

With a 40lb kit, your rifle, you are crossing a bleak moor with your squad. You do thirty miles in a little under eight hours on rough terrain, hiking through the thick heath, jogging along tarmac country roads. When your group slows an officer shouts at you. When one of your group falls behind you fall back with him, grab his arm and hurry him along. It is the hardest thing you have done in your life, yet you could do more still, half as much again. You watch the others struggle, their movements loose, uncontrolled, but you do not.

After all the time in your cell, insensible monk, there is a day when you step out from the back door into warm air, find yourself beneath a darkening sky and feel stray, heavy drops of rain and you are blinded by the colour and detail and depth of the outside, the garden. It begins as chaos, a mosaic of shapeless colours, then the scales fall from your eyes. A square of green grass, fastigiate, full-leafed trees, wet earth. Bees weave between the raped mouths of flowers. Dizziness spins you round. This is how it was to be alive, once.

Before you leave, you talk about marriage, agree to wait until you return. She will make the plans, send the invitations, inform your families. You make plans. Then, the night before you go you drive north, marry in a register office, just the two of you, young and surprised and laughing. You buy a ring on the way, and they alter it to fit while you wait and she asks what you will bring her back. Peace, you say. Freedom of the Western World. Low oil prices, you say, so you can drive into the country and fuck all day.

Sometimes the days pass in flurries, sometimes they just die, the sun setting even as your eyes blink open and you rub the coarseness from them. Perhaps you dream some of these days, it makes so little difference. Perhaps you are a butterfly, dreaming you are a man, dreaming of a life that could not be conceived of. Awake, you cannot conceive of your own life, because it is beyond your capacity to imagine. And yet how many people have already travelled here and learned to understand the demons that afflicted them? Enough. Plenty. Elsewhere, people suffer. Some do not.

While you wait for the hospital to run tests, she suggests you look for some alternative therapy. You talk to several, until you are convinced by a homeopath, who tells you he can help you. He gives you aconite, arsenicum, belladonna, carcinocen, cheladonium, china, colchicum, echinacea, gelsemium, ignatia, merc sol, phosphoric acid, psorinum, sulphur, on tiny lactose pills coated with these things in millionth dilutions. Your doctor gives you less: restrained disbelief, a shrug. The tests are inconclusive, proving nothing. Your body is full of shadows. You climb the stairs one at a time. You have not run for months.

The turkey-shoot commences. Billion-dollar firework shows. Media-live adverts for Western military hardware. You have bombs which create burning vacuums, suck the air from people and fill their lungs with fire. Creative destruction. You trail your great art project up the Basra Road, leaving bodies burned to sculpture, lives wrapped in a thin film of peelable darkness, crispy bark. Their mouths open. The darkness cracks and flies. From tanks and planes and jeeps you fire bullets and shells coated in depleted uranium. It cuts through pretty much anything. There aren't any scientists here to explain what it is, how it works.

She has long brown hair and bright white teeth, pointed, evenly spaced. Her eyes are pale blue, except when her pupils dilate and a flare of brown explodes there. She was a teacher when you met her, now she runs her own business. She has grown up, and become a woman in the time you have known her, just as you have become a child, an old man. While you were away she learned to spend her hours at work, and she will not change now. She breaks your heart with all that she still is and you are not.

Six months in the army, and you have found your home. The rules are familiar to you. You can see how the game is played, and you play it well. You have found your like, and they have accepted you. You belong. You are part of something here, you are separated from the rest, and the only thing outside the fences is the young girl you left behind, the girl you can return to when you have leave, when you need comfort. The disappearing line between the two is clear, and you know which is your home, which your rest.

The view from the sand is this: oil fields burn, and are unconsumed; the sky blackens in an inferno of smoke, an apocalyptic horizon. You are a god, treading on ground no longer holy but sullied, corrupt. When you camp the unit sets up chemical alarms, biological alarms. You keep watch. All night long you see lights in the sky, ordinance, flares, chemical light. The alarms trigger constantly. You lay on your back, enclosed in your suit, pumped full of chemicals, pre-emptive strikes against biological warfare. Pills, swift kicks to your stomach. You see angels in the sky above you.

She keeps in touch after she leaves, rings you every fortnight. Some weeks you wait for days by the phone, only for the call to be over almost before you know it. She sends you a card, stiff in the envelope, over-sized. The thin, cutting cardboard is sky blue. Brightly coloured lettering stamped on it reads GWS. You do a double take. You can't believe it. They make cards for this illness, which does not exist, which cannot be treated. You open the card and read inside, 'Get Well Soon'. There is the weak urge to laugh, but you cannot.

In the winter you walk out in the cold on dark evenings and the snow sparks at you from the orange streetlights. You just walk round the block, twice if the cold does not drive you home. You slip on the snow and ice, too light to tramp through this as you once did. Your lungs are vulnerable to the cold air, and you breathe fearfully. Despite the layers of clothing, the fleece, the thick overcoat, warm boots, scarf, gloves, woollen hat, you are cold to the marrow. Inside again it takes an hour, or more, before you stop shivering.

You suffer. This defines everything about you, all you are and all you can and cannot do. You wait for it to end. You learn, finally, that this will not end, that this is all there is. After that there is nothing else to know in this world. You are as wise as any now to the truth of it all, the chemistry and biology, the nature of being, what it is to live. What it is to be isolated, what it is to be experienced. How living is impossible, suffering easy. You wait for death, and wish it soon.

You're strong, as strong as anyone you know, your mind and body both. You have built yourself in this life, and control it, and shape it as it should be shaped. You are married. You have a purpose, a cause, orders to obey, tasks to carry out, the rewards are yet to come but they are there, within your grasp, proffered. You are a soldier, you belong to the army and the army loves you as it loves all its own, it will comfort you and make you stronger and raise you up unto the light. You are a man.

Dog Days on Monkey Beach

The monkeys have been pissing in the drinking pool again. They know how mad it makes me but they do it anyway, just so I have to climb upstream to fetch water and they can throw bananas at me as I go by. Simian humour. They're worse than schoolboys. Usually I let them know how angry I am by yelling at them or throwing stones, but this time I let it go. To be honest I think they get a kick out of watching me howl and jump around. I've seen them almost fall out of the trees with laughing. So instead I just pick up one of the riper bananas and munch on it as I follow the cliff path up alongside the waterfall.

It's a real pain. To get back to the stream above the fall I have to follow a pig path until I'm way beyond the tree line, almost up to the fortress, then clamber back over the rocks, it's not a long trek, just irritating to have to tote water all that way when there's a perfectly good drinking pool a quarter mile from my hut.

It's a hot sunny day, same as it always is, and I stop from time to time to catch my breath and shake the pebbles out of my sandals. Their leather is getting a little worn. I've been trying to go barefoot to save them but you can't do that on the rocks, it's too easy to cut your feet and start leaking blood all over.

I relax as I get higher up, because the view gets better, and though I've seen it a thousand times I never get tired of it. You can see the whole southern side of the Island, the jungle spilling down to the ocean, the white coral beach like a bright skin separating the two. Then there's the light blue outline of the reef curling out in the shape of a snail shell from the land, the waves breaking over it, and the dark ocean stretching out into forever. It's a great view.

Looking up you see the fortress, the highest point on the Island. It's a natural hide in between some worn old rocks. I have a vague idea I spent some time living up there a few years back, there are still some scorch marks from where I built my fires. But you have to be careful building fires on hills. Too much smoke and a passing ship tends to notice and get the idea that you're signalling to them, angling for rescue. After a couple embarrassing misunderstandings I gave up on the fires and moved down to my hut by the beach.

The dead limbs of a large tree stick up from between the rocks. On the very highest of the branches a parrot perches. It's there all day every day and I've never once seen it move. I'd swear it was plastic except there's no way it could have got up there. The tree is dead and dried and completely unclimbable. Anyway, there's no one on the Island to put it up there. One time I sat and watched it for a week just to see if the damn thing would move, but no, it didn't even turn its head. So I figure it's real, just up there admiring the view, taking some sun. Maybe at night it flies off home. It's always too dark to tell.

I've always felt a little uneasy seeing him perched there like a portent, making me think something bad is going to happen. That was the other reason I moved out of the fortress, the parrot giving me the creeps. But then, he's been there for years and nothing bad *has* happened, so maybe I'm wrong about that. Maybe the really strange thing is that he's the only bird I ever see here. The Island's avifauna is really pretty limited. You'd think there was something wrong with the air, except that about a billion mosquitoes seem to have no trouble buzzing about.

I fill up my water sack, a container I sewed myself from the skin of a dead pig Ralph found, then I lug it down the hill and empty it into my well. And then I go to the beach for food.

Some days even getting the basics together can be a lot of work.

The ocean's animated today and the beach is misty with cold spray. I keep thinking about how the waves just keep coming the whole time. Sometimes they quieten down but they never actually stop, and the next day they'll be thundering in every bit as powerfully as before, throwing up all this spray.

But you can't do much swimming. There's only one pool where it's safe and that's not too deep. Just enough room for me and Ralph to splash around in. It's hard to be so disciplined. In the heat of the day when the sun's overhead the water looks cold and fresh and incredibly seductive – some days you'd think you could drink it – but it's really dangerous, it doesn't matter how strong a swimmer you are. I've vague memories of someone getting dragged right out over the reef and away into the distance. To be honest I may be making that up. I don't really remember anyone drowning, it's just a story I've told myself so many times, to remind me of the dangers, that I've convinced myself it happened. The Island's not a place for memories. I don't look back much more than a month or a year. The rest burns away in the sun.

I built a fish trap here, a corral of rocks the tide sweeps in over, and when the water goes out I get a small harvest swimming around in the trap. There are a million kinds of fish. I see something new with every tide. But I know that some of them aren't going to be too good to eat, so I stick to a few recognizable sorts, the long dull grey ones which are much tastier than they look, and then the brown mottled ones, with the flattish bodies, they do fine if there's nothing else. I used to experiment with the shellfish too, but had a very ugly week after one bad batch, so I'm less adventurous these days. I splash around in the trap and manage to drag out a decent sized grey. Then I go back to my hut. The airy strains of Hawaiian music grow stronger as I approach. Ralph is fast asleep in the shade outside. He's sleeping on his back, all four paws twitching in the air. He snores gently, his dog body limp and furry. It's incredible the shapes he gets into when he sleeps, I'm amazed he doesn't wake himself up. I resist the urge to tickle his tummy.

I get the hot rock stove going. It's only midday but it takes an age to heat up so I have to think ahead. My plan for the rest of the day is to tidy my hut and write some postcards. It's a small hut, and not exactly messy, but I move things around from time to time just to keep things fresh. For the last few weeks I've had my desk in the middle of the room, but it's gotten a little crowded, so I want to push everything against the walls and create a little space. I re-hang my hammock in the far corner. The hut concedes the emptiness a little reluctantly.

But it feels much cooler when I'm done. I sweep the sand out the door back onto the beach. I kick out the cockroaches, though they'll come right back. I've basically got used to the creepy-crawlies, and usually ignore them – for one thing I smell pretty much no different from the beach these days and the mosquitoes mostly give me a miss. And the cockroaches, well, it's not like you can kill them, the little armour-plated bastards. I tried stamping on one the other day and my foot just rebounded back up. They're like little metal helmets with legs, walking nuts.

The last thing I move is my shell. It's a great shell, a bit big maybe, an enormous conch I picked up off the beach a year or so back. I went through this whole phase then when I collected shells. You can get completely wrapped up in a hobby like that, getting up every morning to patrol the beaches and see what the ocean's lined up for you. There are a few miles of beach along the south coast alone, so it was pretty much a full-time job. I'd do a sweep with each tide. I got so obsessed with the routine I had less time to get food for myself and Ralph, and we didn't eat so well during that whole period.

But then one morning I got up and looked around my hut and was just appalled at the clutter. There were shells everywhere. Until then I thought I'd been good at only keeping the best ones, but even with being so selective I must have had hundreds of them, and my hut's really not all that big. So I cleaned it out. I took the shells and laid them along the beach and let the tide take them away. You have to do that, I think. It's not right to hoard these things, there's no need, if I want to see nice shells I can just get up early and walk along the beach. I don't need to own them.

I did keep one this conch though. It's all I can do to lift it. I think if the sound of the waves weren't so overwhelming anyway you could put your ear to it and hear the ocean.

I sit at my desk, brush a few grains of sand from the surface. I close my eyes, listen for a moment to the waves and the lilting guitars. Then I pull open the desk drawer, take out my pencil and root around for postcards only to find I've run out. All I have is an old pad of tatty writing paper and some discoloured envelopes, from when I used to write proper letters, a long time ago. I keep on with the postcards just to remind myself that there are still some things left between us. I've always wanted to write: *There's still something between us. Okay, it's an ocean, but . . .* I don't write that because I know how dumb it'll sound when she reads it. This is partly the reason I write postcards these days. In letters there's always so much more room to make mistakes, to say things that mess everything up. The best things I wrote her were always the shortest. And with postcards I don't feel quite so stupid when I don't get a reply.

I search my drawer again in case a stray card has slipped down the back, but no, I'm right out. It's going to be one of those days when everything I do needs more work than usual.

I leave the hut and look up with squinting eyes to judge the position of the sun. Mid-afternoon. The shop will still be open. Ralph is curled up in the shade like a doughnut, deep in dreams. Somewhere in the jungle Hawaiian guitars play. I check the hot rock stove. It's warm to the touch. Then I head over to the shop, following a sandy path through the trees.

The girl at the checkout sits on her stool, filing her nails. She looks bored. A quiet day, by the looks, and I haven't called by for a while. I walk in quickly past her, sending a nod in her direction. She barely acknowledges me. I head down the aisle towards stationery.

They sell postcards in small books, so you tear each card from the pad as you use it. They only have this one design, a shot of the beach in bright sunshine, airbrushed so it's all immaculate coral sand and no driftwood or coconuts or broken shells, the jungle lush and harmless in the background, a couple of palm trees swooping out elegantly over the sand. It's pretty dull, but nostalgic if you know the beach.

While I'm there I buy some toilet paper. I mean, I know I could use leaves, it would certainly be a lot less wasteful, but if you've ever tried it you'll know it's not the same. I tell myself that it's the only luxury I really have, and that in the scheme of things it's pretty minor. The weird thing is that they only ever stock black toilet paper. I never saw that anywhere except here. I guess they make it out of charcoal or something. But it's not like the colour matters, so I pick it up anyway.

I take my items over to the Checkout Girl. She puts her nail file to one side as she sees me coming, straightens a little on her perch. She puts my shopping through her machine.

'Postcards?' she says, as it registers with a beep on her machine. 'You should give that up. Don't you know it's over?'

I think about the ocean. 'Thanks for the advice,' I say.

'It's just that there isn't any post any more. Not just for you. I mean at all.'

She spends ages trying to find the price on the pack of toilet paper. Eventually her machine gives a beep and she hands it over.

'See you later,' I say.

She sniffs. I sometimes wonder if I should maybe spend more time with the Checkout Girl, maybe call by on her after work one day. But when you've had a long-term relationship with someone in their working capacity it's difficult to make the shift to knowing them socially. And to tell the truth, I find her a little bitter, always so cynical about things, and not nearly so much fun as she was in the old days.

The sun has got to that point in the sky where it's preparing to drop rapidly into the ocean. When it goes it goes like a rock off a cliff. One minute you're wondering how to spend the rest of your day and the next you're stuck in the jungle complaining about how dark things got all of a sudden. In the last of the daylight I cook my fish on the hot rock stove. I break open a coconut and have a milk. Then I light a candle and write postcards until I feel tired enough to sleep. It's strange, but as I lie curled up in my hammock drifting off to sleep I swear I can smell apples. Probably I just dreamed it.

The whole night long Loneliness scratches at my door. The air is warm enough but I feel cold and shift around in uncomfortable half-sleep. I used to have a blanket but it was always too warm and I put it out for Ralph one day. There are nights like tonight though when I regret that.

The sound of the waves blurs and makes my head spin. In my dreams the palm roof of the hut expands and flattens, pressing down on me, extending into unbearable infinity on every side. And calling outside, waiting for me to open the door, sits Loneliness. He lives over on the dark north side of the Island, opposite from me, but there are nights when the breeze changes and blows cold around the hill and brings him along with it. He always finds his way along the pig trails to my hut. And he knocks, certain that if he keeps it up I'll eventually let him in.

The knocking gets so strong I wake up. I feel so bad that I almost get up and go out to sleep with Ralph, put my arm over him just to feel another body swelling and contracting with breath, another warm and regular heartbeat. But I know that's a mistake. I'll go mad if I start on that, it's too easy to forget who you are. One minute you're hanging with Ralph a bit too much then the next thing you're just another dog on the Island.

In any case, that'd mean opening the door, and I can still feel Loneliness's presence. I've spent so much time on my own I can always tell when there's someone else around. I don't like it at all.

I pull my knees up to my chest and settle in the bottom of the hammock. Everything feels dull and heavy, and I know that I couldn't get up if I wanted. My teeth chatter. I feel feverish and my brain washes with the blurry waves. And at some point I fall asleep this way, though I can't tell the dreams from the waking. Either way, I can still hear the knocking.

And then some long time later I wake, as I wake every morning, to the assured and ceaseless roar of the waves. The sun is up and Loneliness is gone. Lying in my hammock I can hear the faint strains of Hawaiian music. I roll out of my net and drink some water from my well. The guitars play on, beguiling and happy-sad.

You can hear them all the time in this part of the Island and I've never worked out where they're coming from. I decided a long time ago that there must be loudspeakers hidden somewhere in the jungle around here, but I can't find any, however hard I look. I've shinned up pretty much every tree in a half-mile radius for coconuts at one time or another, and there's no sign. You never seem to be able to get warmer to the music, like it's on surround sound, coming from every point at once.

I breakfast on bananas and coconut. But I feel uneasy as I munch away. The night-time dreams are still with me. The hut door must have been loose on its latch because Loneliness crept in through the gaps. I feel like he's been standing over me while I slept, pawing me with his cold fingers. I need to wash the dirt of his touch off. But I feel too chilly for swimming.

So I set off instead into the jungle, in the direction of the waterfall. But I branch off before I reach the drinking pool and head through a grove of spindly palm trees, my sandals slapping over patches of flattened muddy sand. It's a long low part of the Island, tucked around from the rise of the hill. There are secret places in the uneven undergrowth, natural clearings between the trees, low hides under the bushes. Pig trails intersect and interweave. This is where the wise monkey lives. He has a big tree on a sandy plateau. The trunk of the tree forks three ways low to the base, creating a natural seat. Through the trees he has a nice view of the sea over the reef.

I come and see him every few weeks. The company helps. That's a bit unfair on Ralph, who's always around when I need him, but as great a companion as Ralph is he's really the wrong shape. It sounds horrible, I know, but it's good to be among bipeds from time to time.

The wise monkey doesn't say anything. He never does. He's just a monkey, after all, old and arthritic and pretty much stuck in his tree. He sits with a blanket of moss and leaves pulled around him like a robe, as though he were cold. Sometimes he shivers, even in the middle of the day. He gives me a sad look.

'You said it, monkey,' I say to him.

I peel him a banana. He takes it carefully and breaks it into small segments, eating them one at a time. He chews each piece carefully. He offers me the last bit.

'Thanks, monkey,' I say.

He reaches down for a half-coconut shell filled with water and has a slow, awkward drink from it. I lean forward and help him pull his blanket back over his shoulders. He closes his eyes. He looks exhausted. I know he sometimes gets like that when he's digesting food so I leave him to it.

He'll be okay. The other monkeys may be a bit childish, pissing in my drinking pool and throwing bananas and so on, but they do take care of him, and every day you see one or another of them clambering down through the trees to bring him water.

I feel a lot better after that. It's strange, because the wise monkey always seems so sad, but he always cheers me up.

On my way back I drop off my postcards at the shop. I catch the Checkout Girl in mid-yawn when I come in. She gives me a disgusted look when she sees me with my cards but takes them anyway, with a resigned sigh. I can't help but feel she resents her job in some way. It doesn't seem like a good attitude to have. No wonder she looks so permanently pissed off.

I'm a little tired by all the walking, so I doze for a bit then, catch up on some of the sleep I missed in the night. After lunch I take Ralph for a walk. It's becoming a zoic kind of day. I've warmed up with the sun so we go down to the beach and splash around in the water where it's safe. After that I let him choose where we go.

Typically, he heads for the north side of the Island. It makes me a little uneasy going over that way. It's not just Loneliness, I'm not afraid of him during the day, not with the sun out and Ralph running around, it's just that some strange things go on over there, and I usually try and keep to my side. The fortress is as far as I go on my own. But Ralph doesn't seem to distinguish between my side and the other, he happily explores any old where.

The thing is, the Island on the north side isn't very solid. It's like, when a wave hits the northern coast it doesn't break over the beach, but instead the land takes on the movement of the wave. It ripples. I've never quite made it to the northern coast, but you don't need to go all that way to know this, because the waves reach quite a way inland. You notice it almost immediately. The ground ahead of you seems to lift and flow like a strong wind is blowing through the trees and then you feel weightless as the wave goes under you. And the further north you go the stronger the effect gets and the weaker the land is. On calmer days it's not too bad, it can feel quite soothing. But if there's a bit of a storm up, or if you're too far north, you can be thrown right off your feet. And the strength of the waves is enough to actually rip the Island apart and open up holes. The one time I found this out I got stuck on a tiny islet that tore off from the main section, an island floating on an Island, a small patch of turf with barely enough room for me to stand and a thin tree in the middle, water opening up around. I clung to that sapling, terrified it would uproot and the land would melt right away beneath me. Eventually I drifted close enough to a bigger chunk of land for me to make a jump for it. I got back fine, but I've never been so seasick in my life.

We reach the north side, and straightaway I can feel the tow of the tide under my feet. It's been a while since I was here and I'm not used to the movement, I totter a little as I walk. Ralph sniffs around for pigs. The pigs, though, are shy and if they've any sense are miles away by now. Ralph barks too much when he gets excited. He'll never make a good hunter. But he seems pretty happy following the scents they've left behind. I'm not sure what he'd do if he actually met a pig: probably try to make friends with it if he didn't run away. He runs around, pretending he's this close to catching one. He makes me laugh sometimes.

Ralph's a lot more curious about the trees over here than he is about the ones back near the hut. I think they must smell strange. The ground too is different – not the sand and dried leaves I'm used to, but a matted green turf, like grass knitted together. The way it moves with the waves it seems like it's not even solid, a curious plant which grows on the surface of the ocean and clings in one great clump to the Island proper, but a plant like nothing I've ever heard of.

Kicking away with my toe at the grass I don't see the wave coming. It's huge, comes out of nowhere. I see it a second before it hits, the loose turf I'm on suddenly disappearing *downwards*, before launching up, sending me ten feet in the air. A small series of slightly smaller waves follow right behind it. When I've finally found my feet there's no sign of Ralph.

'Ralphie!' I shout.

There's no reply.

'Hey! Come back!'

I'm terrified that one of these days he's going to fall through a hole. It makes me feel quite sick, caring for something so much, and unable to do anything about it when he decides to go off on his own. I think that's the reason I tell myself that he's not really mine and just shares the Island with me. The same reason I don't let him sleep in the hut, though I think he finds it too hot in there anyway. I'd feel terrible if he did get lost out here. I look through the trees, but I can't see very far, and nothing moves.

I feel dizzy, and have to bend over for a moment. It's not just the thought of losing Ralph. There's something else. Something about this side of the Island that seems to affect me if I stay here too long. Like I also become less real the longer I stay, that somehow my personality starts to drift with the tide and pulls apart. I start to feel that I don't really exist. I get a blackness that surges over me and makes me want to curl up and sleep. But I also know that when this happens the thing to do is to get out of here. I think if I laid down and slept I'd be drawn into the place and dissipate and maybe not wake up at all. It's okay for a few hours during the day. It doesn't seem to affect Ralph.

I also have a feeling that there used to be more people on the Island than there are now. My memory isn't too good on this point – all the sun and days adding up, making me forget. But I think that if there ever were more people living here, the north side might well be where they all went. Maybe they heard Loneliness calling out one night, and came to find him, to hunt him down and kill him, armed with rocks and sharpened spears. But if they did, they failed, because Loneliness lives on and the Island's almost empty of people.

Another wave runs through the Island, bringing me back.

'Ralph!' I shout.

Then something brushes against my bare calf and I jump.

Ralph is sitting at my feet, a stick in his mouth. Pretending that I'd thrown it and he'd fetched it. He's such an idiot. He affects not to notice he almost scared me to death just then.

I take the stick and throw it, but it gets stuck in a tree. Ralph gracefully ignores it and goes in search of a new stick and we go on with our walk, though I keep us well within sight of the fortress. I regain my sea legs and move with the sway of the world.

Eventually Ralph tires of sniffing at trees and the Island moving around and pads over to me, quite happily, as if to say: okay, that was fun, now let's go get dinner. So we go get dinner.

I get troubled dreams again when I sleep. Better than the night before. Nothing too clear. Ralph barks once, perhaps still in sleep, and maybe that's enough to keep Loneliness away. My head's a bit scrambled in the morning, as though the waves have been wearing me down all night.

The next day I get an urge to go roll rocks. This happens every so often. I feel like it's part of a ritual I need to observe from time to time, though I've no idea why, just something that's part of my life on the Island. Anyway, it's a lot of fun. I climb up the waterfall, going quietly so as not to attract the ballistic interest of the monkey troop. I make my way up until I reach the fortress. There are plenty of rocks around there, from the fig-sized to the pig-sized.

I heft a rock and send it rolling down the hill. It feels great to see it careering along, flying up in uneven leaps and then shooting off the cliff. It always makes me think how it must be a great feeling to have all that space suddenly open up beneath you, and then to plunge down towards the sea. Not that I want to try it myself, I'm sure I'd just crash into the cliff on the way down, but it's nice to imagine how it might feel. Like leap, bounce, bounce – wooooo! And all that water opening out beneath, arms spread wide.

'Wahey!' goes the rock as it flies off the cliff edge.

I roll another one.

'Woooah! it goes.

The next rock goes 'Hey!' before I've even rolled it, which takes me by surprise. I clamber over to the cliff edge to see where the noise came from. I get a burst of vertigo and have to go forward on all fours. I peek over the edge.

About ten feet beneath me, on a large grassy ledge I never knew existed, two sun loungers are unfolded. The Checkout Girl is stretched out on one of them, reading a magazine. She's pushed her sunglasses back over her hair so she can look me in the eye. On the other lounger a man is sunbathing. A crate of what looks to be apples is sitting between them.

'Are you crazy?' she calls up. 'Quit throwing rocks. You could really hurt someone, you know?'

'I'm sorry,' I say. 'I didn't know there was anyone there.'

'Well exactly,' she says.

Looking over the cliff like this is making me feel very strange. My vision starts to go and I gasp for breath. I feel a powerful urge to let myself topple forwards. I pull back from the edge.

'Sorry,' I say. 'Feeling a little dizzy.'

There's an audible sigh from below.

'We'll come up,' she says.

By the time I've regained my balance and have control over my breathing again they're right up with me. I don't understand how they made it up the cliff so fast, there must be an easy way I can't see.

'Try breathing into a paper bag,' suggests the man.

'I'm fine, thank you,' I say. I look up.

They are, I should point out, completely naked. I'm embarrassed about it like I don't know where to look. It's not that there are any rules against nudism or anything, it's simply not done. Even when I'm sure I'm completely by myself on the Island I manage to keep my shorts on.

It's funny, though, the way her anger makes her body look. Devoid of sexuality somehow. Even though I can't remember the last time I saw someone naked there's something about her flesh that's stark and unhappy. It's white like coconut meat, not at all like I've been imagining.

The man she's with is standing there just dangling himself at the elements. He munches on an apple. He's looking stern too, but in a disinterested, less-than-convincing way, making just enough effort to show he's backing up the Checkout Girl on this one.

'Who's *he*?' I ask.

'Be nice,' she says. 'He's a friend. He does water sports.'

I haven't seen anyone on the Island apart from the two of us for years, and it's a bit of a shock meeting someone else. I really don't know what to say.

Then I notice that in his other hand the Watersports Guy is holding a plastic parrot. Up close it's bright red, with a green chest. I look back up behind me and the branches of the tree at the top of the hill are empty.

'How did you get that?' I say.

'I just climbed up the tree.' The thought of that tree holding the weight of such a heavy guy is impossible to imagine.

'But it's not yours,' I protest.

'It's not yours either,' says the Checkout Girl. 'It was up there before *you* turned up.'

Well. That's not how I remember things at all. I'm certain I was here before she was. But she seems so sure about it, and how else would she know about the parrot? All this sun. It's been frying my brain, messing up my memory. I should take more care, wear a hat.

'Sorry about the rocks,' I say. 'I really didn't know you were there.'

'Well, you should have checked,' she says. I walk away. Behind me I can hear the Watersports Guy offering her a bite of his apple.

I spend the rest of the day pottering around my hut unable to do anything constructive. Meeting the Checkout Girl and her friend has really shaken me up. I don't like my routine

being broken and I find it hard to get on top of what I'm supposed to be doing. Ralph's no help, he just patters around
waiting to see if we're going for a walk. In the end I shoo him
down to the beach for a swim. He's beginning to smell.

The day just wastes away. One minute it's all sun and sand
and the next the sun's hit the sea and all there is to do is go to
bed. I sleep okay. In the morning I lie in my hammock and
think about things. There's a buzzing in the air, like a
headache's waiting for me outside.

I decide I have to talk to the Checkout Girl, find out what's
going on. It's fine for her to have friends over, but maybe we
should have some kind of an arrangement whereby we can
let each other know in advance, take away the nasty element
of surprise. I head over to the shop. The day is bright and
sunny and it's refreshing to be in the shade. Everything seems
to be in its right place. I even hear a couple of monkeys chattering up in the trees, gathering bananas. I get to thinking
about how good things are going to be again. By the time I get
to the shop clearing I'm lost in very pleasant thoughts.

I'm so preoccupied I nearly don't see the Watersports Guy.
He's sitting in the clearing, a little way from the shop in the
shade of some palms, head bent over an object in his hands. I
come to a halt. There's a glint of bright metal, a knife in regular flashes as he works on something. A long straight piece of
driftwood, which he seems to be sharpening at both ends. All
my good thoughts are blown away like spray over the ocean.

Then there's a play of light, the sun coming through the
palms as they shiver in the wind, shuffling the shadows. One
falls over his face and in the sudden darkness there he doesn't
look quite like the man I met on the hill. He looks like someone I've never seen, a stupid thing to say except I know in my
gut that it's true. He looks like Loneliness. Maybe he's
learned how to get out during the day, taking on a different
form and walking among us.

I look around for the Checkout Girl. I can't see clearly into
the shop, but there doesn't appear to be anyone at the check-

out. If he's done something to her I don't know what I'll do. I was so confused by him turning up out of nowhere and being friendly with her it didn't occur to me to ask myself who he was, where he came from. I should have seen it. I should have thought. Maybe the sun has really fried my head.

I back away. I can't go on and say hi and pretend that nothing has happened. I'm afraid of the stake in his hands, of what exactly he's planning to use it for. I back out of the clearing, eyeing him as I go. He doesn't look up. I don't think he saw me, was too busy with his whittling. I almost run back to my beach. I feel something pursuing me the whole way but I look behind me and the path is empty.

In the end I stay away for two days. I keep to my hut and the beach with the fish trap. I make my water last longer than normal. I play with Ralph, same as always, but I don't take him for any long walks. He doesn't seem to mind. As soon as he realizes we're not going anywhere he just yawns and uses the time to get some more sleep. At night when I go to sleep I pull my desk across the hut door.

But those two days go by and my curiosity is killing me, never mind my cowardice. I know I should go over to the shop to see what's going on. I leave Ralph sleepily guarding the hut and I head off. I sweat as I walk, but I don't know if it's with the heat or the chill or the fear. I hear something buzz past me on its way to the beach.

I come carefully into the shop clearing. Oh God, oh God. Outside the checkout the Watersports Guy has driven his stake into the ground. Impaled on the protruding end is the plastic parrot. I think it's meant to be a cheap decoration, something to provide a bit of colour outside the shop. I think it's meant to look like the parrot is perched there. But it's horrifying. It looks like it's been sacrificed. I feel sick. My legs start to shake. Tiny broken shards of plastic from the parrot's base are scattered on the sand around the base of the stake. I reach out to free it but I can't bring myself to touch the thing.

I give the stake a sharp kick but it resists solidly and the parrot just quivers on top. I can't stand it, I turn away.

The shop is open and the lights are on, but when I go inside the checkout is empty and unmanned. The hardware section is right at the back. I just take what I need.

Something has changed when I get back to the hut. Nothing to see, and nothing that's been moved. Just something in the way I feel about the place. It's been my home for so long I've been taking it for granted. But now, for the first time, I look around and don't feel as I did. I also realize how cold it's getting again. I consider building that fire after all. Whatever attention it attracts it couldn't be much worse than this. If I build it on the beach it won't shine so far. Maybe Loneliness won't come near the light, maybe he'll think it's the sun.

I gather wood in the last of the light. A distant buzzing carries over the sound of the waves. I hunt around for some matches and get my fire going. The wood's dry, it catches instantly, taking the flame. I drag a rock over to sit on and warm my hands. It produces a fair bit of smoke, but that won't matter when it gets dark, it'll just be the light of the fire I have to worry about.

I enjoy the unusual sensation of burning the fire gives off. I break open a coconut and have a milk, and watch the night sky wheeling slowly round. The firelight obscures some of the stars, but it's a pretty good night for it. A few shooting stars. Every few months there's another season and you see them rain down. If you watch closely you can see the slow track of satellites across the sky as they beam down TV signals. Nothing that matters to me.

The buzzing is persistent in my ears. At first I thought it was a mosquito having a closer reconnaissance of me, but it's been going on too long, and the sound's definitely coming from somewhere off in the distance. A few minutes later it starts to get louder – a whole swarm, an irritating high-pitched whine. I try to focus on the waves, allowing myself to be hypnotized by the distant roaring draw, the hushing of water on sand.

Amidst the noise of the waves I notice a knocking sound, distinct and wooden. Then a few voices. And finally a more regular series of splashes close to the shore, which culminate in a scraping, grinding rasp. I get ready to kick sand over my fire but I know it's too late now. Looking out beyond the glare of the light I can see the shadow of a boat hull arrived on the beach. I sigh. Here we go again. I stand up.

Three tall men approach, wearing white navy uniforms and looking quite pleased with themselves. They've taken off their shoes and are very obviously enjoying the sensation of the sand between their toes. I can see by his stripes that one of them is a Captain. He takes off his hat and puts it neatly under his arm. He makes to salute, but his shoes in his other hand encumber him and he gives up, changing the gesture into a sweep as though he'd been pointing to the fire.

'Hello,' he says. 'We saw the fire, thought we'd better come and take a look. See if there was any trouble.'

'Right. Well, it's just me. Sorry about that.'

'Oh no, no trouble at all. We just thought, with the light and the smoke, you know. Check it wasn't one of ours.'

'Sorry,' I say again.

They have a look around.

'Nice place,' the Captain says.

'Thanks,' I say.

The three of them look a little uncertain for a moment, then by apparent consensus sit themselves down by the fire. I sigh to myself and go fetch coconuts, so we can all have a milk.

'So how are things?' I ask, when they have their milks. 'I mean, over there.'

He shakes his head. 'Oh, bad,' he says. 'Very bad indeed. You don't really want to know. Of course we could always use more people. Say,' he asks, in a half-hearted press-gang, 'how old are you?'

I lie.

'Too bad,' he says.

They quiz me about the Island. How big it is, how many people live here. Then they talk excitedly amongst themselves, cutting me out of the conversation. I get the feeling they've been at sea a long time. I let them chatter. Their voices drown out the irritating buzz enough for me to forget about it. Ralph comes over to listen and lies down beside the fire. One of the men pets him idly. Then it gets late and the warmth and voices make me sleepy so eventually I retire to my hut. I feel pretty safe with the Navy around so I don't bother to block my door. Ships sail through my dreams the whole night long.

When I wake they're still sitting around the fire. It looks like they've kept it burning all night. For once I don't mind at all, because there's been no sign of Loneliness.

I show them where my well is. They're talking about putting a little expedition together, heading over the mountain and mapping the Island. I tell them about the lack of solidity over on the north side, how it's not safe, how there's really no way of mapping it because of the looseness of it, but they just turn to discussing ways of anchoring the Island to the seabed, or putting some foundations down. I don't mention Loneliness. I tell them about the shop, in case there's anything they need. It's a peace offering for the Checkout Girl, too; some customers. When they leave they ask me for directions, so I send them past the drinking pool, so as the monkeys have some new targets to aim at.

The first thing I notice when they're gone is that the buzzing sound is back, and louder than before. It seems to be coming from the beach. And that's about the moment I begin to feel it's time to leave.

It's not that I mind all the people. I don't. Even the Watersports Guy, at least in principle – if he cheers up the Checkout Girl, then that's a good thing, as far as I'm concerned. But not if he's Loneliness. The Navy will most likely push off sooner or later, as they always do, particularly if they start spending too much time over on the north side. The thing is, it's just beginning to feel like things aren't meant to be this way. I can't really explain it. It's like with a story – there are good guys and bad guys, true love winning out and happy endings, everything back to how it was before. But none of that is happening, things feel like they're changing for always, and it just feels wrong.

Of course, I have one or two concerns. You don't just pick up and leave, not after all this time. And I know Ralph wouldn't take too well to the ocean. I try to imagine it and can't, so I decide to leave him behind. He's not actually my dog, after all, and it's not as though he really needs me to look after him. Having me around has made him lazy, and a little fat.

I get moving. I dig out from under my bed the axe I took from the shop. I remove the leather cover that protects the sharp metal head. I've coveted the axe for a long time but never had a reason to buy it. I test the blade, managing to avoid slicing my finger – I can't stand the sight of blood. Then I go outside to select some trees. I find a sturdy palm tree at the edge of the beach, its trunk straight and round and wide. I tilt my head. With the buzzing I can hardly hear the music, and I begin to miss it, it's the same old story, you only notice things when they're gone. Then I turn my attention back to the tree. I figure it will take me a long enough time to turn it into a canoe, so I should probably get started.

I swing the axe back and give the tree a good whack near the base. The blade bounces straight back off the palm tree like it was made of rubber. I feel instantly discouraged. Ralph comes over and nuzzles my hand in sympathy. Either that or he's hungry. I guess I couldn't really have left him behind anyway. I know I try and pretend that he isn't mine but the truth is he's the only friend I have. I think you just have to assume your responsibilities when it comes to your friends, even if you know bad things are going to happen sooner or later.

Ralph gives a whimper. Something is bothering him. Then I hear it too.

The background buzzing swells unstoppably into a terrible din, like someone decided to chainsaw the entire forest. It completely drowns out the gently soaring Hawaiian guitar. I recoil, actual physical pain in my ears. My legs go weak. I can't think straight at all. I put my hands over my ears and sit down with my back against the tree. The sound is coming from out over the ocean. I can't see anything but it comes closer and closer. Ralph scampers off into the jungle, his tail flattened to the ground. I'm cold with fear, can't feel the sun. And then I see movement over the waves.

The Watersports Guy zooms over the reef on a jet ski. He gives me a wave as he goes past, then grabs the handlebars with both hands while he does a little jump off a wave, splashing back down into the water. He guns the throttle and the engine gives a high-pitched roar, then he cuts a tight turn and zips back in the other direction, out the way he came. The noise levels drop a little and he's out of sight again in no time. I trudge back to my hut, feeling sick inside.

Ralph is settled down on his blanket by the door. With his sharp hearing the din must really have got to him. He curls himself into a circle and with a series of little jerks manages to push his chin right over his back. It can't be comfortable, but he falls asleep right away. I go inside. I pull my chair up to the desk and try to block out the racket. The jet ski chainsaws on. I can hear the Watersports Guy just wheeling round on the water. I take a spare shirt and wrap it round my head over my ears. It doesn't seem to help much. I take a look at the post-cards on my desk. Then I tear one off the pad and start writing and pretty soon I don't notice the noise any more.

Dream #89
02/01/__

Only the truly deranged believe that they are in every way sane. He who has slipped somehow through the safety nets of family, school, friends and social services without leaving the slightest impression does not think himself entirely balanced. He spends a lot of time sleeping, wrapped in a blanket with his right arm bent back beneath him. He is forbidden dreaming, because he himself is a dream. There is a home, but it is not his own. There are streets and night shelters strewn across his memory.

At some stage he meets a girl, and they are shy around each other. For a few, invisible days they orbit at a distance, trying to be likeable and trying too to determine how much they like the other. They beg together as often as they beg apart. They take turns begging the same spot. Their conversations at this point are sporadic, but relaxed. They sit and drink cola from a glass bottle, sharing a straw. She tells him how her father and then her step-father. He tells her about his parents – though he did not know his parents – and how his father once told him – though his father never told him. She tells him about the time she and he tells her about the time he. She asks him why he has a tattoo and he tells her. He has a deeply symbolic tattoo, but it is constantly obscured from view.

Miraculously, they are given housing. The house is huge and empty, a suburban mansion set behind trees. Expressionless, they stand by the porch. As though conceived with immaculate cinematography, leaves swirl across the driveway. It could be a scene from a movie. It is, in fact, a scene from a once-seen movie.

'It's beautiful.'

'I never imagined.'

'I didn't think.'

'So are you.'

When they have sex she is on top and bequeaths something of herself to the earth below, dying a little each time. But no sooner have they moved in together than she starts dating the landlord. She sleeps with him, too, so that she at least does not have to pay rent. The landlord is wealthy and drives an old black car, which looks as though it might be from a movie. The girl and the landlord marry. He begrudges her this happiness terribly. This is not a love story, of any kind.

Eventually he is evicted, with unnecessary violence, for non-payment of rent. He is spending his housing money on heroin. And because he has no housing, he cannot get his money. As if in some Kafka-rigged bureaucracy he argues endlessly with people who are installed behind counters – clean white chipboard counters, remorseless counters.

Time passes. There is a night when he falls asleep with his arm bent back beneath him and does not wake though the circulation ceases. He loses part of his arm and three fingers from his hand, it ruins his tattoo. He is hospitalized and treated with methadone, which he becomes hooked on. His teeth chatter all the time and he smokes dope to stop the shivering. It's poor quality dope, because his dealer is an arse.

His hair has grown long. He tries to learn to write with his left hand, so that he can fill in the forms they occasionally ask him to. *Describe your disability.* In childlike writing he has awkwardly answered, *It's like this.* They will not give him his money. *How does it affect your day-to-day life? Can you stand without help? For how long? Do you have trouble walking? Lifting?*

He falls through safety nets like a stuntman down the front of a building, tearing through improbably positioned awnings. The last one catches him, right before he hits the ground. This last net is a hospital. The hospital lasts for a short while, and then there is a list, lasting for a long time, at the end of which there is a flat in a council block.

His rooms have an ugliness established long ago, then preserved and matured over thirty years. The air is damp and the walls slick. In the flat next door there is another rehoused, who screams in the night. He wonders why he always gets the screamers. He is no longer on methadone or heroin but he is still smoking dope, though it sometimes seems as though it exacerbates the shivering. It lessens, in any case, the unpleasantness.

Because he is lonely in his flat he gets a dog to keep him company, and to ensure he exercises properly. Though the dog is quiet the screamer next door grows paranoid. The screamer, it transpires, is heavyset and dangerous, chemically anguished. He has forsworn his seratonin modifiers. A shadow lurks around his edges in a flickering aura. There is an otherness about him. He bangs on the door of the flat in the early morning and when it is answered says,

'I can hear it. I know you'll set it after me.'

'It's four in the morning.'

'Fuck you! I'm not going to let you. You see this?' He scrapes a knife against the chain. 'I'm going to kill your dog. I've seen it. I'm going to kill it. I'm going to cut that fucking thing up. Just you wait and see.'

He does not open the door in the night again, though the screamer bangs on it at strange hours and mutters menacingly through it. Once, the dog barks and the banging increases tenfold as the screamer nearly has a fit. The dog trots into the bedroom and cowers in the furthest corner, whimpering a little.

Time passes. Some nights later he himself wakes from a bad dream, screaming and shouting.

Once during the day when he takes the dog for a walk to the corner shop to buy cigarette papers, the screamer runs up the stairs and aims a kick at the animal, which impacts minimally, but cruelly none the less.

It takes one more midnight threat to his dog by his

insomniac knife-wielding neighbour before he picks up the lead piping from the conservatory or the candlestick from the ballroom and exits his battered door. The screamer has already retired to his own flat, so he crosses the corridor and tests the hardboard. The door is unlocked and ajar. He holds his weapon in his good hand and it does not shake. Crazed to a point of clarity and calm he marches through to the tiny kitchen, which is empty. The living room too is void of people, though something blue flickers on the television, revealing the dark blank of the bedroom door. He enters the catastrophic room. The heavyset screamer is lying on his back staring upwards, his head upon the pillow in the dark. He is wild-eyed and his mouth is foaming. His jaw gapes, then stiffly narrows. The avenging interloper notes these facts with neither fear nor interest. Aiming at the centre of the pillow he brutally staves the screamer's head in. The shadow there splits open like an apple striking the ground. The pillow darkens further. Until this point in his life he has not killed anyone, nor did he ever expect to.

Only the truly deranged believe that they are in every way sane. Once more he is in hospital, a secure unit minimally designed, with no lead piping and no knives scraping against chains. Three times a week he is taken along to a gym where they sit him on a bicycle and encourage him to pedal. Behavioural, he understands, therapy. He pedals hard but arrives nowhere. The remainder of his tattoo, visible beneath the loose slip of the hospital top, is smudged and inky. On a second bike beside him sits a man who has the following problem: he has no private thoughts. There is a hotline from his brain to his mouth and whatever arises in the former finds expression through the latter. As he cycles he is talking to himself, always talking, in perfect rhythm with the exercise.

He says: *'It's Toyah Wilcox. It's my mum. It's India, it's Sri Lanka, it's all grey. I'm thirty-six. I've done this before. I know how to lift weights. It's like this. I know how to do this. You can't tell me*

to do anything. I'm thirty-six. My mum's coming today, after TV.
I've got two earrings. My earring and my nose ring. My ear's like
this. The Albany All-stars. I've got my scars. Now that's what I call
music. I'm floating, I'm getting higher. I'm lifting weights. Six
minutes. I'm keeping it going. I do this every day. I'm really strong.
Up and down. I'm on the bike, I have to keep going. Do it every day.
Don't listen to what they say. It's ghetto music. It's petal shoesake.
My mum's coming today, just before curry.'

Paula

The car accident which left her paralysed from the waist down also caused her a good deal of internal damage (her liver and stomach half-crushed), engendering a severe poisoning of her blood which in turn led to the amputation, above the knees, of each of her insensible legs; so surviving first the crash itself and then the multitude of ensuing operations was never going to save her from appalling, persistent pain and a subsequent addiction to painkillers. But she did survive – not entirely in accordance with her wishes – and the bullying tactics of her old friends brought her finally out of hospital and back into the student house they shared. She was unable to resume her studies, owing to the insistent pain she felt in the spaces where her legs had been, a pain existing somehow outside the sphere of her own body. Her limbs become phantoms of the operating table. And she experienced pain where there were no nerves for pain to exist. Pain that the doctors told her was in her mind, conditioned, that it would cease in time, though her mind seemed set on hanging on to it. Painkillers reduced the agony to a dull, inevitable ache. And it was this ache, and the invisibility of the suffering, which ended up being worse than the more eye-catching absence of her legs.

She divided her mornings between watching daytime TV – emancipation of a kind – and waiting for someone to get up and help her with her toilet functions. Then afternoons when everyone was out of the house she'd start enumerating the sins of her carers. Particularly fucking Barry's.

Barry having previously been her best friend.

There had been, she came to realize, early signs. Once, when she was still in the hospital and talking to him on the phone, and she was having one of those days when the recent loss of her legs was affecting her pretty deeply, when she was beginning to sense how much of her old life had gone with them, she said:

'I just want to go out dancing.'

Barry seemed surprised by this. 'But where will you go?' he asked, meaning it. Thinking that it was perhaps a good and relevant question. And this memory illustrating for Paula now his lack of concentration, or perhaps empathy, depending on which way you looked at it. Or that perhaps he was merely stranded in a world where desires were simple things, easily fulfilled. This world, she wanted to scream at them, does not work that way.

That had been Paula's first indication that she was going to have to endure, as part of her recovery, a shattering loss of confidence in her friends. Even though it was they who had persuaded her to leave the hospital and live with them, rather than return south to her family. This, she was beginning to believe, had been typically selfish of them – to make a huge effort in persuading her to accept the fact of suffering in her existence, and then to carry on as though she were fine and that nothing of any lasting significance had happened.

A later variation on the same theme would come on one of those nights when her friends, after a good night in together – eating, drinking, laughing – would do a couple of lines each and head out to a club, leaving her to an early night.

Once she cried as they left and Helen, God bless her, noticed.

'What's up with you?'

'I really want to come.'

Helen surprised, in a way which was becoming familiar to Paula. 'What? But you hate clubs now! You wouldn't enjoy it. I thought you'd be too tired to want to come, anyway.'

'I am. I just want to come.'

'But you're too tired?'

'Yes!'

Helen just bewildered.

And Paula, even though she was exhausted, stayed up late by herself and drank, even though it really messed her up, drank until she got really drunk in her left eye – with everything blurred that way, and don't even think about closing the right eye – but if she closed the left eye and looked through her right she was just about sober enough to remember not to take the painkillers, because of all the alcohol. Helen returned early, at 4 a.m.

'Paula? What are you doing?'

'Bit pissed,' she said. 'Might need a hand. Not sure I can walk.' And she laughed.

Helen, during the months Paula spent in hospital, would come in and visit, when she could. Relatively often for her; not so often for Paula, whose life was a little quieter. Which was fine and everything, but Paula, who was relying a lot on her friends being available at the other end of the phone line, always hated Helen for never using the phone, or rather, hated her for having a stupid reason for never using the phone. Which was that Helen had a thing about them, they freaked her out, that she had somehow never got past the idea that there was no one at the other end of the line and that it was the telephone, the telephone itself, that was talking to her.

Barry and Helen had, at Paula's insistence, taken her to a night club once, the one club in town that didn't seem to object to the threat she caused to health and safety (an attitude, it appeared, owing more to negligence than to any particular commitment to accessibility). A bouncer had paused, thought about it, then lifted her up the stairs. A bartender had half-grinned at her.

'Not often we see a disabled lass in here,' he shouted over the music.

And Barry, belligerent, leaned over and yelled at the guy. 'She's not fucking disabled, mate. All right?'

The guy looked down at the wheelchair. Wondered about coming out from behind the bar and punching Barry. Left them without drinks.

Paula tugged at Barry's arm. 'What the fuck was that?' she shouted.

'He called you disabled. Not exactly sensitive, is it? Wanker.'

'I am disabled.'

'No you're not.'

'I fucking am.' She gestured at her legs, absent.

He bent down to her level. 'No,' he yelled into her ear. 'It's a mindset thing. Don't let them label you like that.'

'I fucking feel disabled.'

'Well there you go, you see? Listen, it's too fucking loud to talk about this here. You want to dance?'

Another day, Paula tries to explain this to Barry, that it's not just that she actually wants to go clubbing, not in her wheelchair, it's just that she wants to be *able* to go clubbing, to go clubbing ably, that she knows there's a good reason why they leave her behind, but that being left behind still kills her. That, sure, her spirit of adventure has been dented and diminished, but she could still long for nights out. Surely not so difficult to understand.

'I do understand,' says Barry. 'I just don't think it makes any sense to get upset about things you can't do anything about.'

Before all this, long before, once upon a time, they used to share a bed together, sometimes they'd fool around, and when he slept she'd marvel at his propensity towards beauty, at the beauty which seemed to be stored within him and came released in sleep. Even Barry, with his communist slogans and his hatred of private school accents. Now, he thought she was safe. He knew where he stood with her, now. She'd acquired by then a sex-neutral status amongst her friends, which she greatly resented, despite the admittedly reduced nature of her sex drive since the accident (some days, though, the fantasies – I mean, Jesus. Another ache growing deep between her hips, way down below her belly, the desperate urge to rub. Except this ache, like the other, was only a memory of the real thing, it wasn't really where she felt it to be, and would remain unalleviated by her fingers. She had figured out in any case that these few rare kicks of sexual desire were not really about the procreative urge, a last effort on the part of her body to ensure immortality, gene survival, but were rather indications of the starved self crying out for momentary relief, for a few seconds of forgetful pleasure. I.e. that it wasn't the selfish gene, just the selfish self, trying to throw itself into a cocoon of gratification, as it used to do, as most people did.)

'No regrets,' Barry would say. 'That's how you need to live your life. That's my philosophy.'

'So what exactly's happened to you that you've had to regret?'

'Hey. My life's not perfect, you know. But anyway, that's the point. I don't regret anything.' He's seen TV programmes of kids with disabilities who seemed to live happy, normal lives.

'Right,' she'd say. 'Let's swap. Legs and so on. I reckon I'd cheer right up, and you'd be pretty pissed off.'

'Well, maybe, sure. But I think I might handle it better than you do.'

'Oh you do, do you?' A murderous tone. Barry looked hurt.

And so on, and so forth.

Barry would complain about her moodiness, her ability to switch moods in the time it took him to make even a single observation. And he'd complain how hurtful she could be.

'You're quite passive-aggressive, you know?'

'I am passive,' she'd say, 'because I have no legs. Passivity is implied. And I am aggressive because occasionally I get pissed off about it. If you can't live with it, then fuck off.'

'Okay, okay! But you see what I mean, though? I mean *Jesus*. Where did that come from?'

There were a million things she could have said to Barry to hurt him, because she knew him so well, but she never did, she never did.

'I could say a million things to hurt you,' she said, once.

Barry looked briefly scared. He didn't like these strange conversations which came from nowhere. Why talk about these things? He thought about it a moment.

'But you don't,' he said, as though it were a triumph.

Another thing he used to do – and he wasn't alone in doing this, several of her friends had come up with a version of it at one time or another, it was just that he was the most regular source of it – was when he woke from one of those nights out to severe hangover and skipped work, when he'd sit on his fat lazy arse all day, in the sun if he could, and he'd complain about how bad he felt, how sick it made him feel even to move, and the formula that would inevitably find its way to his lips was: 'Now I know how you must feel.'

Which sounds like sympathy, but of course isn't, because he hasn't the faintest fucking idea of how she feels. What she's realized he's actually doing is indulging in an idea of how passingly bad he feels which is far worse than is in fact the case, and while it sounds like sympathy to him it sounds very much like a fucking insult to her.

Or, and somehow even worse, was when an idea would suddenly strike him and he'd look wide-eyed at her and say in a quiet, sympathetic voice: 'I can't imagine what you're going through.' And he'd be quite over-whelmed by the depths of his brief flirtation with empathy. Then five minutes later he'd forget again. Suffering, though, knew Paula, is hard to keep in mind. Notably when it's not your own.

So occasionally, she would make an effort to remind them.

'I'm in pain here,' she'd say.

'You don't look it,' says Helen. 'You look great.'

'Yeah, you look really well,' everyone else chimes in, momentarily distracted from the TV.

'You want me to cry or something? Shit. Sorry. Never mind. Anyway, it doesn't change the fact.'

'I'll fetch you some painkillers.'

'Can't. Already taken some.' Jesus, but how she hates to bore them.

'Well that'll help.' And the TV was once again God. Her hips, and the carrion below her hips felt like toothache, perpetual burrowing agony.

They gave her drugs to help her sleep, as though she were happy sleeping, as though she would be pain free and whole again. Neither of which was in fact the case; her legs never worked in her immobile dreams, not once. Though she was almost afraid they might. Because of the waking up. You don't, she felt, want to lose your legs more than the once.

But back to that conversation with Barry.

'You had an accident, that's all. It's just your legs, it doesn't affect everything about you. You're still who you used to be. You should be grateful that it wasn't worse. Go out and get a job, be normal again. People do.'

'You think I'm living off this.'

'Nah. Not really. But kind of, maybe – it's not about who you are, you know?'

'It *is* about who I am. It's exactly about who I am. I mean it's fucking precisely about who I am. All that below here? They were things that absolutely fucking *defined* me.'

'It just doesn't make any sense to be so bitter. No regrets, remember?'

'If you're telling me you wouldn't regret it at all, not one tiny bit, if I cut off your legs . . .'

'Yeah, but you wouldn't do that. I mean why even mention it? You're missing the point.' Arms folded, case proved.

I.e., one of her prevailing problems being that they treat her as though she were still her old, pre-accident self, her old self in a wheelchair, which just isn't the case. However well intentioned they are, however much they think that's the right approach. Somehow they fail to notice that the equation is flawed, that old self minus a few key functions minus legs does not equal old self, that the accident, or rather its repercussions, have infiltrated every part of her life and have turned her into another person. The almost unavoidable conclusion being that they have never cared enough to notice important things about her, that they didn't even know who she used to be. She had never felt so alone.

Her counsellor listened to her complaints, employing for the purposes of listening an understanding face, a face that saw all sides.

'Don't underestimate how hard it is for them, seeing you like this. They mean well.'

And this was indeed a further part of the problem. They were well intentioned, but they believed that it was sufficient for their actions to be well intentioned. That if your intentions were good then everything you did was somehow irreproachable, that you didn't really need to pay close attention to the circumstances of actions, and as though actual outcomes were irrelevant.

Paula further confessed to her counsellor the problems she had in meeting new people. She wasn't the person she used to be, and she kept apologizing for it. She was afraid they wouldn't like her because she was less than she had been. 'I used to be different,' she'd say when she met people. 'I used to be fun. I used to be this girl who . . .' Jesus, she felt, she really was no fun any more. Even the friends she had were ceasing to be her friends. Why the hell did they put up with her? How in the hell did she put up with them? It wasn't working out for anybody. She should probably wheel herself off down the road and find some new friends. If it were that easy.

She'd been the same way, of course, and she regretted it now. Reports of suffering had failed to rouse her conscience. Now she couldn't watch the bloody news without crying, and she gave a lot of money from her settlement, and from her benefits, to charities. And she'd look down on her friends, with their growing incomes and expensive lifestyles, and hate them for not giving. Or for making a show of it when they did. And she'd examine with wonder her new-found analytical clarity with respect to her friends. Though she was discovering that there was something very lonely about being an immaculate judge of character, particularly when surrounded by the unreflective: no one understands you as well as you understand them. But it was a funny thing, after all, that in her newly fucked-up body her soul seemed to be getting smarter and purer (barring one or two moral flaws, such as the tendency to over-bitch about the people who loved her, to paint them as less thoughtful people than they in fact were – a flaw she recognized and forgave in herself) while her friends, with their undamaged bodies and unregarded good health, seemed to be getting stupider, their souls impossibly blighted by inattention and selfishness, and she couldn't help but to see them as a seriously fucked-up bunch of solipsists.

She amused herself by thinking up slogans for solipsists. Leave the solipsists alone. Quit bothering the solipsists. Let them get on with their own lives.

She'd have picked self-absorbed over suffering, though, any day of the week. If she could choose. Because the pain, it just kept on coming, remorseless, tormenting, it defined every second, and though, often enough, it was sufficiently dull to allow her to function, functioning ain't living, functioning ain't feeling, and nothing she did was any fun any more. And she'd never wished her condition on anyone, not even half-heartedly, not even once, because she truly believed that no one deserved to suffer that way. But her friends' lack of empathy about the whole suffering thing was beginning to piss her off – particularly fucking Barry's – so she did find herself occasionally now, sitting there with him while he talked, fervently wishing he'd get hit by a bus when he next went out – she used to try to conjure this bus by force of will alone – that he'd wake from his easy, complacent life and see how the world looked to her, how it looked to real people, people who were unafflicted by the illusion that they were immune to misfortune, people who understood that there were no rights to be claimed in life, that no one had a right not to suffer. But he never did get hit, the bastard, he never even fell ill, apart from the hangovers. And it came to obsess her, this feeling, that it would seem only fair recompense for the suffering, that you'd have the power to make someone else feel the same way, experience the same pain, make them understand what it was really like; someone who needed it, someone who deserved it.

Barry

He spent the best part of his life denouncing material goods, railing against the wealthy and powerful, condemning the commodification of life, decrying the ownership of luxuries, taking public transport. He knew those things that were of true value – family, friends, credibility. He considered himself to have a good perspective on Things. He considered himself a wealthy man. He only wished he had suffered a little more.

Until there came a point in time when he realized, too late, that he no longer objected to anyone's possession of goods which made their lives more comfortable, and he began to look at his contemporaries and envy them their expensive lifestyles and the satisfactions they seemed to derive from them. For though there had once been something in his belly which told him that all this was wrong, it had burned away with living. Bitterly he came to believe that as a young man his ideals had been cover for a lack of ambition, and that he had justified his sloth to himself in ways which allowed him to believe he was a good man, just as everyone else does, but why shouldn't he make a living if he could, improve his circumstances, live like everyone else lived if it would just make Things a little better for him and his family, no one could have any right to object to that, could they?

Terry

Even when he arrives five minutes early he worries that he's late. Is dogged by the perpetual feeling that he's missing something, has forgotten something. He glances at the dashboard clock two or three times a minute. Registers the numbers, then panics as they transform into unfamiliar symbols, random arrangements of digital bars. He leans a little forward in his seat, looking up to check the sky, the sun, gauging the weather, estimating the hours of daylight left to him. His hand strays often from the wheel down to his right pocket, feeling for the familiar bulge of his keys, his mobile phone, experiencing a brief, evaporating reassurance at the contact. He looks in the rearview mirror, always expecting someone to be there, to be following him or chasing him, to be calling him back to something. And when there is no one there, he feels that there should be.

He pulls onto the station forecourt and parks behind the taxis already waiting there, sits behind the wheel to avoid having to talk to the other drivers, all of whom belong to the cab firm he used to work for. He recognizes at the front of the line Jack, the jerk. Shouldn't be on the road, that lad, not after the accident. Almost killed some girl, a terrible thing. He slides low in the seat. Used to know him once, and doesn't want to be recognized now.

The presence of the taxis, though, reassures him that there would be a train in soon. There was daylight yet. Whatever time it was, there'd be a train, and if he misses this one, he'll get the next.

Terry Skinner sits in his car and time passes like a vast yawn, buzzing around his head and blurring his vision, as though it were pulling him into sleep, the moment seeming to last so long that he's not entirely sure if he has dropped off for a moment there. His eyes are slow to re-focus. When he comes to, he finds himself watching the train slowing in along the tracks, disappearing behind the station building. Terry looks again at the taxis in front of him. Three of them, the bastards, and the train would be half-empty this time of day. Or was it a weekend? No, not a weekend. He'd be lucky to find a passenger, should have tried the supermarket, a few blocks over, old ladies with shopping, enough of them around. Still, he'd best wait now, just in case.

A smattering of passengers emerges. Some heading to their own cars, some walking off down the street. Three, eventually, finding their ways to the taxi rank, each car in turn loading up, driving smugly off. And just as Terry is swearing to himself and deciding to try the supermarket after all, sloping from the station building comes a final passenger, a young man with mismatched baggage – a rucksack, a carrying case for a suit – looking around, seeing him there, wandering over. Terry grins to himself, gets out and helps him with his bags. Gets back in the car, the young man beside him.

'Coming home?' he asks.

'Yeah,' he says. 'Funeral. My dad died.'

Fuck, thinks Terry. Should have kept my mouth shut. Poor kid.

'I'm sorry,' he says.

'Yeah, thanks,' he says.

They pull out of the station

'Old, was he?'

'Fifty-eight.'

Fuck, thinks Terry Skinner. Not much older than me.

Minutes domino over on the digital display. He feels his hands sweat, slippery on the wheel. He drives to the address, a hamlet a couple miles out of town, pulls over. Six-fifty, he says. Sees a tenner coming his way. Call it a fiver, he says, finding the change. He waits, as he always does, until the front door of the house opens, watches the lad walk up to it, sees the crying woman with the smile on her face almost fall out of the door and wrap the lad in a hug. Jesus, he can almost feel the hurt. Sad to see. He drives off. He drives on.

That evening, Terry Skinner calls his mum. Stays on the phone with her long after he's run out of things to say. Then stays up late, with no sense of what time it is. Feels giddy on the passing moments, until finally he feels tired, and then Terry Skinner goes to bed.

In the morning he wakes to the alarm, same as always, but wakes to a feeling of something being wrong, as though he's been pulled from uncompleted dreams, dreams he should have been allowed to finish. There's the wide white ceiling, oppressive above him, closing in, something of the sense of a nightmare clinging to it, or the remnant of one. He feels exhausted, his skin in a cold sweat. But he pulls himself out of bed, the sweat chilling him further in the air, and shivering, wraps a dressing gown round him. He makes a cup of tea, some breakfast. Feels odd eating the bowl of cereal, as though it's the wrong time of day for it, as though the clock on the kitchen wall has lost time overnight and is running slow. And he looks anxiously towards the front door to see if the post's already on the mat.

After he's eaten he walks down to the shops, buys his food for the week. Decides to leave the car today, can't face driving, maybe in the evening. He gets to work in the garden, to switch off his mind, to keep the hours at bay. And it seems to work because some hours later

Terry Skinner, absorbed in the work of cutting back the bushes in front of his house, is surprised by a voice from the gate.

'Excuse me! Excuse me!'

A young woman with a baby in her arms, her voice well bred, something sharp about it as though the faint edge of panic were always there.

'Could you help me please?'

'What is it, love?'

'There's a man,' she says. 'In the gutter.' She points across the street. He can just make out a pair of legs, sticking out from behind a parked car.

'I've called an ambulance,' she says. 'But I'm not sure he's okay. I've got a baby. I didn't want to go too close.'

Terry Skinner had heard nothing. Didn't understand how he had failed to see the man walk along this way and collapse. How long had he been there?

'Well how did he get there?' he asks.

'He had some friends, I think. But they left.'

Left him? Like this? Not friends. Not friends then. Maybe they were just walking along at the same time as him. Ahead of him, and didn't see him.

The man is on his back. Alive, but appearing dead, the breathing so light that there's no movement of the chest at all. Or perhaps not breathing at all. His face pale, purpled. Phlegm and vomit across his lips. Shit, thinks Terry. He knows he should be shouting in the man's ear, but he can't bring himself to say anything, senses anyway that the man's too far gone to hear him. He's focused, knowing he has to work quickly.

The heart, when he finds it, pattering quickly, minutely. But a heartbeat, yes. Definitely. No breath but a heartbeat. And Terry, worrying for a second that he'll have to put his mouth to that mouth, remembers that he'll have to clear the airway first, and propping one arm, one leg, rolls the heavy body easily into recovery position. Where the man suddenly chokes, spews vomit from his throat. Yellow vomit filling his mouth as though it were a bowl, and spilling like grain onto the floor. His cup o'erfloweth. Then breathes. Breathes ever so softly, thereafter, in and out, breathes. And Terry Skinner watches him breathe.

The ambulance arrives some short while later and he has a conversation with the paramedics which he won't remember. They load the man on a stretcher, drive him away. The siren, as it goes, tears something from the street, leaves it altered, foreign. Terry can't look, overpowered by the sense that something is missing from the scene. Something that explains it, makes sense of it. Something that gives it meaning. And he finds himself looking for reassurance at his watch, needing to know what time it is, where he has to be. As though something had been asked of him and he can't remember what it was, and a terrible feeling of omission sets in him, of his existence being folded up in the wrong part of the universe.

And this is how the panic attacks would come on.

And he'd hang on until they passed.

Terry Skinner will come to wondering what happened to that guy, if he was simply drunk and cleaned up in hospital and back on his feet the same day. Or if it was his heart, if it had failed and the man had never recovered. He wondered too – though he realized it didn't matter to him, couldn't make any difference – if he had saved the man's life. There will be days when the man's life will come to feel like an object Terry can't nail down, an inchoate form flapping in the street around him, when Terry's arms will feel like they're made of air and pass through everything they're trying to keep hold of.

And sometimes Terry Skinner knows that he's a man whose whole grasp on time is slippery. He can sense it, the fabric of it, a substance playing past his face like the breeze, its silky touch causing a giddying feeling to rise within him, the awakening of a strange sense, a sense that should not be awakened, that should have remained inert within him. His whole life has been ordered by time, he's spent his days watching the clocks, obeying the hands. Pick-ups and drop-offs, the minutes of a ride, the hours of a shift. Now the clocks move too fast for him, escape him. By the time he's looked at the dashboard and looked away he knows that everything has moved on, and he needs to look again. And he knows he should have moved on with it, worries he's been left behind, and deep inside he's aware that he doesn't know, doesn't *know*, what day it is, what time it is. The numbers don't satisfy him. But he can feel it move, time, his insides reeling as it swirls past him, fails somehow to be carried with it. Like some kind of temporal vertigo. Because the shape of time, the form of it, is out there, distinct from the lazy approximation of measurement. Behind the screen there's something gargantuan, something monstrous, a behemoth of time, which Terry Skinner believes is out to get him, is out to get us all. And normally we hide from it, by not seeing it, by looking only at the mask, making us think we control it, the way we believe we control anything we can give a name to. But if you were unlucky, you'd be looking at the mask, the mirror, and suddenly you'd see right through. And you'd see, sudden and close up, the beast that had been there all along, its terrible maw, its infinite teeth. And some days the beast threatens to devour Terry Skinner. He sweats. He looks at the dashboard clock ten times a minute and still worries if he's in the right place on the right day. Too much information, none of it signifying anything, solving anything. None of it sure, none of it right. Feeding him numbers, fucking numbers – and what do *they* mean? – leaving him with no way of knowing anything. Nothing felt real to him any more. But he'd try and get on with things anyway, feeling always on the edge of panic; he'd drive along, his eyes squinting, trying to make his thoughts forget about it all, but his eyes betraying him too, and glancing too often at the dashboard, the sky.

And all around him, the monster, time.

It was going to swallow him, swallow him whole.

Winter Luxury Pie

Row One – Baby Blue Hubbard to Hong Kong Long Dong

For the best part of two hundred years the women in my family have run farms. We're a late, great, matriarchal agricultural dynasty. Grandma was the last of the doyennes, what with my father not really cutting it in the gender stakes, and myself not having much of a realm to preside over. But the fun stops here, I'm the last – not because I'll never have children, simply because after this there will be nothing more to bequeath.

I was raised principally as a farmer, but allowed out on odd days to go to school. My parents, traditional and untraditional in equal measure, made it clear that a woman's place was running the family business, for which I didn't need too many brains. Just enough, perhaps. And so I was spared the indignities of home-schooling inflicted with great and sedulous care on my two brothers. Da and Ma both had a fixation with education, which ran against a somewhat inauspicious legacy. Family tradition, after all, has it that F-A-R-M spells 'work'. Jer, the youngest of us, could speak Greek and Latin by the age of five, and solve quadratic equations in about the time it took him to blink. He'd answer in Urdu, and not particularly to show off, simply because that was what he usually counted in. He still has a phenomenal memory, particularly for statistics. He's like a walking Harper's Index when he gets going. Aged eight he came third in the National Spelling Bee, devastating my Da who assumed he'd walk it – and he in fact might have, his failure at the final hurdle being primarily the fault of the announcer, who struggled with *aphaeresis*, unintentionally pronouncing the word as though it were in the plural – Jer misunderstood, and rushed in with an entirely correct spelling of *aphaereses*. He was inconsolable when it was called wrong. Being the only person present who realized the reason for his mistake, he protested in vain.

He's never really recovered from those years, even though he left home and didn't return to the farm until my parents had gone. He hardly ever washes, and has worn the same clothes – the entire set, I mean, socks, pants, underwear, shirt – every day for perhaps a decade. His hair long ago got to the state where it was washing itself. He's quite charming, though given to pressure of speech, and he panics a little in company. He collects tomato seeds. He isn't good at conversation, though he can talk for hours about his tomatoes, or battles fought between peoples long since dead. He has this sad and unfortunate tendency to fall in love with girls who have large vocabularies – pretty or ugly, old or young, continent or no. They run a mile, of course. The last of these was Emily, a girl from the *nice* farm down the road, and achingly beautiful – tall where I'm short, willowy where I'm kinda gnarled. She has a laugh which tames wild horses – mine tends to startle tame ones. Whoever she marries, it's hard to imagine her children being anything other than demi-gods. She actually liked Jer, I should say – it wasn't entirely unrequited. Farm girls after all are used to that kind of smell, maybe even get to like it. Where she got her (admittedly impressive) vocabulary from is anyone's guess. But it all ended over the winter. Jer phoned up – and he *hates* using the phone – to tell me about it.

'I really like you Jer,' she said, 'but dontcha think all this physical stuff is, like, kinda banausic?' He's still not over her. It would have been kinder to have rejected him in monosyllables, really. Of course what he really needs is a girl who won't understand a word he's on about when he goes on one of his rants, who will just smile and go run a bath for him, a girl who's sweet and kind but not too bright, a girl who doesn't use the word *heterophyllous* in casual conversation.

Row Two – Untreated Autumn Queen to Gourdgeous Tricolor

And here the two of us are, back on Grandma's farm. Out through Esperanza ('We're beyond hope,' Jer says), east four miles along the highway. Third right after the gas station – a track more than a road. Past the sign advertising Taxidermy & Deer Processing. Next farm, the green gate, you've got it. This particular farm has been in the family about 120 years, before which we were over in the Appalachians. I guess my ancestors fancied a change of scenery.

My great-grandfather who bought the place committed suicide by drowning himself in a puddle. He just lay down and put his face in the muddy water. There were rumors he'd caught syphilis from a dancing girl up in Taylorville. He never really cut it as a farmer, the lure of the city dragging him ceaselessly away. Alcohol, gambling and dancing girls, the usual vices. Great-grandma never let on exactly what it was, so we're very much down to speculation. She just got on with running the farm – she got that at least from her husband's money – and expanded it into a significant empire. They already had two daughters: Hattie, who lived and worked there for forty years before marrying an India-rubber salesman from Cincinnati and moving to California (I heard once that there's a whole lost branch of the family still out there so I guess that, contrary to what they say, rubber don't bounce back); and Grandma, who never married. She told me once that she'd been in love, and after that never wanted anyone else. When I asked her how it felt to be celibate so long she laughed. 'Well there were *men*, honey, of course. Your father didn't come from nowhere. But they were distractions.

After a month or so I'd get thinking back to Harry. I met some wonderful people, some wonderful men. I just didn't fall in love, and wasn't prepared to settle for anything less. I mean, your father did, obviously, but he's not like us, is he?'

My Da then was another who had his heart broken when young, another who drifted away from the farm. He went off to Chicago, educated himself between working jobs in a tax office by day and a bar by night, and turned himself around. Then having been broken down and torn apart and his heart turned to cynicism and his life to the common bleakness of existence, he met my mother, and without falling in love understood perfectly well that here was a woman who would do, who he could be happy with. Ma was easily enough pleased with him. She came from a poor background, but was possessed of a great urge for self-improvement and was thus entirely complicit in the thorough education of her male off-spring. Da saw too she came from hard-working stock and would make (or at least produce) a good farmer. And unlike his paternal ancestry, he came back to the farm, at least until failing health took him away again.

My mother was philoprogenitive, in both senses of the word. Heterophyllous too, bearing the three of us as though we were different species. Like strikes of lightning hitting the same place we emerged with an unlikely forty-minute gap between first and last, Harry, myself and Jer.

The three of us, some facts: Hair colors: black, mousy and blonde (when he gets round to washing it). Eye colors: Brown, green-in-certain-lights and blue. Heights: 6 feet 3 inches, 5 feet 2-ish inches, 5 feet 6 inches. IQs: 110-ish, mind your own business, 160-ish. Handedness: ambi-, right, left. Careers: lawyer, farmer, none. You get the idea. No palingenesis. You could put the three of us together for photos and it would look like a gathering of the races. However, the family has always stuck together and defended its own.

Row Three – Rupp's Green-Striped Cushaw

In fact the only one we never liked was our cousin on my mother's side, Freddy. There was something in his (black) eyes, something about the loss of his (ginger) hair that we never trusted. By the age of twenty he had just clumps or tufts of rusted fur across his head, a distressing crop he concealed beneath a backwards baseball cap which he wore with accompanying white-trash accent. For Freddy a trailer was just the *height* of sophistication, a great bold step up from the ditch.

He never really made an effort to be liked. Family gatherings when we were young he'd make presents to me of dead birds, telling me they were asleep, and would wake up if I treated them right. I can still feel the slimy guilt of failing them today. He tripped Harry when he walked past, then would offer a bare-faced apology, without much effort at coming over sincere. Harry was so honest he thought it was all an accident, and at the wake when he'd been a bit pressed for something to say, all he could come out with was: 'He was always a bit clumsy, our Freddy.' I mean, *Jesus*. I hated him most though because he put maggots into Jer's cot when Jer was still just a tiny child. So don't get me wrong – we like *everybody*. It's just Freddy. Even his parents, Aunt Jean and Uncle Pete, didn't like him enough to go to his funeral. He wasn't actually their son, of course, had been adopted as a baby when it was clear Aunt Jean's problem with her tubes wasn't going to get fixed. Our side of the family we were always suspicious that Freddy had been put into adoption because his Da had been a serial killer or somesuch and had gone away for a very long time. Not that he was ever told about his uncertain parentage – they were tempted, mind, to use it as a constant disclaimer against anything he did. (That whispered confession: *'Of course he's not really ours . . . '*) Personally I think Freddy knew, deep inside, despite not being overly bright. I don't think it helped. Slow, dawning realization is a killer. It's *always* better to be told. Finding out by yourself is a horrible thing, and even the small lies get found out, in the end. He died at twenty-three from sudden heart failure over in Ariola Square Mall, gasping something about how terribly lonely it was in the dark. The irony of it was that there were probably more people concerned for his welfare at that particular moment, he having collapsed in front of a crowd of surprised shoppers, than ever before in his truncated life.

Uncle Pete almost died of relief, in fact, suffering a stroke the day after the funeral. He lasted another three years, but in poor health. In later years Aunt Jean got so lonely and weirded out that she sat at home by herself waiting for the phone to ring. She got rid of her TV, moved the armchair out into the hallway where the phone table was, and settled down every day to wait for calls. Sometimes she knitted (my inheritance from her – which to be fair was more than I expected – was measured in scarves), occasionally she read one of the free household shopping magazines that came through her door. Of course she didn't tell anyone that she was waiting for calls, and our whole side of the family has a thing about phones, so *we* never called her. I didn't find out about this until her own funeral, when my mother tearfully explained what had been going on. And my mother didn't find out until a couple weeks before that. So who called my Aunt? Well, as far as I understand, aside from pestilent telesales reps (to whom she gave short shrift), she waited for people to call the wrong number. Based on an entirely unrepresentative survey of my own phone, I can't imagine this occurring more than once a month. And when they called, she didn't try too hard to draw them into conversation, it was just, 'Oh, there's no one here of that name, perhaps you have the wrong number? Well, this is 476- . . . No, no trouble at all. Goodbye, now.' For Aunt Jean I guess it was enough, the contact.

Ma told me all this not so as to spread gossip, and not to make my heart blur with sympathy. Merely to say, 'There but for the grace of God and your Da go I.' Married siblings are always grateful, and always a little embarrassed when it comes to get-togethers with unmarried siblings. Harry, happily married for ten years, always stands in front of his wife, Sue, when they call at the door, so as to avoid drawing attention to her or appearing smug. It's astonishing to see. My parents too are apologetic whenever they talk about Harry. 'Of course,' they say, 'he was so *lucky* to find her.' This is to make me feel better, because all girls need to be married.

Row Four – Show King Bag 1, Show King Bag 2, Genital Improved Hubbard

When I was young, and after learning one day in school about erosion, I became pretty certain that the end of the world was nigh. Some say the world will end in fire, some say in ice. I developed this terrible fear that it would just wear away. This was precisely not the kind of fear to mention to my dad – he shouted for Jer and then got us to calculate (without the aid of a calculator – which with Jer around is not so much of a handicap), about how long it *would* take for the world to erode, given a posited rate. *Taking account of the different types of rock that make up the earth.* Taking into account too countervailing processes, such as the diagenesis of sediment. Coming up with a number with a name bigger than I remember somehow didn't allay my fears, but I did learn to keep them to myself next time.

Thanks to working with Jer, and helping him learn the long lists of words which are required cramming for spelling-bee entrants, I was doing pretty well at school. Three concurrent educations – on the farm, in school, and vicariously through Jer, while not exactly giving me clear direction in life, have provided me an essential sciolism.

For a while there it looked like I might escape the farm. The acreage then was shrinking anyway, and everything that remained still being run by Grandma with some help from Ma, and I was able to get to college, a year after Harry, where I majored in French.

My love life has been sparse. Remitting, perhaps, is a better word. The action has always fallen a little short of the required standard, and I never really thought my standards were unreasonable. Let me name and shame, for example, Thom the football player. After pursuing me a couple of weeks he came back to my room one night, a bit nervous and overcompensating with fraudulent assurance. After a while he took off his shirt and did a few push-ups, then asked me if I wanted to sleep with him. Let me elaborate on that one – in fact what he actually did was flex his muscles and say: 'You won't get a chance to sleep with a body like this very often.' I felt terribly, terribly sorry for him. It was painfully clear that no one would ever compete with the love he so clearly got from his mirror. Or take Mike, who one night in bed went through a whole bright pleiad of names before he landed on mine, then later, after a minute's recuperation from a sudden interfemoral intervention by my knee, claimed to have been joking. Neither is my worst experience, not by a clear country mile.

For me there was a boy once. A boy who changed everything while he was around. Everything in my life gained meaning or lost it according to whether I shared it with him. He left. I still imagine myself pointing things out to him as I walk the fields. The cobalt bluebirds beneath the willows. Flame-breasted cardinals on the fence post. One or two rare helobious species visiting from the lowlands, and myriad chromatic butterflies crowding like a ticker-tape parade. It all just seems like wasted beauty, without him. I can't say his name. All I'll say is there's not one of us without shit in our soul, somewhere.

And then lately there's Bob. Persistence is his middle name. Hope, unfortunately, is in fact his last. He wore me down, in a sweet kinda way. It happened one night, as the movie has it.

My last year in college. Thereafter he seemed to assume I was the girl for him. Sometimes he acts like we're already married. I think he's puzzled when I run away, find space for myself, but I think too he tells himself that it's just one of my quirks, just me and not him, and puts up with it. I didn't tell him I was coming back to the farm, and he doesn't know where it is, but it's only a matter of time. With Bob everything is just a matter of time. It all wears away, however long it takes.

Row Five – Stokes' Tricolor to Kitchenette

Home-schooling hell aside, the three of us had as golden a childhood as might be believed. From which I don't retain too much. The lingering, slightly fibrous taste of tomatoes straight from the vine. A happiness which rises only when I'm surrounded by farmland or countryside. Great memories of pre-Christmas pig-slaughtering ceremonies. The ability to operate a tractor. Well-developed upper-body strength from every menial task you care to name – and subsequently a right hook a fair degree more dangerous than you'd expect from looking. In fact I only got good things out of it, my upbringing, while it seems to have finished off my parents. On an organic patch at least the farm-life is a pretty healthy one (no organo-phosphates), once the stresses of actually making a living are removed, but it cut a swathe through their generation.

Da has recently received a new heart. Following the recrudescence of what was always a suspiciously idiopathic illness. The doctors doubted, but could see something wasn't right, so relented, and gave him one. I always wondered if transplants were the one final way to mend a broken heart. Unless the donor's heart were broken too. Either way, I'm pretty clear that there's more to the heart than just a pump.

Da, I think, was never really built for this life, nor any other, perhaps, but circumstances have allowed him to survive more comfortably than he otherwise might have done.

Ma joined him in hospital after her back gave out. For eighteen months she lay flat, the duration of two pregnancies. 'You're *not* getting fat,' was all she really wanted to hear from me when I visited. Post-hospital, she and Da moved to the city for access to reliable health care and firmer mattresses.

Grandma then was ninety-five, the oldest human being I ever saw, and complaining of decrepitude, manifested in her recently acquired inability to climb trees. Grandma had been climbing trees all her life, until a year or two back. It was simply what she did, the way other people worked out at the car plant or one of the gas stations up by the highway. In the end her hips gave out. It seemed entirely possible that she'd levitate up into the branches anyway through sheer force of will, hips or no, and God knows she tried, standing by the trunks of her favorite pieces of living timber, and gazing upwards at a lost world. She battled it for months, then finally admitted defeat. She was never the same after that, and died two months ago, her body in the end decaying enough to catch her unawares, asleep. Not the kind of woman who'd be careless enough to go out awake, Da said.

That meant that we were finally able to put in motion selling the farm, the house, and getting out of the agricultural vice. Debts have been mounting. The last of the animals were shipped out last year and sold for prices lower than we'd brought them in at, never mind the work and feed. Even the guinea fowl are gone. I have a feeling Jer ate the last couple, though he must have had some help in killing them. He has whole strata of earth beneath his fingernails, but won't get his hands dirty by precipitating the premature end of livestock. Pig-killing season he'd stay indoors and cry. Anyways. Just this year's crop to be rid of, then we can all go home.

I feel it's important, however, we get this last bit right. Financially, partly, but also to go out on a high. History deserves it. Which is the reason I'm here doing it all and not Harry, or even Jer. Jer was the first choice, and is probably the only one of us sufficiently versed in agronomy, but he hasn't really got the required concentration. Once he'd run out of projects to keep him interested (re-numbering the rows in Urdu, re-writing all the names as anagrams – projects it didn't take me *too* long to straighten out again), he let it all go to seed. Harry's in Alaska with a family to look after. Ma and Da are up in town nursing their respective ailments (and very much on the mend, now they're settled in their urban idyll). So they called me back to take over. There's a moral there. Try as you might you can't separate a woman from the soil of her destiny.

Row Six – Sweet Dumpling and Small Wonder

I don't mind being here. It's good to be home. It's good to work with living stuff, stuff that's grown from seed and needs nurturing. Good for the soul. And for the first few weeks no one had the number here, because we only really use it for outgoing emergency calls, so they couldn't phone. Bob tracked it down eventually, of course.

'Uh, where *are* you?'

'I'm on the farm.'

'On a what?'

'A farm. We own a farm, remember?'

'Oh. I thought you were joking about that.'

He said he'd come over, but I think he's getting worried whether he made the right choice with me after all. He doesn't think it's natural, going off to live on a farm for a few months. Not that I'm lonely – Jer's still around, cutting an increasingly aristulate figure. He sleeps a lot during the day, and sometimes when I wake in the night I come down to find him researching recondite strains of tomato. He's a terrible insomniac, or rather a very good one. I think lately his emotional troubles have begun having a detrimental effect on his health. He's a sensitive lad, and we brought in a TV – the first TV this farm has ever seen – especially so he could watch it daytimes when he's awake to feel numb and quell the rising nausea.

Evenings we rendezvous in the kitchen, and he cooks dinner. He's a great cook, though refuses to countenance any recipe which involves the butchery of innocent tomatoes. That aside, his chief responsibility around the place is to keep the fire burning there – it's an enormous fireplace, recessed like a small room, the natural claw of the hearth holding a row of smouldering logs we take turns to bring in. A great blackened streak up the back bricks. It's not cold – just coming into autumn now – but we've nothing else to cook on. He counts his seeds sitting in the window seat, his index finger on his left hand separating them with an untypical dexterity. Jer's left-handedness was his one act of apostasy against a rigorous learning regime. When he was young he used to write with the sheet of paper perpendicular to him, his left arm curling round it. Ma and Da couldn't shake the habit, and eventually conceded the point. I thought his being left-handed was cool. I still have an over-riding impression that *gauche* means *cool*, even though I know it doesn't.

From that window though you can see the patch. A six- by four-hundred-yard low-level jungle. I walk up the rows three or four times a day, keeping an eye out for slugs or snails. We're organic here so there's no pesticides, and the alternative preventative treatments are never certain. The patch is like critter central. There are bean bugs, which disintegrate disgustingly to the touch, setiferous spiders – variously-armed with poison spikes or wicked fangs – and evil, invisible, egg-laying monsters known as chiggers. Some enormous praying mantises too, eight inches or so – the kind town-folk see and start raving about first contact and alien encounters. And we get cockroaches. I mean real cockroaches, somewhere near the size of turtles.

Then there are the usual (and preternaturally destructive) snails and slugs. Weird things, when you think about it. A slug pretty much *is* its own foot. Put that in your mouth.

I talk to the crop. Grandma was a firm believer in that. 'Words change everything,' she said. 'So talk nicely when you're on the patch.' Harry once got the hiding of his life when he got his foot stuck beneath a particularly robust root, tripped, fell and swore.

Harry though, I should probably say, was the one anomaly of our impeccably agricultural ancestry, an aberration. A man never meant for the farm. A man born to cliché. Captain of his high school football team, dating (and later marrying) the prom queen, a football scholarship to college, law school. He was resistant to an unusual degree to home-schooling, but evinced a compensating aptitude at sports. Da thus kicked him out of his development program (transferring his remaining hopes in the brain department to Jer), sent him to school, and with the collusion of the head coach there fast-streamed him into the sporting life. He's currently working in Anchorage in a building with no windows on three sides. Sends me postcards of blue glaciers. They already have two kids, twins aged eight and a half, and once a few years ago a fortune teller told Sue that one would go on to get a doctorate in physics, and the other end up in and out of jail for the rest of his life. Both, I would say, are well on their way.

Row Seven – Big Autumn

Lately I have come to wonder if I am becoming like Grandma, who though she was happy and faced up to her losses in life, never really found a way of leaving them behind and moving on. Maybe, I think, I should climb trees. See what it was she found there. I'm not sure though there's anything that could make all that much difference. Leaves? Snails? I can't help but think I'd just get more dirt on my hands, and no less shit in my soul.

And I've come to wonder too if I'm wasting my time dwelling on my family, and these stories. There's a thousand things I haven't told you: that Harry once admitted to me that what he really wanted to do professionally was ice-dance, that he and Sue have been taking lessons four nights a week; that when Da was born he was a twin, and his baby sister died of TB; that Ma once had an affair with a rutabaga farmer from the Two Valleys. That I had my first sexual experience when I was twelve, in the hay barn one sunny summer afternoon, when I went all the way with my best friend, a girl called Carol. These stories don't seem to fit in anywhere else. But telling them keeps me from getting bored, when I have nothing to do for the next few weeks months except walk the rows and wait for the approach of Halloween, when I can finally sell all these damn pumpkins.

Fit

and I woke up, and there were all these people standing around me, and I had no clue what had happened or where I was or how I'd got there, and you can imagine how terrified I was. I was looking at the faces of the people around me, there was something strange about the way their expressions twisted, it wasn't concern, or anything like that. Something closer to horror, but it looked very familiar, and I finally worked out that they were looking like I was feeling. They were looking terrified. A few very odd moments later I realized that they were looking that way because they were afraid of me. Scared little me, with the great big headache. I was thirteen years old. And *they* were the ones who were afraid. Though they, of course, were fine. I have no idea what the fuck that was about.

That was my first big fit. It turned out later that I'd been experiencing quite frequent seizures for years by then, though they'd always been minor. I'd just never noticed. I used to space out at school a lot, sure, but then so did everyone else, it didn't seem like such a big deal. The thing is, though, that even when the fits are minor the brain takes a little while to recover. It doesn't start up straight away, takes an hour or so to return to running smoothly. Meantime everything is sluggish, and you experience difficulties in communicating (again, this seemed not at all unusual in my school). And during that hour you can find it hard to lay down memories. So all through my childhood I was experiencing (without any idea that I was experiencing) these seizures, often at intervals considerably less than an hour. Which explains a lot, because I had always been bewildered when people talked about their childhoods, as though they were accessible again once you'd lived through them. Until then I genuinely believed that everyone just made it all up. I thought it was normal to forget everything you did for the first few years of your life, up until you were, say, twelve. Apparently not. I still have trouble imagining what it must be like.

It also turned out that my case was serious and idiosyncratic enough that I was given a place in a then new epilepsy centre, which has been my home for the last fourteen years, while they've struggled to get it under control. Mostly hit-or-miss trials with the latest drugs. My trouble has been that whenever they found a drug that seemed to control whatever seizures I was getting, I started to develop a whole different kind of seizure. The doctors here were becoming very annoyed, and quite sick of the sight of me too, I shouldn't wonder. Never mind how I felt about it.

It's not the happiest place in the world, any more. The centre has aged badly. The paint on the walls is a bit battered these days, and the doctors are more occupied with ensuring fund-raising targets are met than they used to be, with fulfilling their quotas, reaching targets for treatment. I see a little less of them. When I do see anyone it's usually either my psychologist, who asks how I'm feeling, or the pharmacist, for some new pills. The latest crop of auxiliary nurses seem a little under-trained too, to be honest, and somehow not quite so sympathetic as they used to be. But then I'm not a child any more, so perhaps that's all it is.

I'm the only patient remaining from the initial intake. Everyone else seems to come and go – they get better, or their attacks get manageable. Or in serious cases they don't, and they find other ways out. I've always been on the cusp – every time it seems like I'm better and ready to leave it takes a turn for the worse, and finds some new expression. So I miss some of my friends. There was one girl, in particular, who arrived not long after me. We spent those early, golden years hanging around together, and I came to be very fond of her. It was the strangest thing, but anything connected with her and I would remember it. She was my first idea of what memory was like.

I remember, when she was about to leave, asking her not to go, to stay with me, because I needed to live with her.

'But what do we even have in common?'

'Well, there's the stuff we've both been through, and . . .'

'The epilepsy?' she laughed. 'I'm not sure that's grounds for a relationship.'

'There's other stuff, too.'

'I get a lot of depression,' she said.

'Okay,' I said.

'I love you,' I said.

'Oh brother,' she said. Then: 'Listen. This love thing. We're on different wavelengths, you and me. I don't believe in love. I mean I'll never feel it, not just to you. Happiness, sadness, they're all just chemical. The imbalances in our brain, they make me unhappy. The SSRIs make me happy. The way you feel about me, it's a chemical reaction. It'll pass. Love doesn't mean anything. It's all just chemistry.'

And thinking about it since I've decided that she's half right. It is all chemistry – people, emotions, tomato ketchup. But it's not just chemistry. Things mean things, too. I still miss her, and I still have those feelings for her, so they seem justified, to me.

So many of my old friends have left that I don't know too many of the new crowd. I'm rubbish with names anyway, and it gets really embarrassing when you have to ask someone for the hundredth time. So I stick to one or two people I like and whose names I've managed to get down. There's Mary, a lovely, quiet girl who doesn't talk much, which makes getting along much easier. She does have epilepsy, but not the kind with noticeable attacks. She also has a kind of food-based kleptomania. Every day she has to report to one of the nurses to be searched, and to hand over the food she's stashed. She pulls crusts of bread from her sleeves, a muffin from her smock. She finds for the nurse the scraps she's missed. She smiles proudly, pleased with herself. Then she goes off to steal some more. You have to wonder what happened to her as a kid.

But even Mary has a new friend now, whom she spends all her time with. It's an older lady from the next-door room (don't ask me her name) who had a stroke earlier in the year, and has been getting fits since, severe enough to keep her in here. Now *her* memory is really shot. Her daughter comes to visit and I hear their voices carry through from the lounge.

'*Who* is it?'

'Virginia.' Spoken firmly, but patiently, despite it being the third time.

The old lady thinks about it. 'Virginia?'

'Yes, Mum, it's me. I told you.'

She sounds quite surprised at the news.

'Is that *my* Virginia?'

'*Yes*, Mum.'

And so on.

So aside from Mary, I tend to hang around with Michael – Mikey – the youngest member of our fit club. He's fourteen and I'm twenty-seven, so we get on great. Poor kid, though, he suffers from these really fierce attacks, though luckily they're not so frequent. He has to wear a crash helmet so he doesn't bash his head around too much. I'm not sure it's been thought through, giving a crash helmet to a hyperactive fourteen-year-old. It seems to be asking for trouble. Let's just say that it was tested rigorously before it was actually required. Cracking your head open during an attack is kind of a secondary concern in any case. It's the insides of your skull you want to worry about, the neurons firing beyond their capacity. If a fit lasts for too long your neurotransmitters will run riot and burn your axons right out.

Mikey has the usual short-term memory problems after a seizure, but his memory is basically fine, he has a perfect recall for jokes – he just sits and reads joke books and then will spend, if you let him, all evening earnestly running through the jokes. He never smiles or laughs while he tells them. He's young, though, so though he's going to continue to be pumped full of Felbatol or phenobarbitone or whatever for a few years yet, there's a good chance he'll recover. Though his liver might not.

I had the same. I was on those drugs for years. But something strange happened, of which that first fit was a sign. The frequent, minor attacks gradually turned into infrequent, major attacks. Partial seizures slipping up the scale, becoming generalized. They have no idea why. Bang on the head, maybe. Some minuscule malformation in the brain, a tiny knot of veins. Any which way, it's certain now that I have it for life. The truth of the matter is that I'm ill, that something's wrong with my brain, and it's always going to be wrong with my brain. The pills help, but they're capricious. They won't stop my brain trying to kill me one afternoon when it gets bored and decides to have a fit.

And it's Mikey I'm with this morning, as we're walking round the entire facility, corridor by corridor, trying to think of a game to play till lunch. He's chattering off a whole long list of ideas, and he always chooses anyway, but I'm not really listening. I'm trying to find the source of a strange smell that seems to get stronger as we circle the corridors. What the hell is it? It's incredibly strong, unpleasantly so, and right up my nose. Is that *grapefruit*? I haven't had grapefruit for years.

'Can you smell that?' I turn to ask Mikey. But my words are drowned out by that incredibly loud pounding sound which has suddenly started up and which Mikey, insulated inside his crash helmet, affects not to notice. It's funny how after all these years I can still be so slow on the uptake.

I wake up to find myself on the floor of the corridor, a pillow stuffed behind my head.

'All right there, are we?' asks a nurse after a while. 'What's your name?'

'David,' I say. 'What's yours?'

The nurse laughs. But she doesn't tell me her name.

'What has fifty legs, but can't walk?' asks Mikey.

'I don't know.'

'Half a centipede,' he says. And despite myself, I laugh.

'Michael. You stop bothering him,' the nurse says. 'I've told you before.'

'S'all right,' I say. 'Hadn't heard that one.'

That was the second seizure this week, which is way too many. Stress is generally a bad thing, and all these attacks I've been having lately seem to derive from the stress. And the stress, I'm quite sure, derives from a conversation I had a week ago with my psychologist, Dr Costa. I was so unnerved by it I wrote it down:

'Mr Vaughan.'

'David,' I say, helpfully.

'How are you, David? Are you well?'

'Am I *well*?'

'In general.'

'Uh, I guess so.'

'David.' He looks uncomfortable. 'Well. I've been talking with my colleagues.'

'That's great,' I say.

'And it's our opinion, the opinion of the medical staff that is – the care staff, too – that your illness has stabilized. That you're stable.'

'Stable? Like, consistent?'

'Let's stick with stable. Obviously over the years there's been resistance to a good deal of the medication. But we think that what we have you on now is about as good as we're going to get.'

'You mean I'm not going to get better.' And I'm sad about that. I've lived with it for so long it's just a part of me, something I'll always be. But you always hope it will go.

'We'd rather you think of it as though you were, in fact, in a way, already better.'

'You want me to think I'm well?'

'Not *well* well, perhaps, but, well, *well*.'

A pause, which I'd struggle to describe as anything other than expectant.

'And that you might be happier outside this facility.'

I get an instant buzz of fear. I can feel chemicals surging from my glands, sugar releasing into the blood stream. Adrenaline makes a swift swirl through my chest, and my breathing and heart rate leap up, everything threatening to loop into a panic attack. Against my body's wishes, I force myself to breathe ever so slowly.

'But I'm happy here.'

'Good. That's really good. But you're happy in a limited way. We think you might be ready to face up to a little more *freedom*.' No word has ever seemed to threaten more.

'I have all kinds of limitations. But I like it here. I'm *safe* here.'

'Yes. I do understand. It's just. That it might be time to move out of your safety zone. That there might be more opportunities for happiness if you were, well, a little less safe.'

'Less safe? I could go and stand in the middle of the road, if that would help.'

'Of course not. No. I was just hoping to talk a little with you about why you might not want to leave, I was wondering if we could talk about the fear.'

'We have nothing to fear but fear itself,' I joke.

He waits.

'I get so sick. It's not exactly an irrational fear.'

'No, it's not. Partly, though, it's conditioned by your memories of how sick you were.'

'I don't exactly remember how sick I was.'

'But your body does. Fear is conditioned. And though you'll always be prone to epilepsy, you must know that it's more manageable than it's ever been. Perhaps it's time to stop being afraid.'

'You can't kick me out,' I plead. He holds up a hand.

'We're not kicking you out. You are certainly qualified for the assistance you receive here, and as far as we're concerned, that's the bottom line. But it's something you do need to consider. And we'd help in every way possible, there are mechanisms there for you, help in finding you a home and so forth. You'd remain on our books as an outpatient, of course.' He smiles, trying to lift my misery.

'I'm not ready,' I say.

'Only one way of finding out,' he says.

'Why don't you come back in a week and let me know what you think?' he says.

That, as I mentioned, was one week, or two fits ago, depending on how you like to count. I'm not sure where all the time went.

A few hours later, when I can walk again, though my head is still riddled with aching cracks, Mikey and I go have lunch in the canteen. Standing very still by the table with the orange juice on is Mary. She's looking from the jug of juice to her pocket and you can see exactly what she's thinking. It'll never work.

'Hi, Mary,' we chorus as we pass by. Mikey comically batters his helmet with his fists. She smiles shyly and, looking closely at the floor in front of her feet, goes over to steal some biscuits instead. We have our lunch and I begin to feel a bit better. Mikey spends the whole time telling me jokes, even with his mouth full, trying to find ones I like. I don't know where he gets them all from – he has thousands. Someone must have bought him a new book.

I don't listen too well to the jokes though because I'm thinking about leaving. I've been spending most of the last week thinking about leaving, asking myself: am I well? Am I okay?

And I know that I'm not. It's true that things have been better, the last few months, that the seizures are more controlled. But I still get them. Which is bearable, while I'm here, where no one looks at you as though you're a twitching incarnation of evil on surface the earth. People understand, here.

On the way back from lunch to my room I detour past the front doors, just to have a look. Two big bright glass doors, filled with light. The light in the garden is different; yellow sunshine on green grass. Out front of the building it comes cold white onto the grey pavement. I don't have a problem with being outside. I have a problem with being out front. There's nothing for me there. So I freeze up near those doors. The doors make me afraid. The fear makes me sick.

The sickness makes me afraid.

The fear makes me sick.

It's chemistry. But it's not just chemistry

I have wondered if the over-protective love of my parents – when I was very young, at least – made me afraid. Because I think that this fear, though newly discovered, has always been in me. After the fits, of course, my parents treated me differently. They never, not once, looked me straight in the eye again. What is it about this illness that's so disturbing? A tiny part of your brain is just slightly off, a vein twists round itself here or there, and people who have loved you cut you off, refuse to talk to you. Your friends make excuses and never come to play any more. You hear your parents whispering when they're talking on the phone. So no. Even if it were manageable, and I don't think it is, I'm not ready for all that again. I'm comfortable here. I fit in. I'm going to have to tell them that I'm not ready to go, not yet.

I'm still standing staring at the doors when one of my doctors, Dr Reynolds, saunters past.

'So, you thinking of leaving?' he asks.

'Maybe,' I say.

'Great,' he says.

'You're looking well,' he says.

'Thanks,' I say.

'Any plans for what you'll do out there?'

'One or two,' I say.

Even if I wanted to I can't think about what I might do out there because everything out there feels like fear. Freedom and fear. Fear and illness. Illness and freedom. They all seem like the same thing as far as I can see.

Thinking about it all makes me feel weak. I head back to my room, planning to sleep a little. I like my room, it feels like home. But when I get to the door it doesn't look at all like it should. The dimensions of the room are somehow warped. The bed seems much further away than it usually is; oh, wait, here it comes. Time seems to slow right down. Then it speeds right up, and it takes me with it.

I wake up from my fit on the floor of my room. A small crowd is gathered at the doorway. Mikey seems to be sticking his head through the crowd, as though his head was growing on someone's thigh. I look away.

'What has fifty legs but can't walk?' he asks.

It takes a while for me to untangle the words, and when I do I still can't make sense of them. They sound like blurts of syllables, word syllabub, or word soup, and for a moment I can't connect them to what they might mean.

'Whu?' I mumble.

'No,' he says. 'What has fifty legs but can't walk?'

'I can't walk,' I say. My lips feel strange around the sounds. I think I bit my tongue, it feels swollen in my mouth.

'You don't have fifty legs, though, do you?'

To be honest, I'm having trouble counting them, though fifty would seem like a lot. With fifty you'd think that at least a handful of them might be working, which clearly isn't the case.

'Half a centipede,' he says.

Then adds, seriously: 'That's funny, isn't it? I mean that's really funny.'

214

And I'm gone again.

I have half an idea that I regain consciousness once more, before I wake up properly, because I remember something else. And normally it's all black. Normally I remember nothing until I'm fully awake again. And it might just have been a dream, though in that state I don't normally dream, it's just a big black hole, but I have a picture of Dr Costa's face, close up and looking down from above me. His lips are moving and there's a sound, though the two aren't coinciding as they perhaps should. But the sound, blurred by a heavy bass line, goes: ' . . . perfectly honest, it sickens me. You do everything you can to help them and when the time comes for them to do a little bit themselves they show themselves to be utterly spineless. What? Oh don't worry about him, he won't remember a th–'

When I wake up everything is aching, like I'd passed the last hour or so in a washing machine, on heavy spin. My jaw feels like it's still locked. Two fits in one day is a killer. I have to spend long minutes just lying there, waiting for some strength to return. A nurse helps me sit up.

'You've just had a seizure,' says a nurse. 'You've been unconscious for a while. Can you remember your name?'

'I'm David,' I say. 'And you are?'

The nurse laughs.

A few minutes later Mikey bursts in, very enthusiastic, speaking so quickly I can hardly keep up. 'Oh, man! That was incredible! You were really freaking out there on the floor, I was sure you were going to fry yourself right there. It must have been like bonfire night in your head. You were out for *ages*. They wouldn't let me stay and watch.'

I don't think he's exaggerating because some of the other patients are hanging around outside my door, sneaking glances inside, and I can see that though they usually take this kind of thing for granted – mere party tricks – they're looking genuinely impressed.

'Come on, then,' says the nurse, 'let's get you up.' Grasping both my hands she pulls me a little too quickly to my feet and all the blood rushes from my head. My memory's not too clear about what happens then.

I phase slowly back into myself. My arms and legs feel strangely numb, though at least I can feel them. The surroundings gradually materialize. I'm in an office. Dr Costa is there. He performs a thoughtful strum of his fingernails on his desktop. 'You're making the right decision. I don't think we should waste any time. It was inevitable you'd eventually begin to feel trapped, staying here so long, but I wouldn't have predicted it would have caused quite so much stress. There's every danger, the longer you stay, of increasingly adverse reactions.'

'What?' I say. 'No. Wait. I have to *stay*. I've decided. I mean it's definitely getting worse. I haven't had this many attacks since I was a kid. And it's not even as if they're the little ones – they're serious.'

He waves his hand, a reverse conjuring trick, dismissive. 'Yes yes,' he says. 'But as we were discussing . . .' he speaks slowly and clearly, as though I'd suddenly become stupid, '. . . it seems that the stress you're experiencing . . .' he stresses the word stress '. . . is caused by your presence here. As I have explained.'

'No,' I say. 'No.'

'I did. I just explained it to you. It's just your memory playing up again. You know what you're like. You'll just have to trust me on this one.'

'But it can't be about the place. I've been here for years and it's never been a problem.'

'Yes. But – and now think about this – you have, for all of those years, been very poorly, haven't you? So there's a clear link. Don't know why we didn't pick up on it earlier. Obvious, really.'

The symptoms of panic are returning. I don't feel like I

have any control. My breathing ratchets up, threatens to get out of control. My heart doggedly pounds. I grab a sheet of paper from Dr Costa's desk and crush it into a makeshift bag, then I put it over my lips and breathe in and out, concentrating on the crumpling sound of its inflation.

'All right there?' asks Dr Costa. 'Jolly good.'

'Henry!' he calls.

Henry, one of the auxiliary nurses, a big lad, comes in.

'Help our young patient pack, would you? He's leaving us.'

'Congratulations,' says Henry, and cracks his knuckles.

I manage to get my breathing under control. 'You're just trying to get rid of me,' I say. 'Because you can't cure me. You're fixing the figures. I'm not leaving. Absolutely no way. You can't make me.' Henry comes up behind me and after that I'm struggling to remember what happened.

'Well done,' says Dr Reynolds. He's shaking me by the hand. 'We should have a drink to celebrate, really, except of course you can't, what with the medication.' He shakes his finger at me. 'And don't you forget that! Never mind – I'll have one for you, raise a toast.'

'What?' I say. 'What's going on?'

'Oh look! A few of your friends have come to say goodbye.'

Mary and Mikey are standing in the hallway, noticeably failing to fill it.

'What's going on?' I say.

'We're your leaving party,' says Mikey. 'Bye, Dave! We'll miss you! No, hang on! Wait! We're not all here yet! Where's Ruby?'

Down the corridor comes one of the nurses whose name I forget, pushing a wheelchair with the old lady in it, Mary's friend. He positions her next to Mary and Mikey. They're an odd sight lined up there The old lady seems to wake up, and looks at me.

'Hello,' she says. 'Who are you, dear?'

'I'm David,' I say. 'And you're Ruby?'

Her eyes widen. 'I haven't the faintest idea,' she says, and losing interest, begins to look hopefully back along the corridor.

Dr Costa is by my side. 'So we'll be in touch soon, catch up on your progress. Shouldn't leave it more than a few months, if I were you.'

'*Months*? What? No. This isn't . . . happening. This isn't what we agreed.'

'Of course you're nervous. Who wouldn't be? But it's the right decision. You won't regret it.'

'Bye, Dave!' yells Mikey again, his voice coming from some distance away now.

'But you can't,' I want to say, except the sound seems to be flickering. The things everyone's saying are following half a second behind the time they're being said. My forehead feels suddenly hot. The aura's back, words are jamming, like a stupid stutter.

'But you,' I say. 'But you. But you. But you.'

And I know there's lightning forking somewhere in my brain, an electrical storm widening outwards. That's normally the point I fall unconscious, but this fit feels like it's never going to come on, the aura a wave forever on the edge of breaking. I'm not well. They can't do this. I need help. My face is so hot.

'I'm having a seizure,' I try to say.

'But you,' I say.

I feel a tug on my arm and sense that Mary has sidled up beside me. I start to try to ask her to help me, but she looks at me like I'm not listening to her. And I see that she's pulled out half a slice of toast from her sleeve, which she offers to me. As though she thinks I might need it. As though I were going somewhere. After that my memory's a little hazy.

Dream #113
18/05/___

It was just so vivid and absorbing that I felt I'd woken into it, and that it was everything I'd left behind which was dream, evaporating and unreal. My memory of it is a lot clearer than some of the things I've actually lived through, I can remember just precisely how it felt. It was such a hot night, the thick warm kind of air you can barely breathe, so heavy it's an effort to get it into your lungs and then it just sits there like a weight. I was caught up in my covers. It was stifling, way too hot to sleep. All of this, I mean, while I actually *was* asleep, and dreaming. So. I untangled myself from my covers and carried them with me into the back garden, which was blissfully cool in comparison, and I found a brick wall to curl up on and thankfully fell right asleep. I remember waking up once in the night – though I was in fact still sleeping – to find that it had been raining, and that two sodden cats had tried to crawl under my covers and cling to me for warmth and shelter. I hadn't got too wet myself, so I just pulled the covers tighter over me, then I fell asleep again.

I finally woke – still in the dream, yes – to a muddy dawn. I got down off the wall and headed back inside, only to find that on my way out in the night I'd left the back door of my house open, and the kitchen when I came in was a complete mess like it had been turned right over. It was still incredibly humid inside and I was baking hot again, so I took off a couple of thick jumpers I'd been wearing. In the sitting room I surprised a burglar – he climbed out of a window into the garden, where I, following behind, threatened him with a garden chair. He then tried to escape over the wall, but failed

219

to climb it. Almost instantly the mood of the dream, which had been completely fine up to that point, turned bad, and I realized that I might have got myself into a bit of a nasty predicament. The burglar stopped running, sauntered instead confidently back towards me, eased himself into another garden chair which he set down right in front of me, and opened a newspaper. It was somehow an extremely threatening gesture. All of the control in the situation had passed right over to him, just like that, and I was terrified. He suddenly seemed very powerful. I was too close to him to be able to make a run for it, even with him sitting down, and my legs were shaking with weakness, so I just stood there stupidly, feeling awful.

The way my mind began to work was like this: I was in a dangerous situation, and I'd do anything to get out of there. And I was beginning to feel this desperate hope that this whole terrible scenario was somehow just a dream, though it seemed impossibly unlikely to me at the time that this was in fact the case. But I couldn't see any other way out. And it occurred to me then that dreams often contain errors in logic, in their internal consistency, if only to remind the dreamer that they are, in fact, merely dreaming. So if I could spot any such errors I'd *know* I was in a dream, which knowledge of course would mean it would cease to be scary, and I'd become sufficiently self-aware (I mean really self-aware, not the illusion of being self-aware you get when you don't even know you're dreaming) to be able to wake myself up. So I examined everything that had happened closely, and pretty quickly saw a whole swathe of minor inconsistencies that proved to me that it was, in fact, all just a dream. They were things like the fact that I'd fallen asleep on a narrow brick wall that I couldn't possibly really have balanced on, or that I'd suddenly been wearing all these jumpers that I hadn't been wearing when the dream started. Or that on the front of the newspaper the burglar was reading was an exact photograph of his face, appearing precisely as he did in front of me.

So there were all kinds of things that, when taken together, showed how impossible it all was, and the fear dissipated, and I found I was able to get hold of myself in the dream, return to myself a little, and then from the inside gently nudge myself to wake up, I mean really wake up. And I was quite pleased with myself for being so clever.

It was only much later in the day, with the dream lingering and replaying, when I become slowly aware that I hadn't been as clever as I'd thought. I thought I had spotted all these subtle signs that differentiated my dream from waking, and yet it dawned on me that far stranger things had happened in the dream without their provoking the least reaction in me. These were things like the fact that the house and garden I was in aren't even my house and garden any more. I haven't lived there for twenty-odd years, to be honest, not since I was a child, and yet it still felt like I was entirely at home there, I mean it literally took me all day to notice this. But even stranger was this one: that the burglar, when he ran from me, was a young black man. Then he was a thin old white man when he failed to climb the wall, and a muscled young white man with a London accent when he sat down to read the newspaper at me. Yet this never struck me as being at all strange or unlikely. I completely accepted his metamorphoses, even after I woke for real and got on with the day and remembered all of it. It had a big effect on me, this. I realized how much I took for granted. And it meant that I completely stopped trusting my own perceptions, and more than that, I came to look for the unrealities afflicting my waking life, absurdities of the real universe that I accept without questioning, and I fear that they are many in number, and too strange for me to doubt.

Waterproof

We're in the pub waiting for Harry. Nestor is making his usual complaints about exhaustion in a voice loud enough that we're getting strange looks from the drinkers. Not disapproving looks, just strange ones. I can't breathe for laughing. Shafique and Jay Jay are nodding politely and sipping their Cokes even though I know they're finding it just as funny as I am. It's just that they feel they're supposed to disapprove of this kind of thing, so they hide it. Nestor pauses to take a huge gulp of his own Coke and draw breath. I choke on a mouthful of lager and spew it all over my lap. It's lucky I'm still wearing my waterproofs.

'It's the minerals,' Nestor is saying. 'I think I have malnutrition.'

He's looking paler, it's true.

The weird thing is that Nestor works the hardest of us all and he doesn't wash a single car. He's a legend in the forecourt.

'Today's the day,' he says every morning. 'Today I'm going to wash more cars than all of you motherfuckers put together.'

And then even as we're busy filling the buckets – before we've even begun our daily game of *Wash!*, which we always lose anyway because we're always a man short – the first car pulls in and gives us the signal and Nestor marches right over. And the woman – it's not always a woman, but the first one is usually a young mother coming in for her daily shop right after the school run – takes one look at him and they both get in the car and drive off. Every day, I swear. An hour or two later she drives back up and drops him off.

'Sheeit,' he says. 'I thought that was going to be the one.'

Ten minutes later and he's gone again – new car, new driver. By the end of the day he's even more exhausted than the rest of us.

'Fuck me,' he says wearily, and sometimes you get the feeling he's not even saying this, it's just an echo of what he's been hearing all day. I mean it must be pheromones or something. He's a fucking phenomenon.

'I think you're making it harder than it is,' offers Jay Jay. 'It's not a difficult job. You just have to wash cars.'

'You know I am trying,' says Nestor, annoyed. I think it really bothers him.

Basically there's some kind of informal pimping going on here. Nestor is resigned to getting caught and losing his job over it sooner or later, but Harry certainly knows about it already, because he never asks where Nestor is when he comes to check on us, and my feeling is that the supermarket knows about it too – after all, they've blanket CCTV coverage over the car park, and keep a close eye on us to check we don't steal stuff from the cars. They'd notice this kind of thing. But I think too they know that it brings in business – keeps the families shopping here – and they might as well get a piece of the action. They do have a commitment to Customer Service, after all.

And then condom sales are way up, apparently.

Maybe I'm over-stating the case a little. Maybe Nestor has a lot of friends. Maybe these women just need a hand carrying their shopping and I'm only seeing the sex everywhere because I'm not getting any. It's a possibility.

Meantime we pimp ourselves round the car park. Four teams of washers, each with their own bit of concrete turf to operate on. Two guys (just the one on our team, given Nestor's reliable absence) back at the station (a trolley loaded with water containers, buckets and sponges, detergent and windscreen cleaners) waiting for the customer to come to them. Two out on the make. 'Car-wash-mate?' 'While-you-shop?' There's about a three per cent take-up rate, which we work on hard. There are the ones who claim not to have time, who think they can shop faster than we can clean. We offer to do it for free if we're not finished by the time they get back. They pay up.

Quiet times I wander over to talk to Shireen, the only girl on the teams. To be honest, I don't have much of a social life outside of work. Can't really afford it, is the main thing, but I try never to get too far from my mum's place, either. In fact, Shireen is the only girl I actually know to talk to, so perhaps it's not surprising I have a crush on her. It's doing strange things to my head. I'm so insanely fond of her that in the top drawer in my room at my mum's house I keep an umbrella I bought off her once, which I like just because it makes me feel closer to her. I don't even use it – I hate umbrellas. I prefer to get wet.

Shireen gets a lot of stick because she wears Marigold rubber gloves to protect her hands, but the truth is that everyone else is just jealous because we didn't think of it first, and we're too proud to copy her, even though our hands are getting slaughtered by the job and at least half of us come down with frostbite every winter. And she's a fantastic *Wash!* player.

Every day I go over and ask her to come out with me, and every day she says the same thing.

'I don't think my brothers would like that.'

At least she's beginning to smile when she says it. Shafique knows one of her brothers, and tells me she's not kidding. There was one time, I'm told, when a customer had been hassling her, and fourteen members from her family fraternity came down to redistribute him.

'How many does she have?' I ask.

'Thirty-two,' he says. 'Give or take.'

'Any sisters?'

'You're not getting this, are you?'

Most of the washers are from Africa. Nigeria, Kenya. The car-park banter passes in a hierarchy of indistinguishable African dialects, but Shafique and Jay Jay do Nestor and me the favour of talking in English. Shafique is appalled I only speak the one language ('How do you communicate with other peoples?'), but there you go.

The employment agency the supermarket uses has hundreds of these guys on the books – newly arrived, poor as fuck. Sometimes the only English they've had time to learn is, 'Car wash?' Nestor, though, is from Guatemala – he and I are freaks of employment. The deal with him is that the only way he could find to get into the country was via Africa, and Immigration took him at his word that he was a Nigerian with a skin problem and an odd accent. With me it's just the closest work I could find to my mum's place.

In fact I'm the one white guy in the whole car-wash pool. White guys like me are supposed to collect trolleys. I had to beg them to let me work. 'Don't you want to go on trolleys?' they asked me. I told them I didn't have a driving licence, that I wasn't safe. I have my reasons. The uniform is flexible, for a start. You each get an orange fluorescent waistcoat, a company baseball cap, waterproof trousers. But apart from that you wear what you want.

But anyway, this curious colour divide here: black guys wash cars and white guys collect trolleys. The trolley guys assume they have seniority – after all, they actually work for the store, they get a better basic rate of pay, and they're natives – as far as you can be a native in London. We indulge their innocence. Because what they don't seem to grasp is that we get *tips*. Rounded up pay from mothers too busy dealing with their kids to wait for their change, 50p from a fiver. No one tips them for bringing in the trolleys. And no one is going to pay them on a per-trolley basis. They could push all the trolleys in the world for all the good it'd do them.

Also, that our jobs require an ounce of care and pride and profundity. Listen: dirt is superficial. Our job involves removing the superficial. And that's profound. Of course, as Jay Jay points out, a clean car is a singularly superficial object.

So you remove the superficial and you're left with the superficial. How profound is that? I don't hear any of the trolley guys coming up with anything like that. I guess pushing trolleys is functional, doesn't lend itself to philosophy.

To be honest, though, the washer–pusher rivalry has been on hold a couple of weeks since one of the trolley guys was run over. He was an old guy called Mac, a halfway-house case, a thin man with an alcoholic face, too old for any other work maybe, who found the supermarket to be an equal-opportunities employer, at least in the sense that they don't mind geriatric trolley-pushers. Mac was managing a lengthy snake of trolleys, which accumulate in weight when linked together and are, if not exactly difficult to move, at least difficult to stop on a downwards slope.

He was clipped by a black BMW (*Wash!* 12:8:–14), some idiot driving through the car park at rally speeds. The kind who thinks he's a really great driver.

Fucking drivers.

We just heard the quick flip-thump, not the familiar crinkle of cars crashing, but something duller, a sound instantly recognizable when you've heard it a few times. It gets you right in the pit of your stomach. Then we looked up to see this long line of trolleys driving themselves perfectly between the rows of cars, headed in the direction of the supermarket, filling the air with the terrible clattering of their wheels.

Worst thing about it was that the supermarket manager came on site, had a word in Harry's ear, and we had to give the bloody BMW a complimentary wash. Then we hosed the rest of the gore and bits into a drain. If we actually had a contract, I'm sure as hell that this kind of thing wouldn't be in it.

Harry's our supervisor. He's a fat Hawaiian in a Hawaiian shirt. Likes to stomp around the car park in Bermuda shorts and flip-flops. Only the company cap, fluorescent waistcoat (yellow, for seniority) and clipboard indicate he's doing any kind of a job. Harry's a senior figure in the company. He has contacts, knows people. He oversees four major business forecourts in south London. He doesn't do much when he's round here, though. He keeps an eye on our productivity figures. He gives us marks for our performance. He sacks us if we're caught lazing around. And he sorts out disputes with the customers.

Harry has a bit of a short fuse. Bearing in mind he only oversees work rather than actually doing any, he seems a stressful bloke. The incredible thing about him is that he can't believe he's doing the job he is. He doesn't understand his job, doesn't understand why people want their cars cleaned all the time. 'It'll be dirty by tomorrow,' he mutters as another recipient of our cleaning expertise leaves the supermarket. He seems to think that these car drivers are, essentially, just wasting our time.

He doesn't even understand why people *have* cars in London. 'Insanity,' he says as he watches the cars, every one of them entirely empty of passengers, crawl in queues around the forecourt. On the adjacent main road an empty bus hustles uninterrupted down the bus lane.

To be honest I sympathize with him.

And I can see why the clientele gets him down.

For example. There's one guy who drives in with his white Ford Escort (*Wash!* 15:4:22 (for spoiler and wheel arches)) and pulls over, giving us that upwards, beckoning nod of his head which indicates he wants a wash. He's a bulky, gym-built skinhead from one of the nearby estates, and he brings along his girlfriend, a bony adolescent with dyed-blonde hair and a skimpy top. They don't come here to do their grocery shopping. He sits in the driver's seat, door open. She moves over and sits on his lap. They kiss, if you can call it kissing – it's more like mouth-to-mouth sex, lewd and full-on. I've never kissed anyone like that. I'd be too embarrassed, for one thing.

They stay kissing till the car's clean. Loud music on his stereo, needless to say – so loud I can't actually tell what it is,

I mean, if it's techno or rock or Bolivian folk music or whatever. It's just too loud. The guy freaks out if he gets splashed with water, though that makes it really hard if you're trying to wash it fast enough to keep your *Wash!* score up, I mean he's got the *door* open.

But here's the thing. He's quite happy for the rest of the team to wash his car, but not me. One day I'd just got started on his windscreen when I noticed that he'd removed his tongue from his girlfriend's throat and was staring at me.

'What the fuck are you doing?' he asks.

I'm confused. 'I'm sorry, mate, I thought you wanted a wash.'

He's confused. 'You're a fucking *car-washer*?'

'Well yeah. Sure.'

'You can't do this one.'

'What's wrong?'

''Cause you'll be fucking looking at my fucking girl, that's what the FUCK'S wrong, you fucker.'

'I won't look. I'll just wash the car. I swear.'

'Fuck off. Let one of the you-knows do it.'

'What?'

'Oh for fuck's sake. *You* know. One of the you-knows. Africans.'

I honestly think he drives in so he can have a black guy wash his car just to show them that he has a car and a girlfriend, as though he's rubbing it in their faces. And he doesn't mind them seeing him making out with his girlfriend because they're black and don't count. It's weird.

Shafique thinks it's hilarious. 'Oh, it's so funny. Wait till I tell my mother about this. She's never going to believe me.' Shafique is fascinated by him. He washes the guy's car every time he can, and does it with a big smile on his face. Then he wanders over to the public phone, pulls out his phone card, painstakingly keys in a 38-digit number and chats away to his mum. He has a great laugh. It booms back over towards us, cheers me right up.

Rainy days we get off. Though rain, of course, is a sliding scale. Mist and drizzle we work. Showers and light rain we stand by. Anything heavier than that and we're told to bugger off home. In south London this doesn't exactly constitute a demanding workload, so most people here do other stuff, though I never ask what. Jobs (though there are very few jobs that you can only do on a rainy day apart from selling umbrellas), college. I guess. Personally I usually go home and have some tea with my mum.

Today it's pissing it down. The rain started up early this morning and has settled in since, gradually making itself at home in a familiar and determined way, but we're at work anyway because Harry specifically asked for us.

Of course when we arrived there was no sign of him. And the supermarket is bloody miserable in this weather. We waited at the forecourt for a half hour, sheltering in the trolley section. I was beginning to wish, for more reasons than one, that I was on Shireen's team. Then we left a note on one of the trolleys telling Harry where to find us, and came inside – we'd probably have done that earlier, only the pay's not really good enough that we can just go and sit in the pub all day. Not to mention that there's not much point sitting in the pub all day – none of Shafique, Nestor and Jay Jay actually drinks. Shafique is a Muslim, Jay Jay a Christian and Nestor is worried about his sperm count. The extent to which their lifestyles subsequently coincide is remarkable.

'After sex, you know, I feel like I have been crucified,' Nestor is saying, apparently for Jay Jay's benefit. Jay Jay nods sympathetically.

I like all of these guys, but what I like most about drinking with them is that even though they're on Cokes and I'm on beers they still buy their rounds. I don't think they've worked out that they don't really have to fund my inroads into alcoholism this way. Or maybe they just like to.

'Another round?' I say.

'This one's mine,' says Nestor, breaking off from his monologue. Team spirit, after all. And anyway, Nestor does get the largest tips.

When the four of us first started as a team Shafique and Jay Jay were a bit uneasy about each other. There was a bit of religious tension in the air. Shafique goes along to a local mosque, and has been known to disappear around prayer time – there's a mobile mosque which comes around, an old VW camper van (*Wash!* 27:3:3) which pulls up slightly at an angle in the parking space so it's east-facing. Prayer mats in the back. Quite a few of the washers are Muslims and I understand it gets pretty cramped in there. Given the clientele, though, at least it's nice and clean. And Jay Jay belongs to an evangelical church up in Lambeth. One of the things he does on rainy days is street preaching – I bumped into him on Oxford Street in the middle of a thunderstorm one day and he was shouting like crazy. I thought he was sick or on drugs or something and was going over a little nervously to see if I could help him, but he saw me straight off and came over to give me a big hug. Of course he made me listen for a while, so as I could offer him some advice on what really grabbed the attention of the average heathen, but that was really okay. Nothing he said sounded too crazy. I told him he was doing fine, though no one was stopping to listen. He gave me a pamphlet with cheerfully entitled sections like: *You're A Sinner!* and *Jesus Loves You, Sinner!* And perhaps more appropriately: *Wash Yourself Clean (Of Your Sins)!*

So after work one day Jay Jay and Shafique sat down together to chat about things. Defuse the tension. I think they were ready for a row, both made up to be martyred there and then for their beliefs, if it came to that. But when they actually *talked*, they found that, barring minor dogmas, they basically agreed on everything. The Great Debate lasted all of five minutes before they were stunned into silence while they processed things. And thereafter it was like they'd covered that topic – time to move on. Since then they get on fantastically well. They even call each other Brother. Nestor and I were expecting jihad by the jukebox. Where did all this religious tolerance come from?

Sitting in the pub window, and half-listening to Nestor, Shafique and Jay Jay idly play an imaginary game of *Wash!* with the passing cars.

About *Wash!*. I should explain. To keep up levels of interest at work (washing cars, you may be surprised to learn, can occasionally get tedious) there's a competition going on between the four teams. It has the most intricate set of rules you could imagine, I swear they're completely beyond comprehension.

The basic principle is that your team scores points for every car washed. This all started last year. Before that there had been a regular gambling cartel operating among the washers for some time – simply because it's something to do – betting on cars, nothing too serious, just which colour car was going to be next through the entrance, that kind of thing. Not much money involved.

At least to begin with. Competitive gambling among very bored people does tend to spiral. So the money involved crept up until one day an Ethiopian lad bet his entire season's earnings on red, it came up black, and he ended up being deported. Harry cracked right down.

For a while they tried to continue the whole betting thing except without any money. Playing for pride. But the thrill had gone, so at the start of this season a few of the guys put their heads together – I think Shafique and Shireen were principal instigators – and came up with a new game, *Wash!*, whereby each car washed scores according to make, model and colour. Almost straightforward, if you can remember the scoring system.

But then there are two sets of bonus scores. The first set corresponds to time and place bonuses, for example: anything washed on Tuesday between 3 and 5 in the afternoon (a notoriously quiet time) scores double. And anything washed with no cars on either side of it scores at two thirds (with one or two exceptions). The second set of bonuses are car-related: the number of passengers in the car, what you can see on the back seat, that kind of thing. All these bonuses intersect and some take precedence over the others, just don't ask me which.

My life outside the job is completely taken up with learning the rules. I sit and wait for the bus and tot up the scores of the cars going by. I watch out of my window at the cars on the street below and do the maths. It doesn't make any sense to me at all. I don't even know what the numbers mean.

'What do you mean, "mean"?' says Shafique. 'They're just numbers. They don't mean anything.'

Even when the final scores are in at the start of the next day I don't know who's won until someone tells me.

'Mother of God,' Shafique sighs. 'It's so simple. Just let me score for you today, all right?'

He explains again, and it still doesn't make any sense.

Although no one writes anything down, everyone apart from me seems to be entirely able to keep their own score at the same time as keeping tabs on everyone else's. At the end of the days there are no arguments. These guys are not unsmart. Why they're washing cars and not doing particle physics is beyond me. Some university somewhere must see the potential and start handing out scholarships.

'Okay. 16:5:24.'

'No. Twenty-four? No. I mean, how? *Seventeen.*'

'Why is that seventeen?'

'Allah preserve us. A red 2001 Mondeo with an empty space on either side? With a baby-seat? At eleven o'clock? Are you stupid man? Minus seven. You see?'

Harry has definitely noticed that something's going on, and after the gambling debacle he's keeping a close eye on us, but he hasn't yet twigged quite what's happening. I'm not entirely surprised.

Finally, after our fourth round – four beers and twelve Cokes, though the Cokes are small because they only have

those pikey little bottles – Harry comes in. He looks like he's
been waiting out in the rain. His shirt is soaked, only the garish colours keeping it from being see-through, and his
Bermuda shorts are dripping. He looks uncharacteristically
worried.

'Hi, Harry,' I say.

'You could have left a note or something,' he says. 'We
need to go.'

'Sorry, Harry,' we say.

'Where are we going, Harry?' asks Nestor cheerily. There's
an edge of excitement to his voice from too much caffeine.

'Cleaning job,' Harry says.

We pile outside and into a waiting car. Out of habit, and
despite being the smallest, Nestor baggsies the front seat.
Disturbingly, given his distaste for cars, Harry gets in the
driver's seat. I didn't even know he could drive. Shafique, Jay
Jay and I cosy up in the back.

With a spine-arresting crunch Harry throws the car into
first gear and we make a sharp jerk forwards, then pull away
at a speed which presses us back hard into the seats. As soon
as the g-force lessens off there's the sound of four sets of seat-
belts clicking swiftly into place.

We head south-east, I reckon. More or less. Pretty soon I don't
know where we are. I've lived in London my whole life and
most of the city is still a mystery to me – a mile from my home
in the wrong direction and nothing looks familiar, except that
it all looks a bit like south London. Grey and rained-on. It all
looks a bit like home.

We drive for a long time. The streets edge by. Living in one
neighbourhood you forget how big the city is, it goes on for
mile after mile. And watching the houses go by I get the same
thought I always get when I'm somewhere new, something
I've never quite understood, nor how it makes me feel, the
idea that this patch of land here, that yard – it's all somebody's home. It may be an outlying blip on my radar, but it's

dead-centre on someone else's. It all means something to somebody.

At least it's a distraction. Inside the car we're all getting a little edgy, not least because of our heightened appreciation of a certain salient statistic here – that the longer we spend in the car with Harry driving, the more likely we are to die young.

He seems to know where we're going, though, driving relentlessly on. Out the window the suburbs begin to blur into uniformity. It all looks quite pleasant, not a bad place to live, despite the rain.

Eventually the terraced housing thins out, we take a right turn onto a rough road and enter what looks to be a disused industrial estate. Broken piles of old bricks line the pot-holed drive. There are scattered large buildings, each with an immaculate collection of broken windows. The concrete turning areas are grown over with thick grass.

At the end of the lot, fenced off by a suspiciously tall and professional-looking piece of barbed-wire technology, there's a big old brick power station. Harry drives up to the fence where it runs across the track and toots his horn. We wait. From where I'm squished between Jay Jay and the door, looking along the wire fence, I can see that at the top of every other post there's a security camera. A red light on each one gives an understated, intermittent flash. It may be an optical illusion caused by the blurred light and blowing rain, but they all appear to be focused on us.

Then the section of the fence that's directly in front of us slides soundlessly aside. Harry stays where he is. Nestor looks across at him, with a *Well, boss?* look. Harry has long since ceased looking like he knows what he's doing, which is worrying for the rest of us. But he re-starts the car on only the second attempt and shuffles it forward, juggling painfully through the low gears until we jerk to a halt outside the power station itself.

We get out – the rain has lost heart a little, let up – and wander into the disused power station. There's a great gap in the wall where presumably a door once swung. The building is a cathedral of space, a wire-frame draft of a past coliseum. It's really quite impressive. And considering that there's no roof, the interior is remarkably clean. I'm worrying about the deficiency of empty cans of lager and piss-stains, until I remember about the fence. The concrete floor is solid-looking, and brushed clean. There's a raised section bang in the middle, with a hatch door in the centre of that. It looks like the top of a submarine. It's funny how some of the most interesting things in your life happen when you're drunk. It seems such a waste.

'Here we are,' says Harry, looking relieved. 'Someone'll be along soon.'

'See you later, then,' he adds.

We give him a hurt look.

'I have to collect the money,' he offers by way of explanation. 'I'll pick you up,' he says.

Then he's out of the building, in his car and driving away, surprisingly smoothly, by the sounds, and very quickly too.

'You live in a very strange country,' Nestor says to me when he's gone. 'Strange people,' he adds accusingly.

'Harry's Hawaiian,' I say. 'And you live here too.'

We sit around on the raised concrete step beside the hatch, fold our arms and wait. The drizzle drifts on down.

With a metallic edge to it, and making us all jump, a loud voice suddenly vents from a hidden speaker.

'Please lift the hatch and descend the ladder,' it says.

Shafique is holding his heart, taking deep breaths of air, pretending to have an attack. Nestor giggles.

'Please lift the hatch and descend the ladder,' the voice repeats. It sounds authoritative enough.

We assume it means us, so we stand up. Jay Jay leans forward and with a bit of effort levers up the heavy hatch.

'There's a ladder,' he says, looking down. He sounds almost surprised. 'Do we go in?'

'After you,' says Nestor.

One by one we get a hold of the top of the ladder and start climbing down the tube.

'Please seal the hatch behind you,' the voice says. Nestor, last in, seals the hatch above him.

It's a long way. We climb in unison, to a vertical marching beat, our shoes making a pleasing rhythmic clang on the metal rungs.

At the bottom of the ladder is a corridor, modern and narrow, but tastefully brightened with some well-concealed wall lighting. We wander along until we find a door on the left. There is a note pinned to it. After the impressive trick with the voice and the hidden speakers, this comes across as a little cheap.

Dear Cleaners,

Please enter the changing rooms and put on the protective equipment. Enter the main hall through the big doors. After you have finished, please leave all the equipment as you found it and return the way you came. Thank you.

Yours, etc.

PS Make sure all doors are PROPERLY shut as you go through them.

Beyond the door the changing rooms are fairly standard. A wall of lockers for our things, a shower area, rows of benches with pegs. Hanging on the pegs, dazzlingly bright yellow, are what look to be four chemical warfare suits.

We examine them suspiciously for a while, then realize there's not much else to do. We strip down to underwear and T-shirts, stowing our jackets, shoes and waterproofs in the lockers. I struggle into the contamination suit. Your feet go into the boots, and the rest peels up around you, it's an unpleasantly plastic and sticky feeling. There's a hood with a built in visor-and-gas-mask arrangement which flips down and seals to the front. I centre the visor, look at the ridiculous figures of my costumed colleagues. Nestor looks like a little banana. We laugh at each other, then go to look for the big doors, which we find further down the corridor.

They open through into an immense hall. It looks like an aircraft hangar – big enough for sure, though perhaps a little further underground than is usual – a roof which raises in the centre, an even bigger set of doors at the far end. Huge spot-light beams in the roof, glaring down. And parked in the middle of the huge warehouse space is a massive red tanker. It's the largest truck I've ever seen in my life and it still looks like a toy car lost in a garage. The number plates have been blacked out. Beside us, against the wall, lean four long-handled brushes, and coiled beside them is a hose.

On closer inspection the tanker is not actually red, merely coated in dirt, filthy with a thick crimson dust which seems impacted onto the surface. I stroke a gloved finger over it and it doesn't come away, just leaves a garish blood-like stain on my suit. This looks like hard work. No wonder Harry pissed off.

Nestor closes the big doors and finds a tap where he can hook up the hose. It's a neat device, trigger-operated at the spray end, a high-pressure affair designed to simply blast dirt from the target.

We get to work. Nestor jets the water, which slices into the layer of dirt, and we try and brush it off. He's really enjoying himself. Red mud streams from the surface of the tanker and coagulates round our sewn-in rubber boots. It's hot work while wearing the suits, but with a bit of application, the stuff actually starts to come off. Pretty soon we're covered in it.

'I worked in an abattoir once,' says Nestor conversationally. 'It was a lot like this.'

The brushing takes quite a while. Long enough for me to sober up.

'So how many points for this thing?' I ask halfway through.

Shafique puts down his brush and leans on it. Behind his mask I can see him working it out.

'Never mind,' I say quickly. Sometimes they really take *Wash!* too seriously.

Eventually we're done. Nestor finally hoses the last of the stubborn mud into the floor drains. We even brushed clean the tyre treads – might as well be thorough, after all – and so, quietly proud, we stand back and admire our work. The tanker, it turns out, is a sparkling new silver, unmarred by company logo. It gleams in the bright lights. We wash off the brushes, put everything back where we found it, and leaving the tanker behind us, shut the big doors on it.

Still in our suits we get under the showers. It's a strange feeling. Not really pleasurable, because you can't feel the water, but you get a certain weird satisfaction that you won't have to dry yourself afterwards. Except after we've stripped off the suits we get back under the showers to wash away all the sweat, and it's only after we're done that we realize we haven't been provided with any towels.

Dressed again, but still damp, we hang the contamination suits back up on the pegs. Then, closing the doors behind us, we walk back along the corridor, climb with aching arms the ladder and open the hatch. There's a slight whoosh of escaping air as the seal breaches. We come up into the power station. It's already dark. And very quiet. The rain seems to have cleared up, though. The air is blissfully cool, but with our damp clothes it gets a little cold in no time.

There's no voice at the top, telling us what to do, so we shut the hatch behind us, and stand a moment in the middle of the skeleton building, roofed by clouds, purple in the night. Then we head towards the exit.

The empty night cracks a grin at us.

'Where's our lift man?' asks Nestor. 'Are we supposed to walk home or what?'

Seeing as the power station provides no actual shelter, we decide to wait at the road turning. We worry for a while how we'll get through the fence, but find it half open, as though the power on the door had given out. The cameras hang a little limply on their posts. We exit and make a tired walk through the rest of the site.

As we come back out onto the road proper it starts raining with a rejuvenated enthusiasm. Shafique takes one look at the clouds and says what he always says when it rains.

'You know they should never have built this country underwater. In Nigeria now it is sunny.'

We ignore him. It would be night-time in Nigeria, too.

It's strangely quiet around. There's an odd smell in the air, perhaps marking the demise of a distant drain.

Time passes. We get wetter. There's still no sign of Harry.

'Sod this,' I say. 'Let's go get a bus.' There's a general agreement from the others, so we head off in search of one.

Eventually we reach a main street and find a bus shelter to shiver under. The stream of water gathering pace along the street comes up to our ankles, so we balance on the uncomfortable benches. We wait for a bus, but it doesn't show. Unusually for London, not even the wrong-numbered bus turns up. Not even a car goes by. It's like everything got washed away in the rain. For a fleeting moment, and for the first time in my life, I wish I had my own car. Or boat. A boat would do fine.

'It's like with Noah,' says Jay Jay.

'I noah what you mean,' I say.

But he's too busy scanning the sky. I follow his gaze. Just clouds, rain.

'What are you looking for?' I ask.

'Jesus,' he says.

'Yeah,' I say. 'Amazing rain.'

He looks at me, confused.

Actually, the water is starting to get seriously deep.

Shafique takes out his phone card and wades over to a phone box to try and get us a taxi.

'See if you can get a water taxi,' advises Nestor.

'No answer,' Shafique says when he gets back. 'At this time of night they're never going to come this far south of the river anyway.'

We have a brief discussion about the possibility of stealing a car, which is ended by the realization that even if we could find one, none of us knows how to drive, never mind hotwire it. So with our options running out, and tired though we are, we decide to slosh back along to the supermarket by ourselves.

We follow the signposts for central London. It takes us a good few hours, an exhausting slog along slick, amber streets. In places it looks more like Venice. The rain keeps raining. *I could do this all day, no worries*, it seems to be saying cheerily.

I keep myself happy by thinking of Shireen, and wishing I'd brought her umbrella along for company. Then I get to wondering how my mum's doing. She'll have been up wondering why I'm so late home. I don't usually stay out.

There's the first sign of dawn in the sky, the light merging weirdly with that of the street lamps, an almost tangible glow in the streets. Thoroughly worn out we roll up at the supermarket.

Which is open, though no one's there. The rain has started to wash in beneath the automatic doors. The check-outs are unmanned, and there are abandoned baskets of groceries in the aisles. The car park is half-full of parked-up cars, but entirely empty of people. The drains here seem to be working a bit better, or it's not been raining so much, because the water over the tarmac is a good deal shallower, there are islands of protruding dry land created by the warped surface. We poke around for a few minutes, but nothing turns up. I decide I don't want to be here. I want to find Shireen and take her home for tea, introduce her to my mum.

'I'm off to my mum's place,' I say. Even if everyone else in the world has disappeared off somewhere, my mum's the sort of person who'll still be in, the kettle on.

'Me too,' says Shafique. He's joking. His mum lives in Africa.

But he stays standing beside me. And Jay Jay sidles up too, making it clear we're not going without him.

'Nestor?' I say.

He has a think. 'I'm going to stay,' he says. 'Wash some cars, you know?'

He sounds quite positive about it, so I nod in encouragement. He heads off to get our trolley and we stand there a while and watch him.

For a moment I get a nervous feeling building up in my chest, so I take some deep breaths, wait for it to pass. It's something I used to get a lot. A fear of the future (or *for* it). Panic attacks if I went too far from home, stuff like that. It can really get to you. So the trick, I learned, is to not let it penetrate, to imagine it just washing off – water from a duck's back, and all that. If you have to stay home, stay home. *Don't let it get to you*, has been my philosophy since. Somehow I stopped worrying about those things. Never quite moved out of my mum's place, but we have a good relationship, and renting a place is expensive, so that never seemed like a bad thing. I settled for happiness in the things I had, left the future to look after itself. After all, as my doctor liked to ask me, rhetorically, what's the worst that could happen? I remind myself of this. The nervous feeling goes and I perk up a little.

We push off. The rain thickens again like someone threw open a heavenly tap, so we pull off our fluorescent jackets and hold them over our heads to create makeshift umbrellas. It doesn't really help.

Ahead of us the streets are empty. There's really nobody around. Just Nestor, there behind us in the depopulated car park, determined to get some *Wash!* points on the board, pushing his water trolley down the rows, the green hose sidewinding along behind him through the puddles. He's washing every car left in the place, one at a time, a huge smile of satisfaction on his exhausted face.

Dream #145
30/6/__

But I *do* know what it feels like to be talented, to be special. The thing I was trying to tell you about the music was that I hear it in my dreams all the time – completely original melodies and songs, in a variety of styles; classical, rock, bits of jazz, plainsong, the works. I can usually tell I'm dreaming, so I'm conscious of the fact that the music can only be coming from inside my head. And therefore, I always reckon, there's no way that it will be able to keep on going after it starts up – the invention will have to start looping, repeating on itself, the lyrics, when there are lyrics, will have to dissolve into nonsense. But they don't, they just keep coming. I mean those songs just *unfurl*. The music develops and builds in clever ways that leave me, without any musical training or knowledge, just completely astonished. I mean how the hell does that work?

And it's not that I've forgotten it when I wake, like I only dream that I hear all this beautiful music. I remember it perfectly. I spend the whole bloody day still listening to it echo in my head. Couldn't forget it if I tried. It's just that I have no idea how to put anything down. I'd hum them for you, but really, I can't even fucking hum in key (listen, I'll say, this one's great, it goes: dum da da da da-dum and there's this swelling violin sound . . .). Sometimes I remember fragments of the lyrics and write them down, but it's all useless without the music. I mean if it weren't for the fact that I have no ear for music whatsoever, I could have been a great composer. But for that one minor piece of bad luck, I could have been famous. Fate, that infernal machine of our futures, has fucked me once again.

That's just the soundtracks. Even without them my dreams were always incredibly rich. The way other people would appear in them and be totally themselves, I mean not like my limited comprehension of who they were, but they'd do and say things that I didn't understand at all though I could tell, absolutely, that they knew what they were on about. Sometimes working out on waking – after remembering, puzzling over it – why they had acted as they did, discovering that there were perfectly rational emotional grounds for their action. And not saying anything they'd said before, but being completely original and funny in ways I'd never be. As though my head could contain their entire selves, or at least, everything except the physical stuff, which I suspect is not so essential anyway. Never mind the sleepwalking, my body doing its own thing entirely, acting out completely foreign desires and motivations, and which made me realize that there was a whole reservoir of stuff going on inside that had very little to do with *me*. So what I mean to say is that I understood fairly early that people aren't these neat conglomerates of simple stuff ruled over by the conscious, but that all kinds of odd things are going on with them, most of which they're not even aware of, or believe in.

Right, I'm coming back to that. So the last dream I had, the one I was telling you about before, the dream that I couldn't help obsessing about, the dream that eventually sort of ended up with me being sent here; the one in which I was on a school trip to a science laboratory and I got bitten by a radioactive spider. I know, yes. But it felt so real. When I got up it really felt as though that spider bite had given me special powers – I just felt so amazingly alive and special the next morning. And I know it was just a dream, I always knew, but it was such an incredible dream that it felt totally like a part of my life, something I'd lived, and it was so different from anything else I experienced what else would you expect me to do but go on about it?

Sure, I may have come across as being a little manic, I understand that. But I don't think you can just write it off as being representative of any intrinsic insecurity about my lack of talent, or as you put it, my underlying *powerlessness* with respect to my life. I don't feel like that at all. I have always felt, inside, to be quite special. Particularly while asleep, or on a morning when I was still savouring whatever dream I'd had. Even the nightmares, really, they had such a brilliant intensity to them – they scared the shit out of me sometimes, but I've never felt so alive. Now, of course, as part of the deal we made that means I can keep going to school, I'm on these drugs you've prescribed, which have – admittedly – suspended me talking quite so animatedly about spiders and superpowers and so forth, and have largely too stopped me minding the fact that everyone has been so off about the whole thing. But they also stop me dreaming. I go off into a black hole every night and wake up what feels like instantly, though it's the next morning, feeling like something's been taken from me. It's like half my life is being stolen. So what I'm trying to explain to you is that I'm beginning to feel precisely those feelings of powerlessness you've just been talking about, due to the fact that I'm not dreaming any more, which is precisely because of the drugs you've prescribed. It forces me to live in this bleaker world, unpainted by all the stuff inside my head, and it feels like I've been cut off from my own unconscious, severed from the great reservoir.

There are benefits, I'll admit it. I don't get that recurring sadness that I used to. Also, some of the music would get stuck in my head all day and I'd be whistling it tunelessly and it would be extremely irritating all round, so that's gone. Certain things too are more manageable – the pills seem to regulate my mood and energy, which is definitely better than the sudden highs and lows before. Don't get me wrong, I appreciate all of that. It's just that, though I feel all fuzzy now, I *know* that something's wrong, I'm grieving for something, albeit in an oddly painless way. And I appreciate that you're so concerned about my happiness, but I can't help but think your priorities are a little skewed. What's so great about happiness? I can say honestly that, yeah, I've probably never been so consistently happy my whole life. I feel warm and fuzzy and loved, and nothing hurts any more and I don't worry about anything or obsess about anything, and I'm not plagued by thoughts of suicide or car crashes or train wrecks and I have all this energy for sports and for being outside and I don't feel the same overwhelming hatred of all the other kids that I used to, or any of that. But Jesus I miss my dreams, they were more beautiful than anything I had in my own life.

Dead Ancients Trilogy

1. Archimedes

Archimedes runs on a surface turned by his movement. Each stride of his frantic dash sends the ground on which he is running behind him at a speed in direct proportion to the power he exerts in pushing. As his feet leave the ground the operation of inertia causes it to continue to move beneath him, even though the forces which propel it are momentarily removed. Archimedes himself, except for his wild flapping run, does not move.

He looks like a circus performer walking the ball beneath him, or a hamster on a wheel – except that he is running on the outside of the wheel, which turns under rather than around him. The view is significantly improved, the wheel falling away rather than curving up and over.

He has lifted his robes to his waist so as not to stumble when they become tangled with his legs. His long white beard has been thrown with similar intent over his right shoulder. The legs protruding from the lifted robe are long and hairy, but rather muscular. His knees are thin, but his calves and thighs massive, giving his legs the shape of elongated hourglasses. If they were not moving so fast and blurring a little to the eye of anyone who stayed level with him, an observer might comment on the bluing and prominence of the veins on his calf. He's a wiry old man. His sandals flap a little as they kick back.

Behind him the sun rises. Ahead of him his shadow stretches out, immensely long. At normal speed the shadows of his legs disappear in turn into the distant, larger bulk of shadow, and then flash back towards him as his foot nears the earth, before shooting off again as that foot leaves the ground, an effect like that of two enormous pistons flickering down towards him. Beneath the shadow, the earth is moving, causing a rippling visual effect he entirely fails to notice.

To his eyes the horizon is an imperfect plane in the distance blurred slightly by movement, like an oscillator registering peaks of static, tending towards level. In fact the horizon is not a plane, but a circle of constant size with Archimedes as its centre. The visible earth is not flat but a slight dome. The sky above is not a dome but a pellucid sphere viewed from beneath. The stars are held in four dimensions, like bubbles trapped in ice.

He is a lever, moving the first in a series of gears. The spinning of the planet exerts a gravitational force, which bends the space-time continuum in the cosmic neighbourhood. Space is pulled past the planet, along with the stars and planets that occupy it. The operation of gravity and the equilibrium of forces stabilize the path of the planets and moons, as they curve elliptically around him. The sun is moved in a neat orbit, passing from behind him until it goes almost directly over his head, then starts to get into his eyes. With his spare hand, the hand not clutching his bunched robes, he shades his eyes. It's a difficult running position, and his face is concentration made flesh. His tongue sticks out of the side of his mouth, and he's bitten it, once or twice. The whole solar system falls into place around him, then the galaxy, obligingly, behind that. Smaller wheels turn larger wheels. Once the universe gets up and running, the machine works smoothly, despite the crankiness of the operator.

The movement of the spheres changes the nature of the spheres. The distribution of sunlight and the variations in distance from the warmth produces reactions of minerals, gasses and enzymes – something complicated – which result in the formation of atmospheres, terra-climates, and hey presto, suitable conditions for the emergence of life. Archimedes' running alters the surface of the ground he runs on. From time to time there's a noisy splash as one of his feet lands in water, but the foot is dry by the time it hits the ground again, this time in the sand of a desert.

The plants the runner is now forced to dodge as they stream towards him breathe in carbon dioxide, breathe out oxygen. Archimedes breathes in oxygen, breathes out carbon dioxide. It's a fantastic relief for him. He thought he was going to have to hold his breath for ever. Some surprised-looking plankton watch as he blazes past, puffing away, his eyes shaded, robes raised, beard like a jet trail out behind him, legs turning over at incredible speed.

If Archimedes were to stop running, he is aware, he would not move with the earth. No, the earth would stop with him, following the generation of a sufficient amount of friction between the two. The thought of trying to slow down the earth by slowing down his run, or even back-pedalling, is beginning to concern him, because he's not sure if he would survive the effort. If he dug his heels in, his feet would probably be worn right down to his knees before he managed to get to a standstill.

Looking around for a fixed point to grab hold of, so he can keep his feet off the ground long enough for the world to stop turning, he forgets to keep an eye on where he is running, trips over a burgeoning rhododendron bush, and is thrown head over heels on the spot, crashing against the onrushing earth, bashing his head and shoulder then over onto his back where his wind is knocked from him, up on his feet again before cutting his knee badly on the next tumble, barely getting his hands down in time to prevent his face hitting the ground, and so on. After a few spectacularly painful flips he and the ground get back on terms. The universe shudders to a halt. Time and life are momentarily suspended.

'Oh, bugger,' says Archimedes, lying on his back, his beard across his face.

He picks himself up, pulling his robe straight, and rubs his bruised elbows in turn. Glancing over his shoulder he sees it is almost sunrise. Above the horizon in front of him there are still stars low in the sky. There is a pleasingly random quality to their distribution. He amuses himself for a short while in picking out patterns by joining the dots together.

He takes a cautious step backwards and the earth shifts in equal measure. He takes a step to the side and there is an equivalent and opposite movement beneath him. Hurriedly he brings himself to a halt. After that last disaster running forward he doesn't like to imagine how it might be if he picked up any speed in a sideways direction. His knee twinges, and he flexes it carefully, like an athlete. He rubs his sore head, and blinks a few times.

'Well,' he says, and looks around again.

He performs a little shuffling with his feet, putting both feet together and then twisting slightly so that he has a new direction on the earth ahead of him. The universe assumes a new slant, a minor adjustment in its alignment.

He takes a deep breath, and ponders on the conservation of energy. He imagines a wheeled vehicle which he could operate with even less loss of energy, a gear that will turn the world for him, remaining unmoved. He comes perilously close to inventing the exercise bike before he recognizes that the lack of building resources would scupper any such plans.

Archimedes begins a slow walk. Getting started is almost as hard as stopping. He puts an enormous effort into the first pushes. Then things get a little easier, and after a while he picks up into a brisk jog.

2. Pythagoras

Triangles schmiangles. I made my name with squares. In want of the general solution, here's a brief demonstration. We take a right-angled triangle whose two shortest sides (a, b) are in the ratio 1:2. We draw in the squares of the sides, and because the ratios are so simple, we can add by sight one or two additional lines to divide our squares. Use squared paper, if that helps:

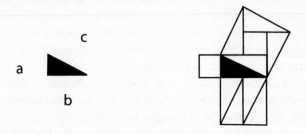

And, like, ta-da: *a* squared plus *b* squared equals *c* squared. QED. You can count the pieces (four triangles and one square on each side of the equation) and tally them up, if you don't believe me. It's tremendously neat. My wife it was who got that one. I merely helped a little with the algebra. The whole school was wonderfully appreciative of the effort. Triangles are the problem, all hypotenuse and question. Squares are the solution.

Squares are perfect, and triangles full of flaws. Take a square. Perfect, non? Identical sides, identical angles, everything in ratios of unity. Then draw a diagonal. Two triangles, right?

Now here's the problem: the ratio of the diagonal of the square to its side is not a ratio of integers. It's not even a neat fraction or recurring decimal. I can't begin to express my frustration with this one. As it is, it makes me edgy, and quite a few people I know, too. Given us all some sleepless nights.

We've been sitting on it for a while now, keeping it quiet. If people start to find out, all hell's going to break loose. There are going to be some pretty strong questions asked, and we're going to look miserable and stupid when we sit there and shrug apologetically. There's just no reason to it – it's completely irrational. Makes you think, though – if only it had been exactly one and a half. Or 1.4, I'd have settled for that. That would have made sense. But no, the ratio of the diagonal of a square to its side is root 2, or to you: 1.4142135623730950488016887242096980785697 . . . Goes on *forever*. Sometimes the Gods really piss me off.

3. ?

Everything I do from this point onwards is new. Not one of these words that I am thinking has crossed my mind before, neither has one of the breaths that burst from my lungs previously done so, nor have my steps landed in these apparently well-worn grooves; not before now, for this moment alone, and never again thereafter. The world is a labyrinth of originality, and I am trapped at the branching of a billion new possibilities every second.

This knowledge instils in me a terror of the future. If I were in charted territory, if I had been here before, I might find some reassurance – if there were only laws which ordered the change. But it is all new, and what is there to prevent the world from altering so that I no longer exist? To stop the sky falling on my head? I believe that my feet are planted firmly on the ground, but what if I were suddenly to lose my mass and be swept away on a breeze, to find myself reformed by the infinite twists of the merciless winds? Perhaps yet I might become one of the tiniest insects that burrow in the sand beneath me, and never know what I had been before. I am consumed by self-doubt, which gnaws at me like a hungry dog on a meatless bone, for I have no way of telling if any of this has already happened. Change alters my past (or what I believe my past to have been) just as much as it threatens the now, and the now plunges into the then without pausing to wait for me. Our freedom is perfect, infinite, horrifying.

I want to cry out 'Stop! Wait just a moment!' so that for a brief while I might take stock of things as they are, before they are subject to the changes that time brings so quickly with it. I want to be able to stop and not need to breathe and be able to see things in stasis, unmoving so that I can know where they are without having every second to keep an eye on them, to track their alterations and movements. I want to be able to delve inwards and find ideas and memories that will not slip away from me and to be able to say with certainty 'I *am* . . .' But there are no things-as-they-are, only flux, one endless becoming, passage from the now to the then, which is never what it was. Nothing is certain, and every moment that I live, with each new breath or step or thought, may well be my last. It is scant comfort that so far there appear to have been certain continuities – after all I remain myself, with the usual number of hands and arms and eyes, and believe (but how would I know?) that my stream of thought is to some extent a natural progression, not characterized by sudden leaps or gaps. No, this does not change the bare facts of my situation one iota. I am teetering on the edge of pure chaos, powerless to prevent my fall.

And there is no succour – I cannot turn my head away from the flight of the birds and look to the solidity of the ground for reassurance, for that too is subject to flux or else the shadows of the birds flicker oppressively across the land beneath me. To close my eyes represents no refuge, for colours shift and meld, and my mind is all the more ready to conjure up pictures before me. And to sleep is hellish – an indescribable agony, where even the pretence of regularity of change is thrown clean away, and the chaos is total. I have not slept for months. But then again, it is increasingly difficult for me to perceive a difference between the states of wakefulness and sleep – each represents a falling into a future, a battering by the change of all around. Panic crowds me round, and I tremble or shed new drops of sweat in a wave of sickness, which comes constantly, changes always, and never leaves. I will be driven mad.

I am terrified of speech, paralysed by the thought of words flowing out of control from my mouth, syllables and sounds askew, meaning run amok. Granted, I have no one to talk to, but if I had what certainty is there that I would not launch into a fury, frothing up curses and swearwords like barbs, driving them from me by my shouting and yelling? Even when I speak to myself the process is so fearful that the intended words garble, losing their meaning as my mouth contorts around a sound which barely progresses beyond a harsh scream or moan. If I try to begin a word I find myself launched into panic, uncertain of what I have said, unsure what noise to make next. To try to speak one word after another, and to put meaning into those words, is to strain my mind and body to the limits of their comprehension, to try and accomplish something which I cannot do. All language is a chaos, a disorder, and I cannot put it right; not within me, at least, and I am terrified by the prospect that others will bring it into my life.

Talk? I can barely move. Each new footsteps lands unbearably on rock which immediately becomes forever changed, or on sand, when a thousand grains move with each step, displaced and never again to return to their positions except in some new configuration. The sand is the worst in many ways. Unlike the smaller particles of dust, the shifting sands are eminently visible. Billions of particles move around without me seeing them but the sand is terrifying in the vastness of its simple changes. On a large scale the dunes move back and forth across the rock base, occasionally reaching to the foot of my hill. They then retreat back the way they came, but never in the same pattern. Even here I am denied regularity, consistency and some firm hold to grasp and thereon rest my expectations. Perhaps it would do no good if they did move uniformly. I would be forced to the conclusion that what was happening was a coincidence of simply staggering proportions, or would be obsessed by an urge to see just what the difference in each movement of the dunes actually was, for it would surely be there. But nothing is sure, nothing is certain, and I can take nothing for granted. And then each dune is composed of an enormous number of individual grains which not only move in infinitesimal contortions but rub against each other as they do so and by this change their shape and the way they blow in the wind, and thus the way the dunes shift and the way the grains move and rub against each other, the way they blow in the wind and so on and so forth. It is just too much for me to bear – as if I have been put in this place to be punished for some horrible crime, condemned to suffer endless flux, to be shown firstly that change is constant and inexorable, and then to be assailed by it, immersed in it and to have it (quite literally, when the wind is swirling and strong) shoved down my throat and be left to choke on it.

My muscles, though aching, are growing harder and stronger and my back and neck are becoming heavily tanned. I am growing older, with the dark curls of my hair showing a touch of grey. My hands are calloused, and almost unfeeling. I am pale with the thought of the abyss of courses which may run at any given moment, and made quite ill as if I were at the top of a hill, and suffering from appalling vertigo. I am sick and afraid, and sick of being afraid, and unable to do anything else except think about all the possibilities that exist at any one moment. To fear the future is to be afraid of the now, because the now does not exist.

To repel my fear I do what anyone would do. Attempt to forget about it. Provide myself with distractions. Form objectives. I immerse myself in routines which occupy my concentration, anything to stave off reality, the despotic demands of originality. I have focused on the object nearest to me which seems to change the least – a huge rock, a great boulder, almost unmovable and able to resist to a degree the infernal processes of weathering and erosion. From this rock I can find some small point of continuity, a beginning from which I can build up a lifesaving routine, something which is mine and will not be infiltrated by the pervasive and alienating metamorphosis of all around. This rock, then, is my salvation. It will see me through. And that is why I flex briefly the weary muscles of my shoulder and legs, spit on my hands to aid my grip, set my feet firmly onto the ground and rest my palms against the smooth hardness of the boulder and then begin to strain, to push, to hold in equilibrium for a moment my force against its mass, and then to slowly, painfully, roll the weight up this narrow groove towards the top of the hill, which I shall never reach.

Acknowledgements

Thanks and love to Natalie Castellanos Ryan, Glennis Hobbs, David Malone, Christie Marr, Molly McGrann, Alastair Nelson, Alejandra Rojas, Kevin Conroy Scott, Sue Scott, Sam Taylor. A huge thank you to everyone at Faber, particularly Kate Burton and Angus Cargill, and to everyone at Rogers, Coleridge and White, not least Deborah Rogers. Thank you Trevor Horwood.

Thanks, for publishing some of these stories elsewhere, to Dan Crowe and Zembla ('Molloy Dies', *Zembla* 5), and to Toby Litt, Ali Smith and the British Council ('Deep Blue Sea', *Picador New Writing 13*).

'New Orleans Blues' is for Jess Hadley; 'Winter Luxury Pie' is for Katherine Ibbett.

The rest, though particularly 'Deep Blue Sea', are for Lee Brackstone.